"Johnson, _____ you shot my brother in the back!

People on the sidewalk stopped. Morgan halted and turned to see who was talking. One man stood alone in the middle of the dusty Cheyenne street. He motioned at Morgan.

"Yeah, Johnson, you bastard. You heard me. Are you man enough to take on a real man face-to-face? Or do you need ten of your riders with you to cut down all the honest men in town first?"

Morgan looked around. Everyone had faded away from him. He stood alone on the boardwalk.

"Are you speaking to me?" Morgan asked.

"Damn right. You know anybody else standing in your shoes called Slade Johnson?"

"That isn't my — "

"Come on! Come on! Stop stalling. I've got you without your dozen side-guns. Just you and me. Go ahead and draw. I'm gonna love every minute of killing you. Die slow, you bastard, Johnson, die slow."

GUNSLINGER'S SCALP

BUCKSKIN

KIT DALTON

LEISURE BOOKS   NEW YORK CITY

A LEISURE BOOK®

March 1992

Published by

Dorchester Publishing Co., Inc.
276 Fifth Avenue
New York, NY 10001

The name "Leisure Books" and the stylized "L" with design are trademarks of Dorchester Publishing Co., Inc.

Printed in the United States of America.

GUNSLINGER'S SCALP

Chapter One

Lee Buckskin Morgan stared across the poker table at the one man he had to beat. Rawlins was big and unshaven, had on range clothes and a much-worn hat. One eyelid sagged a little from a knife scar and a dead cigar stuck out of the corner of his mouth. He squinted against the glare of the three coal-oil lamps, and at last nodded.

"Hell, I'm in. Got too much in the pot not to go for it." He threw a $50 chip in the pot and watched two other men still in the game. Both shook their heads and dropped their cards face-down into the pot. The dealer looked at Morgan, who nodded and put in a $50 chip.

The dealer flipped out the last pasteboard face down to both players left in the game of seven card stud. Morgan shifted his new card through the two concealed ones as he considered his hand showing and the rough man's display. Then he took a look at his new card. His expression didn't change. He watched the last man in the hand look at his new card. The roughly dressed player's eye-tick popped once, then remained still.

The scruffy man snorted and checked his chips. He was high on the table. He bet $20 and looked at Morgan.

Morgan slid out two blue $100 chips and added them to the pot. "Your twenty, plus another hundred and eighty." The man with the drooping eye frowned.

"Two hundred? That's six months' wages for a workingman around here."

Morgan said nothing. He put his cards on the table and lit a thin, long, and black cigar. Morgan was in his late twenties, six feet tall and 185 pounds. He had brownish blond hair that he wore a little longer than a businessman would, sharp brown eyes, and was clean shaven.

No one around the table said a word. At last the dealer took control.

"Will, time's up. Either call the gentleman or fold."

The big man named Will pounded his fist onto the table, then dropped his cards facedown in the pot. He stared at Morgan, his face turning red.

"Nobody wins that much without something being wrong!" the gambler snarled.

Morgan raked in the pot and looked up.

"Did you say I'm not playing fair?" Morgan asked, his voice low and deadly.

"Hell, no. Not saying that. I'm saying you're a cheating bastard and I won't stand for it." The seated man's right hand darted for his side and he got his six-gun out of leather, but before it cleared the top of the table, a shot blasted under the playing surface and a .45-caliber round dug into the floor beside the big man's chair.

"Hold it, Will!" Morgan barked. "The next one goes in your belly and you'll die with more pain than you ever thought could happen. Ease your right hand up on the table. Careful. I don't shoot as well left-handed and I might miss your belly and shoot your balls off by mistake."

Will brought his hands to the table slowly. He lay down the six-gun and moved his hand away from it.

"You're lucky to be alive, Will. Most men who accuse somebody of cheating around here either kill somebody or get killed themselves. You're damn close to being the second kind. You want that?"

"No. Hell, no, but you cheated. You must have cheated. How else you win the last four big pots? Sure, you bailed out on some small ones, but the big ones you won."

Morgan sighed. "Why do I always wind up teaching you dumbasses how to play poker. Show me the hand you folded on."

Slowly Will reached to the table and turned over his three hole cards. He still had four cards showing, a pair of aces, a king, and a four. His three hidden cards were a seven, a king, and another ace.

"Full house," Morgan said. "Good hand, even for seven card. You want to see what I'm holding?"

Showing on the table in front of him were a pair of deuces, a five, and a seven. Three of the four were diamonds. He turned over the three hole cards one at a time. He had another deuce to make three of a kind, then an eight of diamonds. The last card he turned up was a seven.

"I had a full house too, deuces and sevens, but yours would have beaten mine."

"Goddamn!" Will shouted. "You bluffed me."

"Right. You lost your nerve. I didn't cheat here or on the other three hands I won. I had the best cards on two of them. On the other one I didn't but I bluffed out the doctor. Poker isn't only the cards you get. It's how well you can bluff that wins at poker. Learn to play the game at the dime-limit table before you come up here and lose a year's wages on two hands."

The dealer scowled at Will. "Damnit, Will, don't just sit there sulking like an idiot. Apologize to a real poker player here and learn something. Next time you try to draw your hogleg at my table, I'll gun you down myself."

Will rubbed his face. At last he nodded. "Yeah, yeah. Okay. I was wrong. You didn't cheat. Sorry."

Morgan chuckled. "Don't get mad, learn from it. I lost a fortune at poker after I thought I knew how to play."

The game was over. Morgan cashed in his chips, put the roll of bills in his pocket, and reloaded the spent round in his .45 Colt Peacemaker. He checked the saloon, then went to the door and stepped outside quickly.

He looked both ways on the street, saw no one who might be waiting for him, and walked across the hard-surfaced Omaha, Nebraska, street and down half a block to his hotel along a concrete sidewalk. He still wasn't used to such a thing in a town like this.

When he got his key out of the hotel box, the night clerk handed him a folded message. He went to his room before he read it. At his room door he listened, then tried the knob. Locked. He opened it quietly and swung the door inward until it hit the wall. No one was there.

He went in, lit the lamp, and closed and locked the door. Then Morgan dropped his low-crown brown hat with the red diamonds on a black headband on the bed and took out the message.

It was a telegram from his contact in Denver who picked up mail for him and stalled bill collectors when needed.

"TO: LEE MORGAN, PLAINSMAN HOTEL, OMAHA, NEB. ACCOUNT OVERDUE. WIRE MONEY. MAN IN GRAND ISLAND, NEB., WANTS YOUR HELP TO FIND A LOST CHILD. CONTACT ALONZO J. BISHOP, GRAND ISLAND HOTEL."

He sat on the bed and read the wire again. A missing child. Might not be much of a problem. He could use the work. Morgan checked his gold pocket watch. It was ten P.M. He could send a night wire until midnight.

Morgan left the hotel and walked four blocks to the telegraph office. The clerk hardly looked at the wire, tapping out the message on the key automatically. Morgan's wire said:

"TO: ALONZO BISHOP, GRAND ISLAND HOTEL, GRAND ISLAND, NEB. LEE MORGAN AVAILABLE. CHARGES $5 PER DAY PLUS EXPENSES. CONTACT AT PLAINSMAN HOTEL, OMAHA."

The next morning, Morgan was up, shaved, dressed in his town clothes, and heading for the hotel dining room for breakfast when the room

11

clerk called him over. There was a night telegram waiting for him. He opened it and read it.

"TO: LEE MORGAN, PLAINSMAN HOTEL, OMAHA, NEB. COME AT ONCE. TIME IS IMPORTANT. YOUR FEE SATISFACTORY PLUS BONUS. HURRY."

Morgan changed his mind about breakfast, went back to his room, packed, and checked out. He caught the morning train out of Omaha with five minutes to spare and had breakfast on board.

The dining car was almost filled and the steward guided him to a seat across from an attractive young woman at a window.

"Miss, he said I should sit here. Is it all right?"

She nodded. "Yes, it's crowded. Perfectly fine." She smiled when he sat down and ate daintily at her roll and coffee.

He had sausages and hot cakes and coffee, and when she was finished she watched him.

"It's always interesting to watch a hungry man eat," she said.

Morgan looked up. It was the first thing she had said to him since he sat down. He smiled. "It's interesting being the one doing the eating as well. These are good hotcakes. Have you tried them?"

"No, I usually don't eat much breakfast."

"That's why you stay so sleek and slender," he said, meaning it.

She blushed. "Really, that's not something . . ." She sighed. "Well, thank you. Are you going far?"

"No, just to Grand Island."

"I'm going farther. I'm coming from Chicago. It's been a long trip."

His breakfast was done. She started to rise and

12

he stood and helped her. She turned, then looked back. She moved closer to him.

"Could you help me with something? I have a suitcase lock that just won't budge. It's down this way."

"Of course. Anything for a lady in distress."

She flashed him a smile and went ahead. Morgan appreciated a well-constructed female, and she certainly was. Slender waist, hips not too wide. She was taller than he had guessed. She must be five-six.

They went through the dining car, into a coach car, and on to the front of that and into the compartment car. It had small rooms built along one side, with a narrow passageway on the other side. She stopped at the second room, put a key in the lock, and opened it. She smiled and motioned him inside.

The compartment was a small room, with a bed, a chair, a small stand for washing and a window. She closed the door after him and he heard the lock click. He turned quickly but she only stood there smiling.

"There really isn't a suitcase lock," she said softly.

"I hoped there wasn't," Morgan said.

She stretched up and kissed his lips, then put her arms around his neck and kissed him again. Her slender body pressed against him from hips to chest. His arms came around her. The train swayed around a small curve and they leaned against the door for support.

Her lips left his and she grinned. "That feels good, the way you're pressing me against the door." Her hips ground against his and he bent and kissed her again, her breasts straining against his chest. He broke off the kiss and they sat down on the double bed.

"I didn't just take a chance who might sit across from me," she said, looking up at him. "I paid the steward five dollars to seat you there when you came in. I described you to him, and he found you."

He frowned and she kissed away the frown lines. "Don't be suspicious. I saw you when you boarded and decided I wanted to see more of you."

She reached over and began to unbutton the fasteners on his shirt.

"Why?" he asked.

She caught one of his hands and put it on her breasts. "Because I'm rich and I usually get what I want, and I decided I was tired of staying in this room alone, and wanted company, but not just any company would do."

"And I'm the honored one," Morgan said. His hands worked through the blouse buttons and her soft wrapper and then fondled her bare breasts.

"I hope you're not angry with me."

"I'm never angry when I'm playing with a woman's breasts."

She finished unbuttoning the blouse and shrugged out of it, then out of the wrapper she wore, and her breasts surged out, saucy, with glorious pink areolas and darker red, thumb-sized nipples.

"Oh, yes!" Morgan said softly. "The beauty of a woman, such wonders." He bent and kissed them and she purred softly, then pulled him down on the bed on top of her.

"There's no rush. We have almost four hours

with stops and all before we get to Grand Island," she said. She pushed him aside and sat up and undressed him, right down to the new short underwear he wore. She crooned when she found the mass of brownish blond hair on his chest.

She squealed when she pulled down his underwear and his erection jolted upright, hard and ready for action.

"Oh, my!" she said, eyes wide. She slipped out of her skirt and bloomers and curled up naked on the bed beside him.

"Now is when I get shy," she said. Then she laughed and rolled on top of him and began to nibble at his man breasts. He rolled her over and pinned her arms at the sides of her head and kissed her gently.

"Slowly," she said. "I want it to last. No, I don't want to know your name, and you won't know mine. Just something delicious that happened when strangers met on a train. I want to remember it that way."

She turned away from him and he curled his body next to hers and then, gently, softly, sweetly he seduced her. She reacted slowly and then with a growing passion, and when he poised over her with her long legs spread wide, she pleaded for him to enter her.

"Now, sweet man, now! I can't wait a second longer. Push him into me until he won't go any farther! It's going to be so good. I may faint from the ecstasy."

She met him then as he thrust into her and she shrieked in delight and some pain, and then they worked together and it was several minutes before she touched his shoulder and they paused. They looked out the window.

"Three hours more," she said, and asked to be on top the next time.

Four times they made love, and then he came away, kissed both of her flushed breasts, and bit her nipples until she yelped. He dressed quickly and looked out the window just as the big steam engine at the head of the train began to slow.

He was dressed and watching as the train pulled into the station. He kissed her once more at the door. She stood there still naked, still glowing, and the blush tingeing her neck and chest.

"I'll never forget you. I'm going to Cheyenne. If you're ever there, don't try to find me. I'm another person in Cheyenne."

Then he had to run to the coach car to find his luggage. He got the brown leather bag just before the conductor called, "All aboard!"

Morgan watched from the platform as the compartment car came by, but he didn't see anyone looking for him in the second window.

Morgan asked directions for the Grand Island Hotel. It was two blocks away, so he walked. He left his bag with the room clerk and asked for Alonzo Bishop's room.

"Sir, Mr. Bishop is not a guest here, he owns the hotel. I'll be glad to take you to his residence rooms."

They were on the first floor in back and at one side. The clerk knocked, announced Morgan, and then vanished.

The room was set up as an office. It had an outside window next to a street, drapes, a big desk, two chairs, pictures on the wall, and a huge shaggy buffalo head on the far wall. A man sat at the desk working. He was almost bald. He looked up now and then stood.

"Oh, Lee Morgan, the detective."

"I'm not actually a detective, Mr. Bishop. But I am good at finding people."

"Good, good. Just what I need." He looked up and Morgan saw a small round face with spectacles on it. The eyes through the glasses looked larger than life. Bishop's nose slanted left as if it had been mashed to one side, and bluish veins showed on his temple and across the baldness near the front. The man had almost no jawline, and his mouth had thin lips that seemed determined never to smile.

"Sit," Bishop ordered.

Morgan took the first chair but stayed alert, his back stiff and his gaze straight at the small man behind the desk.

"Morgan, I've heard of you. I know many people in Colorado, especially Denver, so I've heard of you. I don't worry about what you've done in the past. All I want are results."

He stopped a moment and stared at Morgan. "I see you're no Wild West bum. I hate those fringed shirts, long hair, and dirty hats. So all right, I'll tell you about this. For five dollars a day, I better get results."

Morgan stood. "Bishop, I'm not sure I want this job. You tell me what it's about and then I'll decide if I will take it or not. You might dislike Wild West folks, but the fact is I'm not too crazy about slick, fast-talking short, bald men. Now, with that out of the way, what about the missing child?"

Bishop grinned, then he laughed. He roared for a minute, then controlled himself.

"Morgan, you don't bully easy. Good. I think we're going to get along just fine. What do you

17

know about the Indians—the Cheyenne, to be precise?"

"Enough to know not to walk into their camp and ask for a free meal. Is this child held by the Cheyenne?"

"In due time. The missing child is mine, name of Harold Bishop, thirteen years of age. Normal-sized boy, good in school. Has lots of friends here. He's an only child. I thought he was happy here.

"His mother didn't like Omaha. She preferred Wyoming and the mountains if possible. We lived in Denver for a year. She didn't like it there. We came back here. Most of my businesses are here and in Denver.

"My wife is half Cheyenne." He passed a photograph over to Morgan to look at. "She looks as white as the next lady at the Congregational Church Social, but she's half Cheyenne. Her daddy rode in one day to the Cheyenne camp, took a wife, stayed a year, made a baby, and rode on again without losing his hair.

"The small band of Cheyenne were attacked by a marauding band of Dakota Sioux and wiped out. Killed every warrior and all the older boys. Saved the women to take them as wives and slaves, and the children to raise as their own.

"My wife, Willow, and her mother hid from the attackers. They had been out picking berries at the time of the siege. They avoided the fight and the capture. Two weeks later they stumbled into a small ranch in southern Wyoming. The owner had lost his wife in childbirth a month before. Willow's mother cared for the child, and the rancher and she eventually married him. Willow was always considered to be white.

"Twenty years later I met her at a dance in

Denver and married her. I had no idea at the time she was half Cheyenne. Her mother had died, and her foster father treated her like a young white lady.

"A year ago, my wife told me she was returning to the Cheyenne tribe and taking my son along. He's only one quarter Cheyenne and looks as white as you do.

"I prevented her from going. Then three months ago she slipped away to Cheyenne, Wyoming, and after a week of talking with some half-breeds there, located a Cheyenne tribe and asked to join it. They accepted her and the boy. Now I want them back."

"You've talked to the Army and the law people in Cheyenne?"

"Yes, they said they could do nothing. The woman is half Cheyenne, and she went in of her own free will. They can't mount a rescue since she doesn't want to be rescued."

"So you want me to walk into a Cheyenne camp and take the woman and boy out by force?"

"However you have to do it. I don't ask questions. I just pay for results. Oh, five dollars a day, and when you have Harold back in my house in Omaha, you'll get a five-thousand-dollar bonus."

Morgan stood and walked around the room, then went to the window and looked out on the street. He turned, shaking his head. "I can offer no guarantee. It depends on the situation up there. In some of that area the Army is constantly harassing the Cheyenne, driving them toward the reservation. It might be impossible even to find your wife and son now.

"If I can find them, it might be totally impossible to get either of them out. The boy went willingly, you said?"

"He did. The last time I talked with him he said it would be like a vacation from his studies at school. I have him at a strict private school so he'll be ready for Harvard University when he's eighteen. He wants to be a scientist."

"They both could refuse to come back. I'll have to go to Cheyenne and talk to some people there. If I think there's a chance to get them out, I'll wire you. Then you send me five hundred dollars expense money and I'll do my best."

Bishop nodded. He reached in his desk drawer and took out a stack of bills. He counted out ten $50 bills and handed them to Morgan. "No sense waiting on the expense money. If you decide you can't do it, wire me the remainder of the money."

"Do you have a picture of the boy?"

Bishop gave him one.

"I'd like to keep this with me. Now I better see about the next train west."

"Night train leaves the station a little before eight this evening. You should have no trouble being on it."

Chapter Two

Since it was still morning in Grand Island and the train didn't leave until eight that evening, Alonzo Bishop gave Lee Buckskin Morgan the use of a hotel room for the rest of the day. He cleaned up, had a bath in a real stretch-out tub, and then went out for a good lunch. When he came back to his room, he noticed that the door was unlocked and slightly ajar.

At the same time he smelled smoke. He rammed the door open and stopped in amazement. The inside of his room had been turned into an Indian tipi. There were two poles with buffalo hide over them. In the center of the room, under the partial tipi, sat an old Indian man dressed in faded, worn buckskins. His hair was pure white and he looked up at Morgan.

"Come in, come in. Welcome to the Cheyenne

Nation. Come and sit and we will make many words together."

Buckskin sat cross-legged opposite the old Indian. The smoke came from a small fire the Indian had made in a large metal pan now between them. He fed a few sticks into it to maintain a small blaze. Most of the faint traces of smoke escaped out the window.

"I am Gray Bear, of the Cheyenne Nation. I come with big talk for you. You are Buckskin Morgan. My people know of you. We respect you because you respect our ways and our traditions."

The old man leaned forward and let the smoke rise over his shoulders and his face. He leaned back, nodding.

"The Great Spirit says that you are on a mission that may not be good for the Cheyenne. You have been hired to go to the place of the Cheyenne and find a small one known as Mighty Dawn. His mother is Willow and his father the man who owns this hotel, Alonzo Bishop."

Morgan spoke for the first time. He watched the wrinkled old Cheyenne and knew him to be a town Indian who had somehow heard of his new job.

"Why is the Great Spirit concerned with one small boy who is only one-quarter Cheyenne? Don't the Cheyenne have worry enough with the Pony Soldiers who chase them from one camp to another trying to force them back to the reservation?"

"I only know what the Great Spirit tells me in the smoke. He says that the small one, Mighty Dawn, is destined to become a great leader of the Cheyenne, and will lead them out of these troubles and across the great border into the far reaches of the north country, and there we will prosper and increase in numbers and strength and live as our grandfathers did in the depths of the mighty forests."

Morgan nodded. "For many years the Cheyenne have had such a dream, but their leaders have not made the trek north. They have a chance to go each summer, but they dally in summer camps or on hunting trips searching for the buffalo that are vanishing from the plains and the woodlands. Why does the Great Spirit think this mostly white-eyes boy can move the Cheyenne Nation north when your best leaders of the People of today can't do it?"

The old Indian shook his head. "It is sad that the Great Spirit did not tell me the answer to your question. I know only what he says. I am to tell you that you must not go to the land of the Cheyenne. You must not attempt to remove Mighty Dawn from the Cheyenne camp. Some great ill will fall upon you if you try this." He closed his eyes, lifted his head to the ceiling, and said half a dozen words in the Cheyenne language. Then he looked back at Morgan. "Our talking is finished."

"Old Grandfather, it has been good talking with you. I have given my word I will go to Cheyenne lands and search for the boy. I must be true to my word. Now I need to find a barber. I'll be back in half an hour."

Morgan had a trim on his hair. He wore it longer than most men, letting it cover part of his ears and almost touch his collar in back. When he was finished and walked back to his room, the

Indian and his trappings were gone. Nothing was missing. The door was locked.

Morgan dismissed it, wondering what he would find in Cheyenne, Wyoming. It was almost 400 miles across the plains of Nebraska and into the edge of Wyoming. Ten years ago by horseback it would have taken him ten hard days of riding. Even the stagecoach would have taken five days of rough bouncing around.

With the modern miracle of the railroad, he would be in Cheyenne sometime tomorrow morning. Amazing.

It was just after ten o'clock the following morning when Lee Buckskin Morgan stepped off the train at the Cheyenne, Wyoming Territory, platform. At least no delegation of Indians met him with lances and war paint. He had not given the visit of the old Indian a second thought. Somehow the Indian knew of the boy. Perhaps he had made friends with Bishop's wife, and had urged her to go back to the tribe. He then would know of her going, and would know about Bishop hiring someone to go get the boy.

Now Morgan looked around, found the best hotel, picked up his traveling bag, and went down the dusty street to the boardwalk and then to the Pride of Wyoming Hotel. It had three stories, fronted the town's 15th Street, and had a wide overhang that covered the boardwalk in front of it. The overhang would come in handy on a rainy day or when the snow piled up in the winter, Morgan decided.

He checked in, asking for a front room on the second floor. The room was much the same as other hotels in the West. Wallpapered with a border two feet down from the ceiling. A bed, a small dresser with a cracked mirror, a wash basin and pitcher made of heavy crockery. The window had soft curtains that looked new and opened on the street.

He paused a moment at the window watching below. Mules and horses pulled wagons and buggies. A team of six mules angled away from the railroad dock with a load of goods heading toward some small community.

He saw a short man with a blanket around his shoulders slip from one street to the alley and wander down it. Yes! He could be an Indian or a half-breed. One of them might know where the Cheyenne bands had their summer camps in this area. They would be well back in the mountains, but were they the mountains to the north or to the west? He changed clothes into his buckskin shirt and tan pants and brown hat with the red diamonds on it and hurried down to the street.

It took Morgan an hour to find an Indian. He was sitting on the steps of a tinware and hardware store at the far end of town. Morgan sat down beside him and the Indian looked up. He was a breed, dark hair and skin and blue eyes. He was also half drunk.

"What's your name?" Morgan asked.

The breed looked up, suspicion in his eyes. "Why?"

"I like to call a man by his name. Mine is Lee Morgan. What's yours?"

"Breed, Jim Breed. Everybody in town knows me."

"You drink a little?"

"Yeah. Why not?"

"Just wondered. You know where any Cheyenne bands are camped?"

"All went to Canada."

"Sure, beyond the big border into the northland. The Cheyenne dream that never will be. How many bands still outwitting the Pony Soldiers?"

Jim looked up, frowning now. "You from the Army?"

"No, Jim."

"Why you want to know about Cheyenne bands?"

"I'm looking for somebody."

"Captured woman?"

"No. A young boy, Thirteen summers."

"White-eyes?"

"A breed, one-quarter Cheyenne."

"Part Cheyenne, to the Indians, all Cheyenne. Part white-eyes, to the white-eyes, all Cheyenne."

"I know. You go back to the blanket now and then?"

Jim Breed nodded.

"How far are they?"

"Can't say. Army hunting. I go now."

The half-Cheyenne stood and walked quickly down the street. Morgan wondered how many breeds there were in town. Might be some town Indians too. He turned and walked toward the center of town.

He had just gone past a general store when a woman gasped and put her hand to her mouth. She glared at him, ran ahead, and caught the hand of her small girl and hurried into a store.

On down the street two men looked at him and froze in place. Both were careful to keep their hands far away from the guns on their hips.

Morgan frowned. What was this? Why was he so menacing all of a sudden? He had just arrived in town. Ahead a saloon door swung open and four men came out, two of them drunk. They stopped and looked at him and the two drunks turned back into the saloon.

The other two stood their ground, hands poised near shooting irons. Morgan didn't even look at them as he walked past. He heard one of them snort.

"Hell, he don't look so damn fast."

Morgan turned into the next saloon. He had no idea what was going on. As always, Morgan surveyed the men in the drinking establishment to check for anyone who might be dangerous. In past years, he'd made enemies and they sometimes turned up in unexpected places.

There were 15 men there, six at the bar, the rest at tables, some playing poker. The closest three men at the bar looked up and when they could see him well, they quickly moved to the far end of the bar.

One man whispered to the next and they watched him. Morgan discounted it and walked to the bar and dropped a quarter on the polished surface.

"Draft," he said. The apron looked at him, his eyes went wide, and then he hurried to the tap, drew a beer, spilling it over the side, and placed it gently in front of Morgan.

"No . . . no charge," the barkeep said, and scuttered away.

Morgan sipped the beer, turned, and leaned against the bar. Every man in the place had been staring at him. Now they went back to their card games or drinks.

Strange, Morgan thought. This was a small town, but with the railroad they must have new people coming in here all the time. He sipped the beer and saw the furtive look of one cardplayer. No, it was more than curiosity, there was fear there. Reluctant respect at the least, fear at the most. It was more then his tied-down holster, much more. He signaled to the barkeep, who hurried up to him.

"Yes, sir?"

"What's your name?"

"Si."

"Si, what's the matter with all these men? They act like I'm going to shoot their heads off."

"They respect the way you can use that hog-leg."

"How can they? I just got into town."

"You been here before."

"You know me, Si?"

"Yes, sir, Mr. Johnson. I sure do."

"Interesting. Keep the quarter, Si. Thanks for the information."

Morgan turned and looked at the men at the end of the bar, then at those around the tables, and walked out of the saloon. Strange. He must remind them of someone. Johnson, Si said. Called him Mr. Johnson. Morgan shrugged. Might make his job easier in this town at that.

He turned down the boardwalk and heard someone call from the middle of the street.

"Johnson, you yellow-bellied rattlesnake, you shot my brother in the back!"

People on the sidewalk stopped. Morgan halted and turned to see who was talking. One man stood alone in the middle of the dusty Cheyenne street. He motioned at Morgan.

"Yeah, Johnson, you bastard. You heard me. Are you man enough to take on a real man face-to-face? Or do you need ten of your riders with you to cut down all the honest men in town first?"

Morgan looked around. Everyone had faded away from him. He stood alone on the boardwalk.

"Are you speaking to me?" Morgan asked.

"Damn right. You know anybody else standing in your shoes called Slade Johnson?"

"That isn't my—"

"Come on! Come on! Stop stalling. I've got you without your dozen side-guns. Just you and me. Go ahead and draw. I'm gonna love every minute of killing you. Die slow, you bastard, Johnson, die slow."

Before Morgan could shout at the man, the stranger's hand darted for his side and came up with his six-gun. Morgan was well behind in starting the draw, but the butt of his hand pushed the handle of his Peacemaker upward, his fingers closed around the grip, one finger on the trigger.

In the same motion his right thumb pulled back the Colt's hammer to full cock. By then the muzzle of the weapon was out of leather and Morgan pushed it forward and lifted it in a point-and-shoot motion so fast that it was automatic and almost too quick to be followed by the naked eye.

The other man had drawn first, but Morgan's .45 belched smoke and a tongue of flame and the man in the street never got a shot off. His body slammed backwards three feet from the force of the big .45 round. He spun as he fell and ended on his back, a growing stain of blood on his shirt-front over his heart.

"Lord A'mighty! Did you see that Slade draw!" somebody shouted.

"He drew first," Morgan said. "You all saw him draw first. I had no choice but to fire at him."

"Yeah, Slade, but that was Harry Cowdering," somebody in the crowd shouted. "He was a rancher, not a gunsharp."

"His fault he's dead," Morgan said. "He drew down on me. Now somebody get the sheriff."

A man stepped from the crowd and strode forward. He was half a foot shorter than Morgan, slender, and wore a gun and a star on his chest.

"I'm Sheriff Goranson, Slade. I saw the whole thing. Much as I hate to admit it, you're right. You tried to stop the man from calling you out. Only time I ever seen you do that." He pointed at two men in the crowd. "You and you, carry Cowdering down to the undertaker."

He walked up to Morgan. For a moment he frowned. "You cutting your hair different, Slade? Don't bother. Come down to the office and sign a statement. You're cleared this time. But I can't say much what the folks hereabouts might do if you try to stay in town overnight."

"Slade Johnson. Is that supposed to be me, Sheriff?"

"Has been since you blew into town six months ago. You gonna change your spots or something?"

"Sheriff, my name is Lee Morgan. I come from Idaho."

The sheriff stopped and looked at Morgan. "Slade, you call yourself whatever you want. Don't make no matter to me. You just sign the paper Slade Johnson and I'll be happy."

The sheriff scratched his jaw. "Your manner

sure has changed. Downright meek you are now. You get religion or something, Slade?"

"That must be it, Sheriff," Morgan said. Right then all he wanted to do was sign the paper and get out of the sheriff's office. He was here to find the kid, not play games with some local fast gun. In the office the sheriff wrote out a statement saying that the other man drew first and it was self-defense. Morgan signed it. He put down Lee before he remembered, then continued with Slade Johnson and the sheriff was satisfied.

"I knew you were in town the minute you stepped off the morning train, Johnson. Do the town a favor and keep on going. Don't know where you put your men, but pick them up and ride out, west or east. Hell, ride north if you want and help the Army run down the redskins."

"Just might do that, Sheriff."

"Wouldn't plan on staying in that hotel room tonight. Second-floor windows got busted out by dynamite bombs in this town more than once. Lots of folks around here would have a real hoedown celebration if'n somehow you was to turn up dead."

"Thanks, Sheriff, I'll remember that." He walked out to the street and cut down the first alley he came to. It paralleled the main street. He checked the back of four saloons before he found him. Jim Breed had been thrown out of a saloon, probably after mooching too many drinks from customers.

Morgan knelt beside him, shook him awake, and watched as the liquor-loaded Indian blinked open his eyes.

He came closer to sober by several notches, his

eyes wide now as he realized who he was looking at.

"Slade, didn't mean no harm. Never bothered you none, Slade."

"Jim, why do you think I'm Slade Johnson?"

Breed's brows raised. "You right tall, kind of skinny. Got same hat with black band and red squares. Who else wears a hat like that?"

"So, I guess I have to kill you, Jim Breed." He drew his .45 and the Indian scooted back, his face working, sweat popped out on his forehead.

"Don't got to kill Breed."

"You didn't tell me what I wanted to know earlier this morning. Remember?"

"Jim no-good drunk. Not worth shooting."

"Probably. Still I could use the practice. Haven't killed a man for fun in two, three days now."

"Jim knows where there's one Cheyenne band. Summer camp, long time use."

"Might buy your life, Jim. How far?"

"Two days' ride. Into mountains."

"You have a horse?" Morgan answered his own question. "You want a saddle? I'll rent us some horses. We'll leave first thing in the morning. No, we'll get outfitted and leave as soon as we can. That way you'll stay sober. No more booze. Lead the way to the livery stable."

It took nearly two hours to rent two horses and saddles and gear, then get some trail food and cooking pans. Morgan slipped into the hotel and took out his traveling bag. He left it at the freight-line office in storage.

He was passing the biggest saloon and show hall in town when he saw a drawing of a girl in the window. She was tall and blond and something about the drawing stopped him.

Gunslinger's Scalp

The broadside announced that Miss Peaches La Belle, direct from New York's glittering stage, would be singing and dancing at the Pride of the Prairie Saloon starting tonight. He looked at two tintype pictures below the drawing.

The same friendly blonde he had met on the train stared back at him. She'd said she was coming to Cheyenne. She'd also told him not to try to find her, she would be somebody else.

When he got back from the mountains he would look her up. He had some questions to ask her. After that, you could never tell what might happen.

Morgan took a back street to the livery where their horses waited. Jim Breed had just finished tying on the blanket rolls when Morgan walked up. He unfastened them, went through them and then the saddlebags, and took out one pint of whiskey.

Jim grinned and shrugged.

Morgan tossed the bottle to the stable hand. "Keep this for me until we get back," he said. Then the two mounted up and rode.

"Two days to the camp?" Morgan said.

"Might be longer without the whiskey," Jim said.

Morgan eyed him a moment, then scowled. "If it is, Jim Breed, you won't have to worry about riding that horse back. You'll be walking without your boots."

Chapter Three

They rode the shank of the afternoon due west into the Laramie Mountains. Just before dark, Jim found a small valley next to a trickle of a stream. It had been grazed down and Morgan could tell that a small band had camped here for some time and moved on.

"How long ago?" Morgan asked.

Jim shrugged. "Ain't too good at that kind of thing. Maybe a week, maybe two. We'll stay here tonight and then swing south."

"Into the Rocky Mountains?"

"One mountain looks like another mountain to me, unless it's a sacred mountain."

They built a small fire and Morgan fried bacon and sliced potatoes in a skillet, and they munched on rolls spread with a strawberry jam from a jar to go with their boiled coffee.

"Almost like a damn restaurant," Lee Buckskin

Morgan said. He handed the empty tin plates and skillet to Jim, who stared at him.

"You ate, now wash the dishes in the creek. Use sand for soap and get them clean."

They slept that night under the stars and a few scrubby pine trees.

"Where you figure they went?" Morgan asked the breed as the fire died.

"South, they go south, the Army go north," Jim said. The next thing Morgan heard from him was a long, low snore.

With morning breakfast out of the way, they rode. They made good time through the foothills and a long, low valley, then came to the rising slopes and the far-off sight of the Rocky Mountains.

"A two-day ride?" Morgan asked.

Jim Breed shrugged. "Depends on the horse. Some run, some walk."

Morgan nodded grimly. To an Indian a two-day ride might take a week or a month, depending how fast they rode, how many times they stopped, and how many interesting things happened along the way.

They rode all day generally south. Twice they stopped at small streams and Jim looked them over carefully, trailing a mile each way along the water looking for sign. Then they moved on. The band had not stopped at either place.

It was just before dark when they came to a third stream. Morgan figured they must be well into Colorado by now. He had watched the landfalls and terrain as they rode. He could come back to this spot alone if he had to.

Jim returned from his downstream search and nodded.

"Band stopped here for two, three days, maybe a week ago. Still moving."

The next morning they paused on a slope of a ridge and Jim Breed listened. He got off his horse and tied it and moved up the slope cautiously. He went about 50 yards and Morgan dismounted and followed him. Near the ridge line he motioned Morgan to stay back.

Jim crawled to the top of the ridge and looked over. A moment later he motioned Morgan to come up.

Below them was a valley two miles long. It had a chattering stream through the middle large enough to water a hundred horses.

Toward the far end in a green carpet of trees, a dozen plumes of smoke lifted slowly into the sky.

"Cheyenne," Jim said.

"How can you tell from here?"

"Smokes spaced out along river." Jim grinned. "Been following Cheyenne trail all day."

"I'm looking for a half-white-eyes woman and a quarter-Cheyenne boy of thirteen."

"Leave horses here," Jim said.

A half hour later they had worked their way cautiously through brush and cover until they were within 200 yards of the Indian summer camp. About 30 tipis spotted the sides of the stream. At the far end of the camp a rope corral of sorts had been rigged and horses were penned there, plus another 40 or so grazed in the end of the valley on spring grass.

Six or eight young boys rode ponies around and through the camp yelping and staging mock attacks on the women and the other children. Morgan could see few warriors.

Gunslinger's Scalp

A two-man hunting party rode in from the north, a deer slung between them on a long pole. A shout went up from the village and the women clustered around.

"Look for women with no men," Jim explained.

Morgan took out the pictures of Willow and the boy and showed both to Jim. He looked at them and grunted.

"Woman looks all white-eyes," he said.

"She's half-Cheyenne. The boy is half of that half-Cheyenne."

Jim turned over on his back and chewed on a stem of grass.

"Aren't you going in and talk to your people?"

"Need a why. They ask me why you here. You like town white-eyes so much, why you back here?"

"Tell them for whiskey."

Jim laughed softly. "They don't have whiskey. Whiskey with white-eyes in town-town. Why am I find Gray Owl band?"

"You left your horses with them?"

"Got no horses."

"You left your woman here."

"Got no woman, no family."

"White-eyes chased you out of town?"

Jim grinned and sat up. "Yes. I come to eat. I hunt for the no-warrior women!"

Jim turned over and looked at the camp again. He searched until he found a lookout this side of the tipis. He pointed out where the guard stood.

"He a boy, fourteen summers. Watch for Army. I go. You stay here."

Morgan watched the Cheyenne town half-breed work down the slope through the better growth of pine now and smaller trees. He moved like a shadow. After he was a hundred yards forward, Morgan stepped out, following much the same route Jim Breed had taken, moving as quietly as he could. Not breaking a branch, not stepping down until he was sure his boot would make no noise.

He paused and watched Jim step silently in front of the guard. The Indian boy yelped when he saw him. They talked a little and then Jim walked openly the last 100 yards into the Indian camp.

Morgan moved around the lookout, working closer to the camp. When he was 50 yards away he paused and watched the tipis. He had no way of knowing where the woman and her boy might be. She didn't have a warrior, so she would have to do some service or marry a warrior to survive.

He settled down with brush and weeds covering him, and looked out at the camp. He counted 32 tipis. That meant 32 warriors. These men were classified by the Army as renegades. The Cheyenne had been ordered into the reservation. About half had gone in. The rest had fled into the hills, scattering so it would be harder to find and capture them. The warriors were fighters, and Morgan had dozens of reasons not to be caught by them.

He had no idea how he could contact the woman. At first he thought he might slip into the camp after dark and talk with her and the boy. Present the offer that he had worked up for the woman. Maybe she was tired of the hard work of a Cheyenne woman by now. The Indian women did all the work in camp, from scraping the hides of the animals to cooking and making clothes, to packing and moving the tipis and setting them up again.

Perhaps she had forgotten how hard a Cheyenne woman's life really was. Warriors spent their time either raiding other tribes or whites, or talking about raiding and bragging, or riding around on their war ponies trying to look important on the pretense of guarding the camp.

Morgan had decided he would offer her $1,000 in gold to come out of the camp and return the boy to his father. If she didn't want to go back to Grand Island, she could take the money and ride the train to San Francisco, buy a house, and start a boardinghouse.

But how did he get to the woman?

He saw Jim moving around in the village. He still wore denim pants and the checkered shirt with the cut-off sleeves and a cast-off, filthy Western hat that had once been brown.

Jim talked to several of the men sitting in front of their tipis, then went to another tipi where he lifted the tent flap and spoke. A moment later he vanished inside.

Morgan marked the tipi. It was the fifth one in from the nearest end of the camp. It was directly beside the stream and even from this distance looked old and worn. It might be a discarded tipi cover that someone had saved for a bride or a charity case.

So she was here! The boy must be with her. Finding her had been his biggest worry. Now the next one came. How could he get her and the boy, or at least the boy, out from the middle of an angry bunch of Cheyenne warriors?

He checked the tipi again. There were tipis on both sides of it, so he couldn't just sneak in out of the woods and cut a hole in the back and slip inside. Not a chance.

He would have to talk Jim Breed into bringing the woman and the boy out into the woods so he could talk to them. Maybe they could go out collecting berries and roots.

Just before the sun went behind the hills, Morgan saw the breed leave the camp and strike out into the hills. Morgan cut him off before he got back to the spot where they had spied on the camp.

"You found her," Morgan said.

"You watched me."

"True. Will she come back, or will she let the boy come back?"

"She laughed at me when I asked that," Jim Breed said. "She wondered why husband wait so long to send someone."

"How can I get to talk to her?"

"She say she want talk you. She go tomorrow digging roots and picking berries. She go north. We find her alone."

The two of them walked back to their horses and made a cold and dry camp. They didn't want the Cheyenne smelling smoke in an area where there shouldn't be any. They ate biscuits and jerky for their meal and drank cold water from their canteens.

In the morning, they left the horses where they were and walked to the north of the camp, found a place they could see the slopes leading upward, and waited.

About ten o'clock they saw three women working up the slope finding berries.

Jim pointed. "One in blue hat."

She was smaller than he had expected. Wore

a Cheyenne buckskin skirt and an Army shirt and the blue fancy woman's hat some warrior had looted from a ranch or farmhouse.

She chattered with the women with her, then pointed them one way. She went the other way. When the women were out of sight, Jim stood up and waved. She came toward where the two men waited.

Her eyes were startling blue when she looked up at Morgan from three feet away.

"So Bishop finally sent someone," she said. "I hope he paid you well, he can afford it. Mighty Dawn and I are not leaving. We like it here. Tell him that. Tell him I have a husband who knows what it means to love his wife every night. Be sure that you tell him that."

"You know the Army is hunting down this band of Cheyenne, Mrs. Bishop," Morgan said. "You and your son could be killed in the first fight with them."

"We're Cheyenne, we'll take our chances."

"Why?"

"Why not? I'm half-Cheyenne. I like the freedom of the band. I like to know that I'm living close to Mother Earth and Father Moon. I love my heritage."

"You married?"

"Yes. My husband, Wounded Elk, would kill you slowly if he caught you. Then he would beat me and I would deserve it."

"You like being a slave to your husband? Like doing all the work, making the meals, moving the tipi?"

"It is my place to do the work. I am a Cheyenne woman."

"You're also white."

"That part of me is dead."

"What about the future for Harold? I hear that he's bright in his studies."

"He was. He likes it here. Someday he will lead this band. He speaks English and Cheyenne. He can parley with the white-eyes. He will be a great Cheyenne chief."

"If he isn't slaughtered in a raid by five hundred soldiers."

They stared at each other.

"Can I talk to the boy? He must be almost fourteen by now. Maybe he wants to go back to Grand Island."

"I won't let you talk to him. No."

"You're afraid to."

"If I scream right now, there will be ten mounted warriors here before you can spit twice. Then we'll see how sassy your mouth is."

"If I'm going to die, you'll be the first one to go. Then who'll take care of Harold? I'm thinking of the boy's future."

"You're thinking of the bonus Bishop offered you to bring him home. I know my husband, whoever you are. I know him too well."

They stared at each other for a moment. He was surprised how small and delicate she looked. He didn't see how she could erect a tipi and do all the hard work that was needed. Her face was much darker now, probably from the sun, but he suspected she might have used some dye to darken it as well to make her look more Cheyenne.

"Look, we're both happy here. Just go back and tell Bishop that. I have nothing against you for trying to do a job. But it's a job I won't let be done. Harold is happy here. He's learning new things, he's discovering his heritage, and he's fascinated with the Cheyenne way of living. I have only his best interests at heart. I would do nothing to jeopardize my only son."

Morgan nodded. "Except expose him to warfare with the whole U.S. Army and Cavalry." He shrugged. "Then there's nothing more for me to do. I've made my pitch, done my try. Now I'll report that you and the boy won't come and for me, that will the end of it."

They heard someone coming and the two men darted into the heavier growth. Willow began searching the ground for the sweet/tart evergreen blackberry vines that grew low to the soil and produced delicious berries for half the summer.

The other two berry-pickers came through the brush and saw Willow, and the three of them turned a new course hunting the elusive low-growing blackberries.

Morgan let out a long breath. One of the other Indian women had stepped within six inches of his leg. She hadn't seen him. When they were sure the women were gone, they rose from the ground and worked cautiously higher on the slope, and then to the left and back toward their horses.

"You will try to see the boy?"

"Yes, but not now. She'll keep a close rein on him for the next week. In a week we'll come back and I'll talk to the boy one way or another. I owe my employer that much at least."

"We go back to town?" Jim asked.

Morgan nodded. "I'm afraid so. At least we found her and you have good enough standing in the band to come and go freely. That will help a lot the next time we ride out here."

It took them two days to get back to town. The morning of the second day, Jim Breed saw a pair of jackrabbits. He slipped up on them and from 20 feet shot one with Morgan's revolver. They stopped and cleaned and skinned the rabbit and roasted it over a fire, then ate until it was all gone.

Morgan wiped his hands on the long grass and looked at Jim. "How did you learn to slip up on a rabbit that way, Jim?"

The shorter man laughed. "Cheyenne half rabbit," he said, and they both laughed.

They were back in town by four that afternoon. Morgan carried his hat as he went back to the freight office and ransomed out his traveling case. He took out another hat from his case, a small billed kind, and put it on. From a kit he took a pair of wire-rimmed glasses and put them on, then changed his shirt to a city kind and checked himself. Now he didn't look at all like himself, or Slade Johnson.

He walked across the street to the hotel, registered as Lamont Jones, and was shown a room on the second floor front. So much for fooling the local folks. He had a week to spend in town before he could try to contact the boy. He sent a telegram to Bishop reporting his progress. He had found Willow and spoken with her, but not the boy. He'd try again to see the boy and bring him out if he could. It would take at least a week more.

That out of the way, Morgan went to the best-looking restaurant in town and had supper. He was nearly through when he saw a tall blond woman come in and sit by herself next to the window. He knew that walk, that long blond hair. The woman on the train who now called herself Peaches La Belle. He quit his supper and walked up to her table and cleared his throat.

When she looked up he took off the glasses and smiled. "The train's dining car is crowded tonight, miss. I wonder if you would mind if I shared your table?"

She looked at him quickly. "Train? I don't . . ." She stopped. A slow smile slipped onto her face and she nodded. "I told you not to try to find me."

"I didn't try to, you simply walked into my life again. I've already finished my supper."

"By now, you must know why I thought I knew you. You look so much like Slade it's frightening. You could be his twin."

"I know. I've already killed a man who thought I was him. Are you really singing and dancing at the saloon?"

"Oh, yes, really. I work . . . various places." She looked around. "Please put your glasses back on. It helps. I can't be seen with you here."

"Then where?"

"You don't understand. I can't see you, be with you. Not in Cheyenne."

Morgan frowned. "You're right, I don't understand. My real name is Lee Morgan."

"I'm sorry I can't explain. Call me Shirley. Peaches is my stage name. I can't explain. Will you please leave?"

"I'd rather cause a scene. I will if you don't tell me when and where I can see you again."

"All right. But I can't explain. Tonight, after the show. The Pride of Wyoming Hotel. Room 222."

"I'll be there. Midnight?"

She nodded. He stood, pushed the chair back in, bowed slightly, and walked out of the restaurant. What a strange, beautiful girl. What was she hiding from? Why couldn't she be seen with him? Was it because he looked a lot like Slade Johnson? That must be it. Maybe she was afraid of Johnson. Maybe.

He walked the streets for half an hour and nobody mistook him for Slade Johnson. The cap and glasses and shirt helped. If he had a stick-on mustache he would wear that.

Back in his hotel room, 228, he broke down his Colt Peacemaker and cleaned and oiled it. Then he reloaded it with five rounds and filled two empty slots in the loops in his gun belt with the .45 cartridges.

He wrote down in a small journal, which he'd bought for his current job, the progress to date. It made writing a report later much easier. He put down the approximate location of the Cheyenne band and the name of it, the Gray Owl band.

Time seemed to drag. He had nothing to do until midnight. Twice he tried playing some solitaire, but the cards were not going his way.

He went for a walk about ten o'clock and watched a poker game for an hour, then went back to the hotel. He made it a point not to go into the Pride of the Prairie Saloon where Shirley sang.

Morgan went through his traveling bag and tried to arrange things. Then at last it was midnight, and he locked his door and walked down the hallway to Room 222.

Morgan knocked and heard a voice say something inside. He turned the knob and opened the door.

46

Gunslinger's Scalp

The thundering blast of a shotgun roared like a dozen steam engines all at once as it went off. Morgan staggered backward as half the world fell on top of him and he knew he was slamming into the hall. Then it didn't matter anymore because everything turned black, as black as death.

Chapter Four

Mighty Dawn sat near the stream watching the boys riding their ponies through the camp. He was learning to ride, but most of the Cheyenne boys his age were much better at it than he was. They told him they had been riding ponies since they were five years old. This was much different than living in Grand Island.

He didn't have his own pony yet but his new father, Wounded Elk, said that on his fourteenth birthday he would be given one. Mighty Dawn practiced riding every day. He had to borrow a pony to do so, but he was learning.

The girls his age were playing a game of hockey on the open space beyond the stream. They used curved sticks and hit a ball made of leather and stuffed with horsehair and pebbles. It was a foolish girls' game.

Mighty Dawn had heard his Indian name since

he was a small boy, but he wasn't used to it yet. Sometimes he wished he was back in Grand Island. He did miss his school. Science fascinated him. He wanted to know more about why things worked, and why the stars and the moon came out every night. His mother had said that would wait. They were here to learn all they could about being Cheyenne.

He knew some of the language that his mother had taught him. For three months he had sat at the feet of an old warrior who taught him how to speak the Cheyenne language. He had learned enough by now to get along.

One of the boys, who was a year older than he, ran to Mighty Dawn and slid down beside him.

"Come play a game with us," the Cheyenne boy said.

Mighty Dawn nodded and jumped up. It wasn't often the others asked him to play. He had no real friends among the boys his own age yet. It would come in time, his mother kept telling him.

The boys walked over to where a dozen others had gathered. They were divided into two lines facing each other. The boys were from 12 to 14, some nearly as big as grown warriors.

"What kind of a game?" Mighty Dawn asked.

His new friend gave him a strip from a buffalo robe and wrapped it around his right forearm.

"Easy game. We line up and then run at each other and try to kick the other team to the ground. The robes on our arms help take the kicks."

"That's all?"

"No, when we kick one down then we all jump on him and pound him with our fists until he bleeds or gives up."

"Won't the others on his team stop us?"

"They'll try. When one boy gives, up, he's out of the game."

"What if he won't give up?"

"Then we make him bleed. When he bleeds, he's out of the game too."

Then it was too late for any more explanations. The sides lined up and the boys glared at each other. One boy on each team shrilled out a Cheyenne war cry and the two lines charged each other.

Mighty Dawn was a little larger than the boys his own age, and heavier. He charged a boy and ran into him, then kicked at his feet. One foot lifted and he blocked it with his arm, then kicked at the other foot, and the Indian boy fell down.

But before Mighty Dawn could pounce on him, the boy sprang up and shouted something. Another boy darted in to help the first and both attacked Mighty Dawn, driving him back. Then he missed one kick and felt the sting on his shins and before he knew it, the boy knocked his other foot from under him and he sprawled on the ground.

He wore only the traditional breechclout and moccasins, and now tried to squirm away from the pair of brown bodies that fell on him. He knew not to cry out for help. The fists of the other boys pounded him. He doubled up his own and smashed one into the nose of one boy and saw him fall away.

Now it was more even. He rolled over and pinned the boy below him. He pounded on the smaller boy's shoulders and his face and then saw blood pour from the downed boy's nose. He leaped up shouting in victory, and the bleeding youth stood slowly and then ran to the stream to wash off and stop the nosebleed.

Before he could celebrate, another youth charged into him. Mighty Dawn fought with him. The youth was strong and wiry. They kicked and punched each other, but neither could get the advantage. Then the boy who had come and talked to Mighty Dawn at the creek slipped up from behind and kicked both feet from Mighty Dawn's opponent and he crumpled into the dirt.

Both boys fell on him, pounding him until he screamed in rage, and when he could stand it no more he shouted that he gave up.

When the two victorious Cheyenne youth stood, they saw that only three others were still in the game. Two of them were from their side, and they ran the last enemy across the creek and then hooted at him and the other losers and gave a shout and a cheer of victory.

When the cheer was over, the boys all went to the creek and sat in the cold water and washed the dirt and dust off their bodies. They splashed each other and continued to hoot at the losers.

"You fought well today, Mighty Dawn," his new friend said. "I am called Yellow Feather." The Cheyenne youth was 14, as tall as Mighty Dawn and as strong. They sat on the bank of the stream drying off in the sun and talked until it was almost dark.

"Do you want to ride my war pony tomorrow?" Yellow Feather asked.

Mighty Dawn nodded. "Yes, let's meet early in the morning so we'll have all day." Mighty Dawn went back to his stepfather's tipi feeling better than he had in weeks. Yellow Feather had the fastest and biggest pony of any of the young boys.

Tomorrow Mighty Dawn would get to ride it!

When Mighty Dawn entered the tipi, he saw his mother lying on her pallet. It was not like her to lie down during the day. He walked over to her and she stirred and tried to sit up, but sagged down.

"Mother, you're hurt!" Mighty Dawn said in English. She shook her head, shushing him.

"No English," she said. "I was just a little tired."

"You work too hard here. At home we had servants to do the work. Now you work harder than our cook and cleaning woman together."

"It is the way of the People, Mighty Dawn. It is the way. Now, bring me a big bowl of water from the creek so I can get our evening meal ready."

Before Mighty Dawn could move, Wounded Elk came in the tipi and threw down his buckskin shirt and his bow.

"Food, woman. Where is my food? I'm hungry." He saw her on the pallet and scowled. "Sick again, wife? I made a mistake to marry a woman who already has a child. Now you won't get pregnant for me. I can always dissolve our marriage or take another wife or two."

He looked at her, then at the boy. "Ah, Mighty Dawn. You are starting to live up to your name. I saw your game today by the river. You bloodied two and made one give up. Good work. I remember the game well. The boys who won the most times always became leaders in the band and the whole tribe. I have some good news for you."

He looked back at his wife. "Woman, get me food, now. There's a council tonight I must sit at."

Gunslinger's Scalp

Wounded Elk took the lad by the shoulders and steered him outside. They sat in front of the tipi and looked at the stream.

"This is good land. We must keep it for the Cheyenne until the moon fails to rise. We must protect it. Tomorrow we will go on a raid. The white-eyes have put a trail through the mountains from one of their small villages to another. A box pulled by six horses goes over the trail once a day.

"Tomorrow we will stop it and close the trail and keep the land for the Cheyenne. Tomorrow the council has agreed to let you and Yellow Feather come along with us on the raid to hold our horses and to gather wood. It will be a fine experience for you as a future leader of our people."

"A raid? I'm to go along?" For a moment Mighty Dawn could not speak. Then the words tumbled out too fast. "I'm excited about it. It's been my wish now for a month. But what shall I ride? I have no war pony."

Wounded Elk turned and pointed to a tree just behind the tipi. Tied to it was a brown pony with four white spots on it. The pony had a hackamore on it and a surcingle around his belly and back.

"Go ahead, take a ride," Wounded Elk said.

Mighty Dawn's face broke into a wide grin and he raced toward the horse, then remembered and walked slowly up to the animal. He patted his flank, then scratched the long brown neck, and at last petted the animal on the neck and rubbed behind his ears.

"His name is Thunder because he was born in a furious thunderstorm when the gods of the wind were fighting. He's yours."

"Great! Thanks! Can I ride him?"

"Until it gets dark." The Cheyenne warrior stood there watching the youth with the horse. A moment later Mighty Dawn vaulted to Thunder's back, picked up the braided hackamore, and rode away.

Inside the tipi, Wounded Elk watched Willow working on an Indian stew made of a rabbit he had brought home that morning.

"When is the food?" he demanded.

Willow looked up. "Soon, husband, soon."

Wounded Elk reached down and backhanded her across the face, toppling her over near the fire.

"Next time have my food ready when I get home." He went outside and watched his son ride the painted pony. The two soon worked well together. A bond had been formed quickly. The boy would do well on the raid tomorrow.

The next morning an hour before daylight, the warriors and the two youths met at the horse corral. All were ready to ride. It would be only a one-day raid, so the warriors carried no food or water. They knew these mountains from many summer camps.

They rode steadily for four hours. The tough little Indian ponies didn't ever seem to tire. Yellow Feather and Mighty Dawn rode behind the rest of the party. It was their job to report anyone who lagged, or if someone's horse went down. They each had small packets of food. Their mothers had insisted that they take food along. It was pemmican and some tough venison jerky.

The boys rode quietly, awed by the simple fact that they had been chosen to go on a raid with the warriors! That was the hope of every boy their age in camp. It meant that they had been watched by the men and deemed to be ready to take the first step toward becoming warriors.

Nowhere did they see any buffalo. One sure way to gain status from being a mere boy to becoming a man was to kill a buffalo single-handed. Now with the buffalo vanishing from the prairie and the mountains, they would need a new animal to be killed by the young men.

Yellow Feather finally spoke. "You know we won't take any part in the raid."

"My father told me. We hold any horses that need to be held. We get firewood and run errands and bring water. Whatever needs to be done."

"This is woman's work!" Yellow Feather said with disdain.

"Still, I'd rather be doing it here than playing silly games back in our summer camp."

It was slightly before sun-overhead time when the party stopped. The boys crowded up close and listened to the leader of the raid, Gray Owl himself. Gray Owl was nearly 55 summers, but he still led the band on important raids.

"The river is below," Gray Owl said. "The wheeled coach comes along the track they have made near it. They come upstream and go somewhere to the sunset. They must not continue. The coach will bring more settlers, and diggers of Mother Earth, and more of the white man's buffalo animals, and the Cheyenne will know no peace ever again.

"Here we make our stand. Here we say this is our land. You may not come through our land."

He pointed to a thin line of a road that led along the length of the river that they could see.

"The coach crosses the Red Bird River. There

we will capture it." Gray Owl nudged his pony with his knees and the trained war pony stepped out and angled down the steep hillside, then cut back the other way, working down the quarter of a mile to the river.

They were there well before the coach would arrive. All the ponies were watered and allowed to graze for a few minutes. Then the warriors checked both sides of the stream for places to hide in the thick growth of trees and brush.

"No warrior must attack until the wheels are all in the stream," Gray Owl commanded. "Then we will capture the horses and the large coach will be ours." He looked around at the men. "There will be many prizes and captives for everyone."

The warriors divided themselves on each side of the river. It was little more than a creek, Mighty Dawn decided. Here it was 20 feet wide but no more than a foot deep any place that he could see.

He and Yellow Feather waited in some trees 50 yards back. They had no horses to hold. They were commanded not to participate in the fight unless the warriors were outnumbered or in danger of losing. The boys had only their small bows and arrows.

The boys were on a slight rise and saw the stagecoach coming first. Mighty Dawn had never ridden in one. He knew about the train, but not a coach pulled by horses. There were six horses on this one and it rolled along at a fast trot even though they were moving slightly uphill.

On the roof in front sat a driver holding long reins and another man he had heard called a shotgun guard. He couldn't see a shotgun. Bags and bundles were tied on a rack on the top of the rig and a boot in back had been roped shut, evidently holding more passengers' bags.

Until now, Mighty Dawn had not realized that there would be white people on the coach. It had been so wonderful to get to come. Now he knew that the people would be white-eyes, whites like himself—well, three quarters of himself.

He knew that the Cheyenne were kind and thoughtful people. Hadn't they taken him and his mother into their band, even though they both were half-breeds? Any captives would be treated kindly, he was sure. Ransomed perhaps for much money or for rifles and a herd of cattle. Yes, that was it, a herd of cattle.

Then the coach came closer and he could see the man on the top. He held a pipe clenched in his teeth, wore a black hat, and caught the 12 reins in his hands like he had driven six up a hundred times before.

Mighty Dawn looked at the edge of the trees where he knew there were six mounted warriors waiting. Three of them had single-shot rifles, and four of them six-gun revolvers. The rest had bows and arrows and the long lances with steel tips on them.

Yellow Feather's eyes sparkled. "It won't be long now," the Cheyenne youth said. "The horses are in the water now. They're walking across the water not knowing how deep it might be."

Mighty Dawn shivered. Suddenly, he was frightened for the driver and the guard and the passengers inside. Some of them would die, he was sure!

Then the rig had all four wheels in the stream. Piercing Cheyenne war cries shrilled through the calm and quiet of the Colorado mountain valley.

Two rifles fired and the driver slumped in his seat. The shotgun guard grabbed the reins and tried to keep the horses moving. Two arrows hit him, one in the side and one in the chest, and he toppled off the high seat and into the water.

Now all 12 Cheyenne warriors galloped out of hiding. The six-guns spoke and several rounds went through the windows of the rig. Two warriors kicked their ponies up to the struggling harnessed horses, caught their halters, and pulled them to a halt.

For a moment all was quiet. Then a gun fired from inside the coach and a warrior spun off his horse and died as he fell into the water. Twenty, then twice that many shots and arrows thundered into the coach through windows and doors.

Gray Owl held up his rifle and the firing stopped. Slowly the door on the coach opened and a man stumbled out. He had a revolver in his hand. The closest warrior slammed his war axe into the man's skull, cleaving it in half and dropping the white-eyes into the stream. Mighty Dawn shivered. Another white man had died! He hadn't counted on this.

All was quiet again. A warrior rode near the back of the stage, stepped from his pony to the rear boot, and jumped to the roof. He leaned over the top and looked inside. Then he stood and did a little dance on the roof and shouted that there were no more men inside, only three women.

Warriors rushed the coach. Whoever captured a prisoner owned that captive. Mighty Dawn had learned that during his stay. But there had been only one raid before and they'd brought back ten horses and no captives.

A warrior leaped inside the coach and came out with a white woman. She had blood on her dress. Her hat had fallen off and she screamed at the warrior and hit him with her free hand.

Two more warriors dragged women from the coach, led them to the shore, and then pushed them to the ground to examine their prizes.

Mighty Dawn could not follow all of the talk. Other warriors led the horses out of the stream, pulling the stage with them to the near side, and promptly began cutting the animals out of their harness. They would make good additions to the pony herd. Mighty Dawn heard one warrior say that his captured horse would be good for pulling the travois on their next move.

Yellow Feather and Mighty Dawn led their ponies and walked down the 50 yards to the scene. They watched from the edge of the woods.

One warrior looked at his captured woman. She was taller than he was, broad-shouldered and with a heavy body. He screamed in delight.

"I will make her my second wife and if she doesn't get with child in a year, she will be my slave instead."

He stripped the top garments from the woman over her shouted protests. Quickly he had her naked to the waist and the other warriors cheered in approval.

The second warrior checked his captive. She had deep red hair and was short, but sturdy. The warrior nodded and hoisted her onto his war pony. She slipped off the far side and ran. The owner of the prize caught her in ten steps and slapped her face one way and then the other.

She sat where she fell, and tears streamed down her face.

The third warrior stared at his woman with a scowl. She had an arrow deep in her shoulder. She sat and stared at the distant hills as if none of this had happened. He tried to make her stand up but she ignored his threats and his hard slaps.

She was thin and looked sickly. The warrior screamed at the rest of them that he had drawn the worst of the lot.

"I offer her for sale. Two horses, anyone? Surely one of you fine warriors can part with two horses for such a fine piece of woman."

"If she's so fine, you keep her," one warrior shouted.

Now the others who had not captured a woman or a horse tore open the traveling bags and boxes on the coach. One box had a lock that was promptly knocked off with a heavy rock. Inside was nothing but oblongs of green printed paper. The warriors took handfuls of them and threw them in the sky and watched them break apart and scatter and flutter to the ground.

Mighty Dawn edged down near to where the paper was and looked inside the box. There were still stacks of the paper there. He asked if he could touch it, and a laughing warrior said he could have the rest of it.

Mighty Dawn recognized the federal bank notes as soon as he saw them. The money meant nothing to these Cheyenne. He looked at the stacks of bundles of $20 bills. He had never seen so much money in his life. He took five of the bundles and pushed them inside the shirt that he wore. He still burned easily in the sun and his mother insisted that he wear the shirt.

Gunslinger's Scalp

Yellow Feather came up and frowned.

"The squares of paper, we can use them for a new game," Mighty Dawn said. Yellow Feather grinned and picked up the rest of the bundles of $20 bills and pushed them in a pouch he carried over his shoulder.

The warriors laughed and played with the clothing and treasured possessions of the four passengers. One woman pleaded that she be allowed to keep her carpetbag, but the warriors ripped up her dresses, and one put on a red hat and wore it proudly the rest of the trip.

Mighty Dawn wouldn't look at the bodies of the three men who lay in the water. It had happened so fast he hardly thought it was real. Only it was. It was the way of the People. The Cheyenne warriors lived to fight. That was their only skill in life, their only reason to be alive.

That was why they had not gone to the reservation. A place where they could not raid and fight and wage war would be a hell on earth for them. Mighty Dawn knew this. He and his mother had talked about it on the train as they rode west.

The belongings had been trashed and scattered and looted for anything that might help the Warriors. Two shirts and a man's hat were saved by one warrior. He proudly put on the red shirt and the black hat and rode around standing on the back of his war pony for everyone to see and applaud.

Gray Owl gave a signal and the warriors got ready to move. The dead warrior had been carried from the river. Now he was wrapped in a blanket and tied over his war pony. It would be led back to their camp.

The two warriors who had strong women mounted their ponies, then scooped up the women and straddled them over the pony in front of them. With both arms around the women, the warriors were ready to ride.

The third Cheyenne, who'd captured the woman who was thin and wounded by an arrow, watched her now with new interest. She wouldn't react to anything he did. He ripped her dress down the front, exposing her breasts, but she remained calm, looking at the horizon.

The warrior gave a terrible scream of anger and rage, and drew his knife and slashed the sharp blade across the woman's throat from one side to the other. Blood gushed in pulsating spurts from her neck. Then the woman fell over on her back. Before Mighty Dawn could run for his horse, the white woman died. He stared at her, so shocked he couldn't move. How could the warrior kill her that way?

The death of the captive did nothing to dampen the high spirits of the raiding party. They whooped and hollered as they began working back up the slope the way they had come down.

The men who captured the horses had them tied on lead lines behind them. The horses were used to going where they were led and followed sedately.

Both the white women screamed and tried to get free. One soon lost her voice. The other one gave up and quieted down. Mighty Dawn decided she must be saving her strength until she had a good chance to get away.

Mighty Dawn rode at the end of the party. He knew they would break into four groups to return to camp to throw off anyone who tried to track them.

He waited, and when he was sure where the white women were, he picked another group to follow so he would be far from them. He couldn't wipe out of his memory the expression on the woman's face when her throat was slashed. It didn't change. She must have been out of her mind. Yes, he decided, that was it. Mighty Dawn still trembled when he thought how easily the warrior had killed her.

The warrior could have left her there. Someone would have found her. No. He was a Cheyenne warrior. He owned the woman because he had captured her. By Cheyenne custom he could do anything that he wanted to with her. It was just bad luck that he had captured a woman of no value as a hostage, as a wife, or as a slave.

Mighty Dawn scowled at the thought. His mother had said it enough lately. It was the Cheyenne way. It didn't matter if it were right or not. It was the Cheyenne way, and that was the deciding argument in all things.

For the first time since he arrived in the village, Mighty Dawn wondered if he wanted to spend the rest of his life as a Cheyenne warrior. So far it all had been a wonderful outdoors summer vacation. Today things had changed. Everything was different now.

For a moment he felt the packets of $20 bills inside his shirt. There must be 100 bills in each packet. He had five of the bundles. He was good at figures and did it in his head. Each packet would make $2,000. Five of the stacks of bills would be worth $10,000. He was rich!

But a Cheyenne warrior couldn't use money.

It was simply so much paper. He would keep it, deep in a hidden place where it would be safe. Perhaps someday he could use it.

On the long ride home, Mighty Dawn tried and tried, but he could never erase the sight of that woman with blood spurting out of her throat. He shivered, shook his head slowly, and caught up with the warrior he followed toward the band's summer camp.

Chapter Five

"Hey, mister, you all right? Hey, wake up. Come on, you don't look hurt none too bad."

Sounds came, but they meant nothing. Lights blazed into his eyes, then were gone. The sounds again. Slowly he understood that the noises were people talking. Words. A few isolated words filtered through.

"Hey, mister!"

This time he heard it distinctly. So he wasn't dead. Almost dead. Still alive! The lights came back. He blinked and slowly the maze of light and dark turned into shapes, wavering and shifting, some upside down, some double where only one should be.

Lee Buckskin Morgan shook his head. He lay on the floor, just where he wasn't sure. The hallway, the room? He had been going in Room 222 when the universe exploded right in his face.

Then he remembered the blast, the unmistakable sound of a shotgun going off. Once you've heard that sound from the muzzle end, you never forgot it. Why wasn't he dead?

"Son, can you hear me? Your eyes are open, are you awake? I'm a doctor, young man, now talk to me."

He understood the words this time. A doctor. The wavering shapes settled and then firmed. He saw the ceiling. Yes, he lay on the hall floor at the hotel. A face moved into his line of sight. A big face with oversized spectacles and a nose with hairs in it.

"Talk to me, son. Talk to me."

Morgan blinked and a groan seeped out of his mouth.

"Well, we're making progress. What's your name?"

"Morgan. Yeah, that's me."

"You hurt bad anywhere?"

He took a deep breath and the stabbing pain drilled through his chest.

"Ribs," Morgan said. "Why am I still alive? Shotgun."

"Yep, seen it before. The shooter inside couldn't wait for the door to come all the way open. Buck fever, I'd say. His first time trying to kill a man. Most of the slugs from the double-aught buck went into the door. Jolted it off the hinges and it hit you in the chest and smashed you back six feet into the hall."

"Who?"

"Don't know who the shooter was. Time folks in the other rooms got out here, they said the window in Room 222 was open, and it's an easy jump to the first-floor porch and then to the ground. He left the Greener inside. Had another round in it. Buck fever, I'd say."

"Who's registered in the room?" Morgan asked, feeling better and starting to get mad now.

"Nobody. Clerk says it's empty. Doing some repairs in there, he said."

"Needs some more work now," Morgan said. He tried to sit up. Strong hands helped him. His head felt like a top on a string. He put out both hands to steady himself. One found the wall.

"Kind of dizzy?"

"Right, Doc."

"How are the ribs?"

"Hurt a bit. Not broken. I've had broken before. Shoulder hurts, but I'll live."

"Damn lucky. You remind me of somebody, but I don't recollect who. You want me to tape up those ribs?"

Morgan shook his head. "Makes them hurt worse. I did that before. Sheriff here?"

"Nope. He said if nobody was killed he didn't want to be bothered."

"Figures. Thanks, Doc." Morgan dug into his pants pocket and came up with a $2.50 gold coin. He gave it to the medic, who nodded and stood.

"I'll give you a hand. Might be on the wobbly side for a day or so."

Morgan looked down the hall. A dozen people stood there watching. Most had on nightclothes or dressing robes.

"Hell, he ain't even dead," one man said, and turned back into his room. The others decided the excitement was over and slipped back in their rooms.

Morgan stood with the doctor's help, put one

hand on the wall, and then turned to thank the medic.

"You still remind me of somebody. I'll think of it. You have a room on this floor?"

Morgan pointed down the hall and walked with loose-jointed knees to Room 228.

The doctor looked at Morgan from behind his glasses. "You need any laudanum to get through the night?"

Morgan shook his head. The doctor was older than he had thought at first, over 60, but sharp and energetic.

"I'll be fine, Doc. Long as the man with the double-barreled calling card don't come back." He fished his key out of his pocket, unlocked the door, and went in. Only then did Morgan hear the medic move on down the hallway.

He hadn't even started thinking about why the lovely blond lady who called herself Shirley wanted to blow him to pieces. Had she pulled the trigger, or had it been a man she hired? He wasn't sure but he'd find out.

How did she set him up for Room 222? Maybe she knew it was being worked on and no one would be there. Maybe. She could be in Room 322 or 122. Then again, she might just have picked 222 by chance. He'd find out in the morning. He'd tear the damn hotel apart until he found her. Then she had a lot of damned hard questions to answer. He'd slap the words out of her if he had to.

She was a beautiful sexy lady, but that didn't mean a thing if she was the one who'd tried to kill him. He'd find out one way or the other.

He had only moved a step inside his room. Morgan turned and locked the door, leaving his key in the hole and turning it halfway around so it couldn't be pushed out. Then he took the room's only straight-backed chair and pushed the back of the chair under the door handle, leaving it perched on its two rear legs. Now anyone breaking into the room would have to shatter the chair first. By then he'd have put five slugs through the thin door panel.

He didn't bother to light a lamp. A stream of moonlight came in the window. At least this way, nobody outside would know he was here. He pushed the dresser over in front of the window so no one could get in that way. Then he loaded a sixth round in his .45 Peacemaker and settled down on top of the bed, boots and all. He might not sleep much tonight. Better sleepy tomorrow than stone-cold dead tonight.

It was a long night. Once someone walked down the hallway, but the heavy boots kept going past his door and didn't come back. He slept by fits and stops.

When morning came at last, he was bleary-eyed, mean as a she-bear who'd lost a cub, and ready to take on the whole damn world if he needed to.

At six o'clock he opened up a small cafe. The owner/cook glared at him. "You look like you came out on the losing end of a dogfight," she said. "Sounds about like the kind of night I had. You want the works?"

"The works?"

She pointed to a sign on the wall "Three eggs over easy, grated, fried potatoes, bacon, two hot cakes and sausage, three slices of toast and jam, and coffee. Thirty cents."

"Yeah, looks good. Coffee soon as it's hot."

He sat at one of two tables in the small place. Through a door to the kitchen he heard her humming a tune. When she brought him coffee he tasted it and nodded. "What made you so damn happy all of a sudden?"

She put one hand on an ample hip and grinned. "Hey, I'm doing what I like to do. I'm good at it. I own this place free and clear. Why shouldn't I be happy?"

"Yeah, good for you. Now when is it my turn?"

"Just as soon as you get some of my food into your gullet. Always makes a man feel better." She grinned. "Food and a good romp in bed usually does it for any man."

Morgan laughed, feeling better already. "At least you're frank about it."

"Why not? Most women love to make love, they just don't think they should talk about it. Like now. I don't know you, maybe you'll wait and jump me from a dark alley somewhere. I wouldn't like that."

"Never jumped a pretty girl out of a dark alley in my life," Morgan said.

"You never have to. Women probably line up at your bedroom door waiting their turn." She grinned and hurried back. "Don't want to burn those spuds."

Another customer came in. The woman hurried out, took his order, and then rushed back to the kitchen. She came out a moment later with two big plates filled with his food and a pot of coffee. Everything promised was on the plates, along with hot syrup and fresh butter. And there was more coffee for his cup.

"Enjoy it," she said, pausing a minute in front

of him. "In case you wondered, my name's Lottie, Lottie Fuiten. You got a name?"

"Lottie, I do." He stood and held out his hand. "Lottie, I'm Lee Morgan." They shook and she grinned. Lottie had soft brown hair that must be long. It was rolled and tied in a bun at the back of her neck. She had pale green eyes and stood no more than five-three.

"Hope you enjoy the grub, now I gotta cook," she said, and rushed back to the kitchen.

Half a dozen men and one woman came in in the next half hour as Morgan took his time eating the big breakfast. Twice more Lottie filled his coffee cup.

She had taken care of the customers, and they ate and hurried out to their jobs. She came back and sat down across from him. One man lingered over coffee across the room.

"Well, Lee Morgan, how did you like breakfast?"

"Good, best I've had in weeks. That's the first half of making me feel good."

Lottie laughed softly. Her green eyes sparkled as she looked up at him. "You asking for the other half?"

The man with the coffee finished it, tossed a nickel on the counter, and left.

Morgan watched Lottie. He smiled. "Lottie, are you offering the other half?"

"What do you think?"

"I don't think you would have mentioned the idea if there wasn't a damn good chance."

"Morgan, you know something about women. Once in a while I get a wild, crazy feeling. Only one thing will put out the fire."

71

"Never been a fireman, but I could try," Morgan said with a grin.

"Morgan, I usually close up after the breakfast rush for an hour or so. That'll be about nine. If you want, you come back about nine."

Morgan tossed two quarters on the counter. "Unless I'm sick or dead, I'll be here. Make it for an hour and a half."

Lottie punched him in the shoulder and laughed. Three more customers came in. He waved and stepped out the door.

Back in the hotel, he put on his billed cap and glasses. He had on a town shirt and brown trousers. He had stored his sack of camping and cooking gear at the livery. Now he wanted to find the blond woman, Shirley.

He went downstairs to the room clerk and showed him a dollar bill.

"The tall blonde who sings in the saloon. Peaches. Does she stay here?"

"Can't say. Boss would kill me."

Morgan moved so the man could see the gun at his hip. He let his hand slide down beside it. "A man can die for all sorts of reasons. I'd suggest you cooperate."

The young man looked at the six-gun still holstered and swallowed hard. "Guess it wouldn't matter. Yeah. She's in 322. She says she likes it high."

Morgan dropped the dollar bill and turned around. "I never asked about her, right?"

The clerk made the dollar bill vanish and nodded. "Yes, sir. I don't even know who you are."

Morgan went to the stairs and took them two at a time. On the third floor, he paused. There was no one in the hall. He walked quietly to Room 322 and knocked.

He heard steps come to the door and then a question. He mumbled something and heard a key turn in the lock. When the door opened an inch he rammed it inward, stepped inside near a frightened Shirley. Her eyes went wide.

"Right, Shirley, you missed me last night with your shotgun. You've got to wait until the door is all the way open. The slanting wood door took most of the double-aught buck."

"I . . . I didn't shoot at you."

"Maybe you didn't. But you did set me up as a target. Why did you do that, Shirley?"

"I . . . I didn't. Don't know what you're talking about." He could see the fear in her eyes. She walked to the window. Shirley wore only a robe and the bed was unmade. There were two pillows and both had been slept on. No one else could be in the room now. He caught her arm and pushed her down on the bed. The robe slipped open, flashing a breast at him for a moment.

"You do know what I'm talking about. Why did you set me up to get killed?"

"I . . ." Her big brown eyes pleaded with him. "I didn't want to, but he persuaded me. I'm not much good saying no to a man when he's making love to me. You know that." She let the side of her robe fall open showing one surging breast, the wide areola bright pink and the darker red nipple rising with her passion.

"Who? Who was here and made you do it?"

"I . . . I was going to meet you down there last night when I talked to you. I really was. Then he made me tell him and he went instead."

"Who?"

"Slade."

"This Slade Johnson I keep hearing about? The one I'm supposed to look like?"

"Yes, Slade. He's my man. He made me tell him." The other side of her robe opened and it fell off her shoulders showing both breasts and the blush of brown hair at her crotch.

"Please don't be angry with me."

"It wasn't Slade who pulled the trigger last night. From what I hear about him, he wouldn't have missed. So he hired someone or used one of his men. Does he have ten men in his gang?"

"No there are only six of them, Slade and his five partners. They're good at what they do."

"Which is what?"

"They're bandits. They rob stagecoaches, trains, and banks. The trouble is they have to move around a lot."

"Where is their camp?"

"I don't know."

Morgan sat down beside her, bent, and kissed her breasts, then began to chew on one nipple. When she was panting he looked up. "Shirley, where is Slade's camp?"

"More," she said. "Chew me until I'm all gone!"

"When you tell me where his camp is."

"Out on the Crow River, three or four miles east of town." She moaned and fell backwards on the bed, pulling Morgan on top of her naked body.

"Now, Morgan!" she said. "Do me a quick, hard, fast one, Morgan!"

"No time right now, sweet-tit. I've got to see a couple of people. But don't go away, I'll be back." He kissed her breasts again, then kissed her panting lips before he eased away and stepped to the door.

"Don't worry, Shirley little darling, I'll be back. It might take me a couple of days, but I'll be back to see you."

In the hall, Morgan looked at his watch. It was a quarter of nine. He did have an appointment. He hated to walk out on Shirley when she was panting and ready, but a man had to keep his word to a lady. He did say he'd be back to see Lottie at nine o'clock.

When he walked in the place, which he now saw was called Lottie's Cafe, there was only one customer. Lottie offered the man more coffee and he declined, paid, and left. As soon as he was out the door Lottie put up her closed sign and smiled at Morgan.

"Damn, you came back. I've had a few who didn't. This way. I've got a small place in here where I sleep some nights when I'm too tired to get home."

It was a room behind the kitchen. He could see three more rooms that were not furnished. Evidently the former owner had lived behind the cafe.

The bedroom did have a double bed, a dresser, and two chairs.

She turned and held out her arms and he pulled her close. She looked up at him.

"Morgan, two rules. First you don't have to tell me you love me. We both know that ain't true and don't matter so no apron strings are attached. Second, we do anything that feels good and don't hurt either one of us. Okay?"

She had been grinding her hips against his, and

the erection he'd had in the hotel room quickly sprang back in force.

"You don't take long to get excited, do you? I like that." Lottie grinned. "Hey, Lee, you ever fucked a fat girl before? We're soft like a pillow and give you a good ride, and most of us are just sexy as hell 'cause we don't get poked as often as we'd like."

Morgan laughed softly and they sat down on the edge of the bed.

"Oh, rule three. You do have to kiss me. I ain't no whore, and I like kissing, and sometimes I warm up a little slow, but not today. Fuck, I'm ready right now!"

Lottie stood and began a wiggling little dance. As she danced, she bounced and shook and slowly stripped off her blouse and then a wrapper under it. Her breasts hung downward from their weight and size. They were huge and had small pinkish areolas and tiny nipples that were starting to enlarge.

"Oh, yes, dance, girls," she said. "Shake them tits and make them bounce and swing and sway. I love the way it feels to let my tits flop around that way. Makes me so hot!"

Lottie pulled at her skirt, working it down until he could see a swatch of crotch hair. She slowed.

"Hope you don't mind. I figured you were coming back so I took off my underthings, left it all hanging in the breeze there case you wanted a quick inspection." She laughed and flipped up her skirt, showing her crotch, and Morgan made a fake grab at her and she danced back.

She pushed her skirt down and kicked it away, then stood there quiet for a moment, naked. She was fat, chunky, with a roll of flesh around her middle and fleshy arms and thick thighs and legs.

"A lot of naked girl here, boy. You want some of this?"

Morgan laughed and pulled off his shirt. She helped him with his pants, and when she pushed down his shorts, she moaned and fell on him, taking half of his erection in her mouth. She came off him and looked up, her eyes dancing now.

"Oh, God, oh, God. I done died and am in cock heaven! Such a beauty. I love cock, oh, God, he's gonna stretch my poor little pussy all to pieces."

She jumped off the bed. "Come on, Morgan, dance for me. I want to see your pecker there shiver and shake."

"I can't dance. Never learned how."

"Not fancy dancing, more dirty kind. Come on, I'll help."

He stood and she showed him how to bump forward his hips and grind them around. He'd seen girls do something like that before but never tried it himself.

After a few tries she shook her head.

"You're hopeless. Hope you're better in bed." She fell on the quilt and held out her arms.

It was an hour and a half later that they lay there, both breathing hard.

"Four times! God, but you are good. And so fast. You get ready to go in a rush. Hey, what time is it?"

She looked at a windup alarm clock on the dresser. "Ten-thirty! God, I got to get ready for the dinner crowd. I'm so far behind now you got to peel the potatoes for me. Don't tell me you don't know how. I ain't got time to teach you. Come on, time for you to peel potatoes."

"How many?"

"Enough to serve twenty hungry men. That's about how many big dinners I serve at noontime. My best time of day. Most customers. Then in the evening for supper I get mostly the unmarried men who got no cook to home."

He peeled for 20 minutes and Lottie said that was enough. She'd already taken half of the potatoes to boil on the stove for mashed potatoes. He had one cup of coffee, kissed Lottie good-bye, and headed out the door.

His next job was to check on this outlaw, the one people said looked like him. Time to have a direct confrontation. He was damned sure what he'd say if he found Slade. He did wonder why some robber would want to kill him. Maybe they wouldn't talk. Maybe they would let their guns do the talking.

Morgan was heading for the livery when a man came charging out of an alley in front of him bellowing at the top of his lungs.

"Get the sheriff! Somebody run and get the sheriff. A woman's been murdered right down this alley!"

Chapter Six

Morgan adjusted his bill cap and glasses and asked the man who had just burst out of the alley screaming what he had said.

"Some woman got her clothes ripped off and raped up there in the alley and then killed dead. Knife kill, ain't pretty."

The man ran on looking for the sheriff.

Morgan and four other men went up the alley. About halfway along, among some big cardboard boxes behind the general store, they found her.

She was naked with her legs still spread and had one breast sliced off and her throat slit. She was one mass of blood, indicating to Morgan that she had been cut many times before she was killed. A body doesn't bleed except by gravity after the heart stops beating.

A crowd soon gathered. Sheriff Goranson came bustling through it, pushing men to one side. He stared at the body a minute, then ordered them all out of the area.

"I need to look around, maybe the killer dropped something. Get out of here." He kept two men to hold back the crowd and then began walking over the area, looking for any clues he might be able to find.

Morgan went back to the street and continued his hike down the block to the livery. Somebody trying to kill him always put Morgan in a bad mood, and he figured to have it out with the bandit Slade this afternoon and end it.

He got the same horse he'd used before, borrowed a rifle as well, a Spencer seven-shot repeater, and a box of shells, and pushed the rifle into a boot he tied on the saddle. Now he was ready.

Morgan rode east at a canter for a mile, then slowed to a walk as he watched ahead along the Crow River. He didn't think the stream had been named for the Indians, probably the bird.

After he figured he'd covered three miles, he paused and looked ahead. He couldn't see any smoke or any kind of buildings. He'd found a small ranch about a mile out of town far off to the left on a smaller stream running into the Crow.

Morgan moved ahead on the horse at a walk, watching to the front and both sides of the trail along the stream. It was a wagon track, but didn't look like it got much traffic. Small creeks ran into the Crow, and the land around was mostly good only for grazing.

He came around a small bend a half mile farther on and ahead he spotted smoke and some buildings. They were set in a small valley on a creek that ran into the Crow. It had at one time been a farm, with a pole fence near a barn, a corral, and a good-sized farmhouse. He stopped in the cover of some trees and studied the place.

Two saddled horses stood at a hitching rail in front of the house. A door banged somewhere and he saw a man in a red shirt walk toward an outhouse.

The same creek that watered the farm also would provide concealment for Morgan. He turned across the Crow River, which was no more than knee-deep here, and came out on the other side with the line of trees between him and the house.

Slowly Morgan worked his horse along the trees, staying out of sight of anyone in the house. Two horses out front could mean some of them were going into town or had just come back.

When he got to the point he had selected, he was about 40 yards from the house and half that distance from the barn. What now? He liked to plan out an attack, to know his moves. Here he was stymied. He didn't know how many guns were inside. He didn't know if Slade himself was there or not.

Morgan slid off the horse, tied her, and bellied down in the weeds next to the far side of the creek where he could watch the place without being seen. He studied the layout.

The barn could shield him from the house if he wanted to sprint up there the 20 yards. But someone might spot him. From here he had command of both front and rear doors to the house.

Now he saw two more horses in the corral. That made four, but most gangs like this would have some spare horseflesh at the home base.

One man came out the front door with saddle-

Kit Dalton

bags. He flipped them on one of the two horses at the rail and started to mount. Morgan put a .52-caliber rifle round a foot behind the horse. The man spun around, six-gun out, saw no one, and raced for the cover of the house. Morgan let him go.

Five minutes went by and nothing happened. Then a man bolted from the back door. Morgan fired low with the rifle and ripped a round into the runner's left leg. He screeched in pain, rolled in the dirt, and crawled back inside the farmhouse.

An upstairs window opened and the curtains pulled aside.

"Who the hell is out there and what do you want?" a big voice boomed from the window.

"I want Slade," Morgan bellowed from his concealment. "Send him out the front door."

There was movement at the curtains, then no response. Two minutes later the front door opened and a man walked out. He was neither of the ones Morgan had seen before.

"I'm Slade," the man called. "Who are you?"

"I'm the guy you killed last night, only you missed. Now you're a dead man."

Slade dove for the front door opening and rolled inside. Morgan didn't even have the rifle aimed at him. Morgan eased back from the edge of the greenery and moved behind a large cottonwood tree.

A moment later four rifle rounds slammed into the dirt and brush near where he had been. Morgan put a round through the upstairs window, knowing that the brush would conceal the exact location of his shot by filtering the blue smoke from the black-powder round.

He slid over so he could see the house again. A man tried it from the back door. Morgan put two shots close to him and he darted back inside.

Morgan realized it was a standoff. He could keep them inside until dark, but then they could get out and ride off, or ride over and challenge him with four guns to one. He shot out two more windows, then called for Slade again.

A voice boomed back at him. "I'm listening."

"You leave me alone, Slade, and I won't kill you. Just because we look alike is no reason you have to die. You stay away from me, or you'll be dead and halfway to Hell before the devil knows you even applied for admission."

"Talk's cheap, Morgan. I know your name. I'll kill you sooner or later, unless you want a showdown right now."

Morgan fired four times through the lowest window that he could see was open. Then he reloaded the Spencer magazine tube that went through the butt plate. It was still early afternoon. He put one more round through the same window, and took two rounds in response from rifles inside.

Then Morgan ran to his horse, mounted, and rode back the way he came. By the time they figured out he was gone, he'd be two miles away. They wouldn't come after him. Slade was here because he was planning a big hit. He could have no other reason. The woman in town, Shirley, could be his accomplice, getting details about the bank, the train, any target he picked. Slade would rob the bank or the train. Maybe the Railway Express car on which the government sent cash from the mints and the printing office to banks all across the country.

Yes, with Slade it would be the Express car. He thought about it on the way. With Slade it might be the bank and the Express car the same afternoon. The train got here about ten-thirty. Must leave shortly after that. He'd hit it on the other side of town out too far for the town to help, maybe five miles.

Morgan rode back to town without pursuit. He felt better. He'd shot at the bastard who tried to have him killed. He'd figured out why he was in town. A sudden thought came to him.

It might be a lot tougher on Slade if Morgan took his woman away from him than if he killed some of his men. Yes, now there was a thought. That would be a job that he would really enjoy. He remembered Shirley and the soft white thighs and her marvelous hanging breasts and the wild way she had in bed. The idea sounded better all the time.

He still had on his town disguise: bill cap, town shirt, and glasses. He could walk the streets and not be mistaken for the outlaw.

In town, it seemed that half of Cheyenne was talking about the woman-killer who was loose among them. He stopped by at Lottie's Cafe for a piece of cherry pie, and she sat across from him. It was the slow time between dinner and supper.

"You enjoy this morning?" she asked, her eyes dancing as She watched him.

"Immensely. You were certainly right about the cushioning."

They both laughed.

"You want to come to my place tonight?"

"Lottie, I'd love to, but I've got to work sometime. I'm a railroad detective here on a case."

"Oh. I've heard bad things about you guys."

"None of them true. We're knights in shining armor. Remember, without the train there wouldn't be any Cheyenne town here."

She nodded. "Yeah, but then I'd have a cafe somewhere else." She pushed closer to him, and her hand under the table and out of sight found his thigh. She stroked it up to his crotch and rubbed.

"Hey, wanted to tell you I ain't never been done so good in more damn years than I want to remember. You gonna be around a while?"

"For a while. I'll be using that back room again. Long as you throw in a couple of pieces of pie."

"Hell, you can have a whole pie tin." She grinned and hurried to wait on somebody at the counter.

Morgan found a new hat at the general store. It was a soft cloth rain hat that he could pull down all around and it covered nearly half of his face. He folded the bill cap and put it in his back pocket and stood on the main street listening to the talk.

Four men had already been questioned by Sheriff Goranson. The dead woman's name was Priscilla Lang. She had been a seamstress for the only women's dress shop in town. She was unmarried and not a beauty, but well endowed with big breasts and a slender body.

"Somebody must have done her two or three times back there, then cut her up good," a cowboy said as he stood on the boardwalk laboring with the makings as he tried to roll a cigarette. "Damn, I been on the range for a while, but not long enough I got to do something like that. For two dollars he could of had a woman over at the Longbranch.''

Morgan went into a saloon and the talk there was all about Priscilla Lang. One drunk claimed he'd done Priscilla all night one time at her house. The other drinkers shouted him down. It was a given fact that Priscilla was a virgin. She'd said nobody could even touch her until she got married. Somebody had touched her all over that afternoon.

Morgan went to find Jim Breed. He'd changed his mind about waiting a week to see the boy at the Cheyenne band's summer camp. They could move, or the Army could find them. Somebody was bound to track them if they tried to do any raiding. He was so close to talking to the boy that he couldn't afford to wait any longer. It would be five days since he had talked to Willow by the time they got back to the Cheyenne camp.

Jim wasn't behind the saloon where he had been before. Morgan scoured the other two alleys, then began working every saloon in town. It was after suppertime when he found him. Jim was so drunk he couldn't stand. He leaned against the wall in the Territorial Saloon.

Morgan talked to the barkeep. "Jim owe you for any drinks he caged?"

The apron scowled. "Who are you, his keeper? He don't do no hurt in here. Known Jim a long time."

"I want to hire him. Okay if I carry him out?"

"Fine by me."

"He have a place he sleeps?"

"No place special. I tried to get him to use the shed behind my place, but he don't much."

"He will tonight."

Morgan lifted the Indian over his shoulder and took him out the back door. The lean-to by the side of the saloon was six feet wide and about that high. Morgan knocked off his hat getting inside. He found a lantern and lit it and then pulled an old tarp down over the open door.

A pallet of dirty blankets showed on one side. Morgan rolled Jim on the ground bed and pulled one of the blankets over him. Jim didn't need any supper, but Morgan realized *he* did. He hadn't had anything to eat since morning besides that piece of pie.

He headed for the general store. He'd buy their trail food tonight and leave it at the livery. Then have supper at Lottie's and get a good night's sleep. First thing in the morning he'd get Jim sobered up and they would ride for Gray Owl's summer camp.

The short Indian and the tall man in the saddle took the same route as they had before, only this time they cut off some corners since they knew where they were going and it made the ride a little shorter. They came to the last rise before the valley and Morgan felt ill at ease.

"Something's wrong," he told the Indian half-breed. "I have a bad feeling about this."

They topped the ridge and looked down into the valley where the band had camped before. Now there was no smoke coming through the trees. They could see no tipis along the river.

"Gone," Jim said.

They galloped for half a mile, then walked on into the former Cheyenne camp.

Even Morgan could tell what had happened. One tipi had not been removed at all. It lay smashed to one side and half burned. A travois lay to one side still harnessed to a horse. The horse lay dead and bloated.

"Gray Owl's people leave in hurry," Jim said.

"Damn fast. They left a lot of things here they must need. Those pots over there, and a lance. There's a bow and two arrows."

They walked the half-mile-long camp searching around where the tipis used to be. The spot where Willow and Mighty Dawn had been was where the burned one lay. There were few useful items left around it.

"Almost packed up and ready to go when they were attacked by a small band of Pony Soldiers," Morgan said. "The warriors probably fought the soldiers at the far end or maybe a half mile from the camp, giving the women and children and young boys time to scatter to the west, over the ridge, taking everything with them that they had ready to go."

Jim looked up. He had collected the bow and two arrows, and found three more and kept them as well.

"Good arrows," he said. "Straight, long, with man-kill points on them."

"Did they get away, Jim, or did the Cavalry chase and catch the women and children?"

"We ride west to find out," Jim said.

At the far end of what once was the Gray Owl summer camp, they found six mounds of earth. They were obviously graves. There were no markers over the mounds, only a small pyramid of stones. There were six stones on the bottom, all touching in a circle, then three on top of those and one stone on top of the three.

"Cheyenne dead," Jim said. "White-eyes bury

them, one Cheyenne Warrior slip back and put ten-stone markers on them. When safe they will come back, dig up their people, and give them a traditional Cheyenne burial high on the top of a hill somewhere."

"Let's get tracking," Morgan said.

The trail wasn't hard to follow. Now and then the drag marks of a travois could be seen. Usually they were covered up by ten to 20 shod mounts. Cavalry.

Ten miles up the valley, over the ridge, through a second valley and over another ridge, they tracked the victors and the vanquished. A mile later the Cavalry tracks vanished.

"Gave up and went home," Jim said. "Figured they killed enough of the Cheyenne for this time."

Now the tracks of the running Cheyenne were plainer, easier to follow.

"Two families, maybe three," Jim said after a half mile. "Band split up into ten, fifteen groups so Army can't follow all."

"They all heading for the same spot or just running?"

"All head for another summer camp. The destination would be shouted around camp as they tore down the tipis."

"What happened back there?" Morgan asked.

"To get that well cleared, the village had two hours' notice. Warriors rode out to attack the Pony Soldiers. Give women time to take down camp."

"The men did a good job."

"Warriors' only job fighting."

"How much farther do you think they went?"

"Jim never been this far into mountains."

They had been climbing steadily. Their horses

89

paused at the next small stream and drank.

"Should we make a stop?" Morgan asked.

"Two hours' light left for tracking."

"We'll keep going."

Over the next ridge they found what could only be the Cheyenne camp. A dozen smoke trails came from a patch of dense woods in a small valley with a stream.

As soon as they saw the smoke, the two riders faded below the ridge line and dismounted. They tied their horses and crept up to the crest and looked down. They were a mile from the smoke.

"Lookouts?" Morgan asked.

"Double tonight. One on this crest somewhere. Jim go down, talk. You stay. Camp here. Cheyenne now shoot quick any white-eyes they see."

Morgan nodded. "Find out if the boy and Willow are still in camp. Maybe they were captured."

Morgan found a spring and made camp. Jim took a handful of crackers and three strips of beef jerky and waved, then vanished in the growing dimness of dusk.

Morgan knew that he couldn't make a fire. He wanted coffee but didn't boil any. Jerky, crackers, an apple, and a can of cold beans were his supper. He stretched out on his two blankets. The nights this high were crisp, even if it was summer.

He wondered how Jim was faring below. Would the warriors be so angry they would kill Jim's white-eyes half? If Jim didn't come back tomorrow by noon, Morgan knew he had to work his way closer to the camp. This had to be the time to talk to the boy.

He watched the stars through the ponderosa

pine and the Douglas fir. The stars seemed to move, but so slowly. A moon came out and tracked across the sky. He wondered about Jim Breed once more. Then he slept.

Morgan came awake but didn't move. His hand under the blanket closed around the handle of his Peacemaker and he strained to hear the sound that had roused him. It came again to the left, then again, and this time he figured it out. An elk or a moose was moving through some brush and the rack of horns scraped and snapped through the dry branches.

The sounds came again, more faintly, then once more and were gone. He relaxed his hand on the six-gun, let the hammer down softly, and closed his eyes.

The screaming, raucous call of a bald eagle from its nest high in a nearby pine tree roused Morgan at dawn. He checked around, saw nothing out of the ordinary, then sat up.

Behind him someone coughed. Before he could whirl a voice came.

"About time you woke up, Morgan. Jim been waiting a half hour for you."

Morgan turned and lowered the .45. "Are they there?"

Jim had a small fire going and the coffee was boiled and ready. The fire must be all right. They would know Jim was out here.

Jim handed Morgan his cup filled with hot coffee.

"Boy in Gray Owl's camp. Woman is dead. Killed in rush to leave other place. She went back to tipi to get something. Her tipi that one not taken down."

"But the boy is fine?"

"Wounded, rifle round through arm, but strong."

"I bet he's ready to come back to civilization."

Jim Breed took a long drink of the coffee, then slowly shook his head. "No. Boy says he now Cheyenne warrior. He killed the Pony Soldier who rode down his mother. Boy found lost Army rifle and shot the trooper off horse, then run in woods."

"Is he serious?"

"Much mad about mother. Say Cheyenne his only friends. Say he is Cheyenne warrior."

"He's no more than fourteen years old!"

"Gray Owl needs all the warriors he can find. Boy has Spencer carbine. Gray Owl says Mighty Dawn is now Cheyenne warrior."

"You said the first time you found the woman Willow had taken a warrior husband. Did he survive the attack?"

"No. Dead. Gray Owl lost eight of his thirty warriors. Gray Owl will stay in valley a week, then move north across railroad into northern Wyoming to join other Cheyenne to fight the Pony Soldiers."

Morgan scowled and threw the last bit of coffee into the fire. "If he leaves this valley, we might never find him again. That means we have to do something right here within the next few days! We have to figure out how I can talk to the boy."

Chapter Seven

Mighty Dawn looked over the battered group of Cheyenne in their makeshift camp high in the Colorado Rockies south of the Wyoming border. They had lost eight warriors. They had not been able to bury their dead in the traditional way. Four women and three children had been killed.

He would never see his mother again! He hated the Pony Soldiers! He was glad that he had killed at least one. He would forever hate the Army and the Cavalry. He had dedicated his life to being a Cheyenne warrior, to killing as many Pony Soldiers as he could. No matter how many, it would never make up for the death of his mother.

He was two months away from being 14 years old, but already he was as tall and broad-shouldered as many of the Cheyenne warriors. He had his own war pony. Every day Walking Bird taught him how to ride better, how to control the animal with the slightest touch of his heels, calves, and knees. He was getting better.

Mighty Dawn had captured a rifle in the wild melee with the Pony Soldiers, but he had only seven rounds for it. He had to get more bullets. It was one of the new rifles the Cheyenne called "shoot many times." He knew it was a Spencer repeating carbine, the shorter kind the Pony Soldiers carried. He must find some way to get more rounds for the Spencer. He had thought of finding the Pony Soldiers' camp and sneaking in and taking rounds away from sleeping Cavalrymen, but he decided not to try it. Anyway, he had no idea where the soldiers had ridden to.

Each day he practiced with a bow and arrow. If he had no rounds for the Spencer he had to use other means to kill the Pony Soldiers. He could use a lance, and now he practiced three or four hours a day with a bow his mentor had made for him. It was as big as those used by the warriors but not quite as hard to pull.

He had no tipi to sleep in. It didn't matter. He had a thin pallet of three blankets and he spent each night in the open under the trees and the stars. Soon he could tell time by the movement of the Big Dipper around the North Star. He couldn't remember who had taught him to do that.

Each day now the council came together and talked of what they should do. More and more warriors wanted to move far to the north, well beyond the tracks of the big steam monster and to the top of the place called Wyoming where they would find others of the Cheyenne Nation. There they could band together and form a mighty army and match the Pony Soldiers and those on foot and destroy them and drive them from the sacred Cheyenne hunting grounds.

Some said there were too many white-eyes in the areas they had to pass through. They would be seen and reported to the Pony Soldiers, who would ride on the great steam monster and find them.

Others said it was worth the risk. Scattered this way, they were always outnumbered and easy prey for the marauding Pony Soldiers.

Their camp was smaller now, and more of a war camp than a relaxed summer one. They had put up half of their tipis, with the others still packed and ready to be hauled away on the travois at a moment's notice.

That way twice as many women could take down the remaining shelters and be ready to move in an hour instead of the usual two hours.

Mighty Dawn went down the creek to the tipi of Knows a Lot and sat down and watched him making arrows. He was the best arrowmaker in the whole camp. Every warrior must know how to make his own arrows, but in times of relative peace, they relied on the chief arrowmaker to do the job for them.

Now he worked hard to make as many fine arrows as he could. Most of the warriors also worked at making their own arrows, but Knows a Lot's arrows would be kept for those important shots when the arrow must fly absolutely straight and true.

Mighty Dawn sat cross-legged in his breechclout, his back now as brown as the other youths'. His hair had grown longer and he brushed it back from his eyes.

Knows a Lot had just taken a bundle of cherry

shoots down from where he had kept them seasoning on a string near the top of his tipi. Mighty Dawn guessed there were 30 slender stems in the bundle. They were all about two feet long. They had all been peeled free of bark and now the wood was dry and cured.

Knows a Lot picked up one of the shoots and studied it. He looked at Mighty Dawn sternly.

"Mighty Dawn, do you know how long an arrow should be?"

"No, Honorable Grandfather."

"A warrior's arrow should be as long as from his elbow to the tip of his little finger, plus the length of that finger." The old craftsman took one of the cured cherry-wood shoots, laid it against Mighty Dawn's forearm, and marked it at his finger. Then again, at the length of his finger, he made another mark.

He laid that shoot down and selected another one. It looked perfectly straight to Mighty Dawn. The old man began to work. The young one-quarter Cheyenne knew that there were few old people in the Indian camp. Most old men and women who could not contribute to the welfare of the tribe were not allowed to stay.

Some of them simply sat down by a small fire and prayed and watched the blaze. Some added small bits of wood to the fire, and when the fire went out—they died.

Only two days ago he had seen an old grandmother who couldn't keep up with the quick march the warriors had set as they raced away from the white-eyes Pony Soldiers. She had wailed, then said good-bye to her only daughter. The old grandmother had no horse to ride. Her daughter's husband had been killed in the attack and his horses run off.

It was her time. She sat down along the trail. When Mighty Dawn last saw her she had stretched out on her stomach and put her nose in the dust. She would soon be dead.

Knows a Lot was too old to be a warrior. But he was the best arrowmaker in the band. He received gifts for arrows when he presented them to a warrior. The gift might be a horse, or a quarter of a just-killed deer. He earned his way and was aided when the band had to move.

Mighty Dawn watched him working on the arrow. He took two sandstone blocks that had been carefully crafted to make a groove in each half. When put together they formed a circle. Through this hole the arrow shaft was pulled and pushed back and twisted and pulled through again. It might take 50 times through the sandstone hole to get the shaft shaved and sanded down until it was the same diameter all the way along the 19 or 20 inches of its length.

Then the old craftsman began straightening the shaft. He sighted down it time and again and after each sighting, he bent the wood slightly with a bone or horn tool that had a hole in it.

He needed to apply grease to some arrows to bend them, and some he heated to aid the process.

When the arrow was straight and the same size all along the shaft, the old Indian took a special tool of bone or flint that had been fitted with a sharp point. He cut a zigzag line down the side of the shaft.

These "lightning" lines were supposed to help the arrow fly straight and true. Some warriors said the lines also helped the arrow to maintain its shape and resist warping.

Now with his sharp knife, Knows a Lot cut a slot down the end of the arrow. Into this notch he fitted the type of arrowhead that was needed. For hunting birds they used small points. For hunting large game such as deer and buffalo, they used larger points made of some piece of metal that they had stolen from a farm or ranch they had raided.

Some of these arrow points were an inch and a half long. The man-killer points were the largest and strongest.

Knows a Lot then cut off the shaft at the proper length for the warrior he made the arrow for, and cut grooves along the tail end of the arrow. Into these grooves he glued and bound split halves of wild turkey or buzzard feathers. The glue for this work was usually made from boiled buffalo hooves. Since the Gray Owl band had not seen a buffalo for over a year, they were forced to use the hooves of deer for the job. It did not make as good a glue but it was adequate.

The arrow was laid aside for the glue to dry, and Knows a Lot began on another arrow.

"Mighty Dawn, I have heard that you are a warrior now. I will make six arrows for you the right length. Practice with your bow hard, so you can use my arrows to defend the band and to fight off the Pony Soldiers who keep chasing us."

Mighty Dawn nodded, trying not to let his pleasure show. A Cheyenne Indian did not show emotion. It was unmanly. He rose and walked away, then ran to where he kept his bow and began practicing again. He could now hit a pine tree from 20 paces away. He had to learn to shoot farther. He went back 30 paces and missed his foot-thick target five times out of six.

He raced to pick up the arrows before someone else found them, then tried again. For two hours he shot the bow until his arms ached. The last time he hit the tree four out of six times. Now he made two marks across the trunk of the tree with his knife. They were man-high and represented a man's chest, a Pony Soldier's chest.

He practiced another hour, and at the end he could put two of the six arrows into the "chest area" on the tree.

Mighty Dawn put his arrows in the pouch on his back that held them tightly and went back toward the tipi of his mentor, Walking Bird. The great warrior had helped him since his parents were killed. He ate at the warrior's fire but slept in the open.

Mighty Dawn was passing another tipi when one of the captive white women ran out of it. Right behind her was Long Knife, the warrior who had captured the tall, blond white-eyes woman from the stagecoach. She had survived the Pony Soldier attack.

Long Knife hit the woman with his hand, knocking her down. She whimpered on the ground. He kicked her in the side. Long Knife screamed at her in anger, telling her never to shout at him again. He kicked her once more, then turned back to his tipi.

The woman, who Long Knife called Loud of Mouth, slumped in the dust of the walkway. She whimpered, her eyes filled with tears. There was a great change in her from the day Mighty Dawn had seen her pulled from the stagecoach. Then she had been well dressed, her hair on top of her head, her face clean and smiling.

Now she was in the tatters of an old doeskin dress, with big holes in front showing her breasts. Her face was bruised and a slash on one cheek had not been cared for. Her hair had been cut off close to her head and her face and arms were layered with dirt.

Mighty Dawn had not spoken with either of the white women before. It wasn't his place or his right. But this time he couldn't help it. He squatted beside the woman.

"Do as he says and he won't hit you," Mighty Dawn said.

The woman's head snapped up. "You speak English!" She nearly cried. "Help me get away! My parents have money. I'll give you thousands of dollars. Help me get away!"

"I can't. I'm a Cheyenne warrior."

"You have blue eyes. Are you a breed?"

"Yes, but the Pony Soldiers killed my mother. Now I am a warrior and I will kill Pony Soldiers." He paused. He had to move quickly before anyone saw him. "Do as he says, please him, and you'll live. That's important right now, to live!" He stood and walked away from her.

Long Knife came out of his tipi again.

"Loud of Mouth, come and fix my food. Quickly, woman!"

The white woman stood and ran into the tipi. Long Knife grinned at the way she obeyed. The whole camp knew she had been difficult. Maybe now she had seen the way. Any new horse had to be broken before it could be ridden.

Mighty Dawn walked on to his mentor's tipi. The plight of the two white women troubled him.

But there was nothing he could do. The women belonged to the warriors who captured them. They were free to do anything they wanted with the women. Some captives became honored wives of warriors. Some bore children, he knew, and others were beaten and whipped and turned into slaves. He shook his head. He was a Cheyenne warrior. There was nothing he could do about it.

In the tipi of Walking Bird, he smelled the evening meal as it cooked over the small fire in the center of the shelter. He had seen Walking Bird return from a hunt with a wild turkey and a small doe. The turkey would be eaten first, and the doe butchered and half the meat given to relatives and half of it sliced thinly and hung on drying racks to make jerky. It would dry in three days of bright sunshine.

Mighty Dawn took in the scene and knew he would never forget it. Living with the Cheyenne had been an entirely new experience for him. He had thought about his Indian heritage, but living in Grand Island, he'd never thought that he'd ever live like an Indian, like a Cheyenne.

But now these were his people. They were being chased by the Pony Soldiers who had killed his mother, and he would fight them to the death! He would fight for the band, for the Cheyenne Nation. He would learn every Cheyenne word so he could speak to the council. He was Indian! He was Cheyenne!

That evening, after the supper, he sat with his small lump of possessions. He had little. He had grabbed a saddlebag off a downed Pony Soldier horse during the frantic, wild battle, and now he used that for most of his treasures. In one side he had strapped down the fortune in $20 bills. They were his and he would never part with them. Someday he or the band could use them.

He had a picture of his mother, and one of his father, in a small family bible his mother had given to him. That and a few mementos from his first days with the band here in Colorado were his only other possessions.

He had a bow and six arrows and Knows a Lot was making him six more—six war arrows! They would have man-kill arrowheads on them!

He remembered again the agony of watching the Pony Soldier charging his mother. The soldier deliberately ran her down with his big heavy Army horse. The shod hooves cut her body in four places, and one struck her head killing her instantly.

Mighty Dawn had just found a lost Spencer carbine. His father had taught him to shoot both a pistol and rifle when he was 12. He lifted the Spencer, levered a round into the chamber, and shot the Pony Soldier off his horse almost before his mount could get untangled from the corpse of the woman beneath its feet.

The soldier slammed off the saddle, hit the ground hard, and rolled once. He sat up stunned. Mighty Dawn screamed in fury at him and fired twice more. One round hit the trooper in the shoulder, the next in his heart, dumping him over backwards into Hell.

Mighty Dawn now sat outside the tipi watching the small stream. Here in the mountains, there was plenty of water. He'd heard that if they went north there would be some long dry stretches. How would they get across? Perhaps they would try to follow rivers to the north.

Gunslinger's Scalp

Mighty Dawn watched the members of the council gather in an open place near the stream. A small fire had been built there and as it grew dark, more fuel would be added to light the proceedings.

He knew they would talk about going north. Every warrior in camp could speak to the subject. Walking Bird came from the tipi and stopped in front of him.

"Are you coming?" he asked. "Every warrior can speak before the council."

Mighty Dawn leaped up, his face expectant, his eyes gleaming.

"Yes, yes, I want to come. I won't speak, but I want to come." He had forgotten. *He was a Cheyenne warrior!* Now he could speak if he wanted to at council!

Three hours later, Mighty Dawn was tired of the talking and arguing by the members of the band. Fourteen different warriors had spoken to the plan to go north. Tonight they would decide. He watched as the last warrior sat down.

Gray Owl looked around at the men. His eyes lingered on Mighty Dawn, then moved on. At last the old warrior picked up a pipe and lit it. He puffed contentedly for a moment, then he held the pipe.

"I propose that we move north within a week," he said. He turned and gave the pipe to the warrior sitting beside him. That warrior nodded and smoked the pipe and the count began.

Ten minutes later the matter was decided. Fifteen of the 22 warriors had smoked the pipe, giving their vote to back Gray Owl. Within a week they would make the long trip out of the Colorado Rocky Mountains, across into Wyoming, and up through more mountains and the high plateau to try to find others of the Cheyenne people who had scattered rather than accept the prison of a reservation.

Mighty Dawn had heard talk of the Medicine Bow, the Green, the Bighorn Mountains. Exciting, faraway places. But there was talk as well of the Great Divide desert where nothing grew and the skeletons of horses and buffalo lost there years ago could be seen. Where were they going?

No one could say for sure. North, just north toward the area known as Montana, perhaps even into Montana. Most thought that they would find more bands of Cheyenne in the Bighorn Mountains, which were over 300 miles away.

After the council was over, the men retreated to their tipis or to their pallets. Most of the warriors slept outside at night. As Mighty Dawn passed Long Knife's tipi, he saw the big blond woman rush out of the shelter. He could hear Long Knife's angry words from inside, but Long Knife did not chase her.

The woman dropped to the ground near a pine tree and sobbed. It was none of his business. A warrior did not touch another warrior's slave. Yet Mighty Dawn paused, then walked toward the woman. He could see no one outside of a tipi or close by.

"You have a real name?" Mighty Dawn asked her.

She looked up startled. He could see a new cut on the side of her face in the faint moonlight.

"Yes. I'm Kara."

"I'm . . . I'm Harold. You must remember, survival is your one purpose. Don't argue with him.

Don't shout at him. You're his slave. He can kill you if he wants to. No one would think a thing about it. I can't be seen talking with you."

Mighty Dawn stood and walked away quickly. A minute later Long Knife rushed out of the tipi.

"Woman with loud mouth, come back to tipi," he said. She didn't understand, but arose and walked back where he could see her. Her head was bowed. She went meekly into the tipi and Long Knife chuckled. Tonight he would break this mare to his own kind of riding.

Mighty Dawn found his pallet, and moved it to where he could look through the tall pines and firs and see a patch of sky. He had a long drink at the stream, then lay down with his head cushioned in his hands and stared at the pinpoints of light high above.

What were they? Stars. But were they suns as someone had told him? If they were suns, did they have planets rotating around them the way the earth and the other planets went around our sun? Were there men and women on those faraway planets that he could only wonder about? What was this world all about anyway?

His father, back in Grand Island, had once told him that he might be part of discovering the secrets of the universe if he went to Harvard University in Boston, studied hard, and became a scientist. Maybe he could have some small part in a great study about the planets.

Mighty Dawn had been surprised when he told Kara just now that his name was Harold. He hadn't even thought about his white-eyes name or his father or Harvard or the planets for a long time.

At home he had a book about the planets. He

stopped. He had said "at home." Did that mean he still thought of Grand Island as his home? Wasn't this his home, his people, his mission to kill Pony Soldiers?

That made him think of his mother and the way that trooper had deliberately ridden her down. Tears seeped out of his eyes. Tears were all right now, no one could see him. No one had ever seen a Cheyenne warrior cry.

He was confused. The thoughts of going to a great university jangled at him, sparked his interest and his imagination. Then it was all blotted out by the galloping of that horse and the shrill death cry of his mother and his own fury and the Spencer rife firing three times.

He lay there wondering. Mighty Dawn knuckled the tears out of his eyes and sat up.

A night hawk screamed in the darkness downstream. Calling to his mate. An owl hooted upstream, and he could hear a thousand crickets chirping, countered by a dozen big bullfrogs along the shores of the stream croaking out their bass notes.

It was all so pleasant here, so easy. He was learning to be a Cheyenne warrior. A warrior did no work. A warrior's job was to protect the camp, to make war on enemies, to go on raids, and to be a mighty hunter and provide food for his family.

Was he all of that? he wondered. Soon they would be moving north, across the railroad tracks. The tracks, he knew, would lead back to Cheyenne, where he and his mother had spent two weeks. The same tracks went all the way across Nebraska to Grand Island and his father.

For just a moment he wanted to go home, back

to Grand Island. Then he heard again the shrill cry of his mother dying and saw the murderous hooves descending, and he cried out in stark hatred. No! He was a Cheyenne warrior and he would kill as many Pony Soldiers as he could!

Chapter Eight

Lee Buckskin Morgan sat there near the small fire watching his half-breed friend, Jim. "I know, I know. You have no reason to go back down to the summer camp. You told me that. But I need to find some way to contact the boy. I'm not good enough to slip up on a camp full of Cheyenne."

Jim chuckled. "That's true. You're a fair woodsman for a white-eyes, but not Injun good."

"So what can we do? It's my job to bring that boy back to his father."

"What if boy doesn't want to go back? You going in there, drag him out by hair, and fight off twenty-one Cheyenne warriors and their wives?"

Morgan shook his head, pushing another small stick into the fire. "There's got to be a way."

"Drive ten buffalo into their camp. They'll welcome you, make you blood brother. This bunch down there angry. Not sure why Army fight them. Want to be left alone."

"I don't have ten buffs. What else would get me, you at least, back into their camp?"

"Could tell them I see Pony Soldiers."

"No. Then they'd pick up and vanish."

Morgan poked another small stick in the fire. It went a ways, then broke in half. Morgan grinned. "What if you broke a leg?"

Jim scooted back from the fire. "No!"

"Not *break* one. How about a bad sprain so you couldn't walk for a day or two. Happens."

"Not to Cheyenne!"

"Sure, but you're only half-Cheyenne. You can turn around now and hike back down there, and when you get near the camp you start limping and then fall down and crawl the last hundred yards."

"Warriors might shoot me for practice."

"You're a blood brother. Won't do that. You get into camp, find this other breed, the boy, and talk. Make friends. When you know he won't give you away, you hand him a note I'll write. I have to have a meeting to talk to this young man."

"He won't leave camp far. Be afraid of you grabbing him and run."

"A practice ride on his pony. He can stay on the animal. I can get close enough for that. Downstream, say a quarter of a mile. They have hunters out?"

"Hunters all the time."

"I'll have to be careful. Can you get down there before dark?"

Morgan spent a half hour writing the note. It had to be just right to entice Harold to come talk to him.

"I know your mother is dead. I'm sorry. I know you're mad as hell. But don't let one wild, crazy Cavalry trooper ruin the rest of your life. Your father wants you to come home. He said you had made great plans for the future. I want to talk to you about it. I won't force you to do anything you don't want to. You're almost a man now, you must decide what's best for you. I hear you want to be a scientist. Hard to do that out here. Please come talk to me. Jim Breed will tell you when and where."

Morgan folded the note and gave it to Jim, who hid it in his pocket, then strode out toward the village. He would make it well before dark.

"Tomorrow, just before sunset, a quarter of a mile below the village on the stream," Morgan said. "I'll be there, try and get the boy to come. Promise him anything. I've got to talk to him."

Morgan watched the short Indian breed nod and walk down the side of the slope toward the Indian village. This had to work. If it didn't, he might lose track of the boy for months, especially if they did move to the north hunting other Cheyenne bands.

Morgan stretched out on a bed of pine boughs and his two blankets. He had nothing to do but wait. Tomorrow at dusk he had to be within a quarter of a mile of the village. Imagine, sneaking up on a hundred Indians. He'd done it before. This time they were angry Indians. He'd have to be doubly careful.

That same afternoon back in Cheyenne, a slender man in a business suit of black, white shirt, and a gray town hat leaned against the wall outside the Pride of Wyoming Hotel. It wasn't a bad little town, he decided, all in all. He had sold enough of his kitchen and farm and ranch cutlery to make a tidy profit for himself, and that would keep the sales manager from threatening to fire him again. He might just look for a new line. But he'd always been partial to fine knives.

It was getting dark. His favorite time of day. He took out one of his new business cards and looked at it.

"Thurlow Deeds. Fine Cutlery. The Eversharp Company. Chicago, Illinois."

It was a good card. Store owners liked to have a card to tack up on their wall. Across the street a woman came from a clothing store and moved quickly down the boardwalk. He liked the smooth way her hips worked under her long skirt, but she was too skinny. He liked a woman with some meat on her bones.

Absolutely no connection. That was his whole secret. Not that he relished it. It was more of a disease with him and he didn't know how to treat it. He didn't even know if there could be a treatment for it. In the meantime, the ailment savaged him.

He turned and walked down the block to the far end. A house would be good, and a bed and some comfort. He had seen a particularly interesting woman come from a house with blue trim just at the end of the business district. At the time he had been working up a final order for the Patrick General Store. It had been the biggest order of his trip so far.

The woman was average height, maybe five-four, a little on the chunky side with a round, pretty face. He had been taken with her at once. She'd come past the store, and before long returned to the house. He'd seen no one else go in or come out of the house while he wrote up the order.

An hour later, Thurlow perched at the front table in the Sisters' Cafe and lingered over a piece of cherry pie and coffee. Still no one came to or left the house with the blue trim.

Later that afternoon, just after he had written an order for the Pride of the Prairie Saloon for an assortment of hunting and sportsman's knives, he walked toward the house with the blue trim and white curtains.

He stopped a man on the street.

"I'm looking for the Wilson house, sir. Is that it, the one over there with the blue on it?"

The man shook his head. "Afraid not. That's the Widow Henderson. Ain't heard of a Wilson family. They new in town?"

Thurlow said he wasn't sure, and turned and walked away in the other direction.

He stayed out of sight in the alley nearest the Henderson house as it grew to full dark. Then he left the alley and walked up the street to the corner and down past the Widow Henderson's place to the alley behind it. Thurlow glanced both ways casually, and when he saw no one on the street, he stepped into the alley and into its darkness behind the Henderson house.

Moments later he stepped up to the porch at the rear of the place and tested the doorknob. It was unlocked, as were the doors of most of the houses in town. He turned the knob slowly, then eased the door inward. It swung on oiled hinges.

Inside the small room, it was dark. A creep of light showed under the door into what he guessed would be the kitchen. The light wasn't strong and he figured it came from another room. Thurlow stepped cautiously across the floor to the door with the light under it and turned that knob. Then he pushed the door inward slowly.

Dim light in a kitchen that came from the living room. Quietly he stepped inside and closed the kitchen door. A typical small-town kitchen with a table and cupboards and four chairs.

He listened but could hear no one. Without making a sound, he walked across the kitchen and peered into the living room. A woman sat in a rocking chair, knitting needles clicking in her lap. She seemed to have a book on a stand, and now and then paused in her knitting to turn a page.

It was so easy that Thurlow felt little of the thrill of the capture. He slipped up behind her, put his arm around her throat in one swift move, and put his other hand across her mouth. Her scream never got through her lips.

Thurlow worked around the chair still holding her, and lifted her out of the rocker. Now he could see her eyes and they held an odd kind of resignation.

A lamp burned with a low wick in the bedroom. He walked her over there from behind and pushed her down on the bed.

"Don't scream and don't say a word, Mrs. Henderson, or I'll hurt you so bad you'll think you're in Hell." His words were soft and gentle, but with hideous undercurrents of evil enveloping them. Her eyes went wide and she only nodded.

He reached out and gently rubbed her breasts. She shrank back.

"Mrs. Henderson, how long have you been a widow?"

Kit Dalton

"Near to three years now," she said, her voice small, fragile, as if it would break if she spoke the words too loud.

"A long time to go without making love to a man. It has been near three years for you, hasn't it?"

Slowly she nodded.

"Then don't you think it's about time?" Gently his hand curved around one of her breasts, and this time she didn't pull back. She mewed softly and began unbuttoning the front of her dress.

He watched. Widows! What a great idea. He'd have to specialize in widows from now on. She unbuttoned the dress to the waist. Then her hands fell to her sides. He petted her breasts through the open dress front and found them covered with a wrapper. As he rubbed through the cloth, he could hear her breathing speed up. Soon she was breathing hard.

He sat on the bed beside her and took one of her hands and put it over the swelling behind his fly. She looked at him quickly and he nodded. Her hand rubbed him tenderly.

She half stood and whipped the dress up from under her legs and lifted it off over her head. Then she found a fastener and slowly undid the long piece of cloth that had been holding her breasts.

Thurlow smiled, bent and fondled her breasts, then kissed each before he stood and stripped off all his clothes. She watched him with curiosity and a growing passion.

He lay on the bed and pulled her over him, dropping first one and then the other breast into his mouth for chewing. She ground her hips against him, and at last gave a little cry. She rolled away from him, pulled off her pink bloomers, and sat there naked and waiting.

He put her on her back, raised her parted knees, and slid into her waiting slot on the first try.

"Oh, my God!" Mrs. Henderson said. "Three years, I don't believe it."

By that time, Thurlow hardly heard her. He drove and pounded and jolted against her, and when his time came he shrilled a cry of accomplishment and emptied himself into her.

Twice more they made love. She became more excited, more passionate each time. The last time she asked to be on top, and he obliged her. He reached below the bed to his pants and took out something, then helped her to reach her climax. He was close enough to match her shrill cry of ecstasy.

At the same time he picked up the four-inch heavy blade from where he had readied it and drove it deep and hard into the center of her back. He pushed sideways with it and then back, severing her spinal cord.

She fell on him, a dead weight, and he rolled her to the side and sat there on the bed panting. There would be no blood ritual this time. This was one to remember, to put in his book and to re-read when things were hard on the road.

When he had caught his breath, he dressed, cleaned the blade on the bedding, and blew out the lamp in the bedroom. He checked to make sure he had left nothing, then blew out the lamps in the living room and let himself out the back door. He stood just inside the porch for five minutes watching the alley and the street.

Nothing and no one moved. He left the back porch, walked to the alley, and went out the long way to the far street, then circled back to the downtown main street and the hotel.

He was in need of nourishment. A fine steak dinner with five kinds of vegetables would be good. It was only nine o'clock. He found a small cafe open that still served supper, and had his steak.

It was better than he had expected. An hour later he dropped into bed in the hotel and went to sleep within seconds.

High in the Rocky Mountains in Colorado, Lee Morgan had slept in almost until noon. He rose, made a small, nearly smokeless fire, boiled coffee, fried bacon and potatoes, and had his breakfast.

For two hours he practiced throwing his belt knife. It was the hunting type with handle, finger guard, and a five-inch blade sharpened on both sides of the end for cutting in either direction.

He picked out a practical distance, 15 feet, and threw at a big pine tree. It had been some time since he had thrown his knife and the first few times were miserable. Then he remembered the right twist and the coordination. He stuck the blade in the tree ten times in a row.

Then he began working on hitting a mark. He cut off a spot on the bark a foot square on the same pine tree and from the same 15 feet threw another 50 times aiming for the square. The last five throws hit the mark and he was pleased.

At two o'clock by his pocket watch, he watered the two horses, retied them on some grass, and headed along the slope toward the Indian village. He planned on going well past it and then coming upstream toward the village. That way he hoped to miss any hunters and find a spot to hide until Harold and Jim Breed walked into sight.

That was the plan.

He was still high on the slope, a half mile above the valley, when he saw movement ahead of him. He slipped behind a big Douglas fir and edged around for a look.

Less than 50 yards ahead he saw two Indians working through the light brush and trees toward him. Both had bows and arrows, and were hunting. He glued himself to the tree waiting. Twenty feet from him, one of them cried out.

Just to the left of them a doe leaped up and took two bounds and was gone in the woods. Both Indians darted after her.

Morgan hurried across the spot where the Indians had had him blocked and watched ahead with more intensity now as he worked past the village and on downstream.

A half mile beyond the village, he turned downhill, running into no more Cheyenne. He found the stream and waited. It was only four o'clock. It wouldn't be dusk for another three hours. He found some thick brush, crawled into it, and settled down to wait.

Ten minutes later, three young Indian boys ran past, laughing and shouting, throwing rocks at one another and cheering when they scored a hit. They splashed through the stream and were gone as they continued toward the village upstream.

An hour after the boys passed, two hunters came along a game trail near the stream. Each carried some kind of big game bird. They plodded along with supper on a rawhide thong over their backs.

Finding enough food to live on out here in the

wilderness would be the number-one demand on the warriors, Morgan decided.

When it was nearly six-thirty by his watch, the beginnings of dusk were showing through the trees. He lifted away from the brush and worked with caution upstream. He came to a bend in the stream and ahead, about 200 yards, he could see the first tipi of the village.

Morgan worked backwards another 200 yards and found a hiding spot. Some wild rosebushes had tangled and matted, but some small animal had burrowed under them and over the years chewed out a path that led to the less-dense interior.

Morgan crawled in and found he could see out, but doubted if anyone outside could see in. There was room enough to sit up and he did so, watching upstream, hoping that Jim Breed could convince the boy he should come see someone from his father.

It could be a trap. There was always that chance. While the Cheyenne hated all whites, they were especially angry with the Pony Soldiers. Morgan had weighed the odds and decided that the boy would be curious to see what his father had to say. Morgan was betting his life that there would not be a war party descending on then as soon as Morgan showed himself.

The time dragged. The murky dusk began to gobble up what was left of the daylight.

Then ahead he saw movement. Two shadows came out of the darker areas and continued toward him. One was taller than the other. They were no more than 20 feet away on the bank of the stream when Morgan recognized Jim Breed.

"Jim, I'm here," Morgan called.

Gunslinger's Scalp

He worked his way out of the wild rosebushes and Jim and the young man in a breechclout came to him. The boy was about five feet tall, broad-shouldered, and tan as any Indian, but even in the faint light Morgan could see his blue eyes.

"You must be Harold Bishop," Morgan said, holding out his hand. "I'm Lee Morgan with some messages from your father."

"My name is Mighty Dawn. I am a Cheyenne warrior and shouldn't be talking with you. What do you want?"

"To talk. I didn't come here to kidnap you. I just want to talk. Your father misses you. He doesn't know about your mother yet. I'm sorry about what happened. Sometimes Pony Soldiers, just like Cheyenne warriors, get a little out of hand."

"No Cheyenne warrior would deliberately . . ." He stopped.

"Harold, let's not argue. Your father misses you. He wonders if you've been thinking about Harvard University. He knows you had been counting on going there to become a scientist."

Morgan saw the boy's brow crease. He frowned. Then he sat down in the grass. Morgan sat down near him so they could talk quietly.

"Yes, I have thought about Harvard. I once wanted to be a scientist and study the stars and the planets. Now I know that was foolish boy thinking. I'm a warrior now."

"What do Cheyenne warriors do, Harold?"

"We defend the camps and the women and children. We make raids against our enemies, we hunt to feed our family, and we capture horses so we can be wealthy."

"Trying to figure out the universe sounds like a much bigger job. Not many people can work on a job like that."

"I am not going home. I belong here with my mother's people. They have taken me in. I must kill nine more Pony soldiers before I will have avenged my mother's murder."

"The Bible says an eye for an eye. A life for a life seems like vengeance enough."

"No, not for a Cheyenne warrior."

"Harold, you know your father is worried about you. He sent me out here to find you. He told me that you can do anything that you want to do if you come home. You can go to Harvard or not, you can become a scientist. You can take over one of his businesses and run it. You can do anything you want to do. He also told me that you'll never have to worry about money. He's rich, so you're rich too."

"That rich part sounds like my father."

"Mighty Dawn. I don't want to rush you. I'll be in the town of Cheyenne for another week. Promise me that you'll talk to me again before I have to go back to see your father."

"I can't promise. We will be leaving soon, moving north. That's all I can say."

"How will I find you?"

Harold grinned. "Your breed will find us. Jim tracked us here after the Pony Soldiers gave up their chase. It's hard to miss the tracks of a whole village. It is said we might spend some time in the Medicine Bow Mountains."

"Promise that you will be in contact with me before you leave for anywhere else farther north. Remember you are three-quarters white. This Indian life may begin to pale and wear thin after a while. It certainly will be a hard winter. No stoves, no heat except a fire. No solid buildings. Remember all the good things you had in your house in Grand Island. I should have brought you some books."

"Books. I haven't thought of books for a long time." He looked into the growing darkness toward the camp. "I should be getting back."

"Surely a warrior can stay out in the night."

"Of course."

"Do you think about home?"

"Yes. Often. Some things that happen here, I'm not used to yet. I went on a raid with the warriors. A stagecoach. The warriors took three women captive. One of the women was small and sickly and couldn't work, so the warrior who captured her tried to sell her to the other warriors. They laughed at his offer. So he killed her. It meant nothing to him."

"The way of the Cheyenne people," Morgan said.

Mighty Dawn looked up quickly. "My mother used to say that. I must avenge my mother's murder. I'll try to see you once more before you go. I must kill more Pony Soldiers."

"Or one of them might kill you," Morgan said.

"A chance I'll have to take."

Harold Bishop stood. Morgan stood. The young man stared at Morgan hard.

"You do this for a living? Hunt people, take messages?"

"Yes."

Harold nodded. "I'll try to get in contact with you before the week is up. Send Jim. I'll get him into camp anytime."

Mighty Dawn turned and ran into the darkness

before Morgan could say a word. He was at least half Cheyenne already.

Jim came out of the gloom.

"You heard?"

"Yes. Let's get to camp, then you decide what to do."

Morgan pondered it as they hiked the two miles back to their camp just over the ridge. They started a small fire, cooked some more of the bacon and potatoes and coffee, and ate biscuits and some of the jam.

Morgan stirred the fire.

"I've got to report back to Bishop what's happened. Ask him for instructions, offers to the kid. That means I can't be here to shadow their move. You'll have to do that. In the morning I ride back to Cheyenne, and you watch the Gray Owl band. How soon will they move?"

"Within two or three days."

"If they light in the Medicine Bows, they'll be within a day's ride of Cheyenne. Come in and tell me where they are. By then I should have word back from Bishop."

Morgan frowned as he said it. He was taking a big chance letting the kid get away from him this way. He'd talked to him. He hadn't convinced him to come back. Next time would be his last chance.

Chapter Nine

Buckskin Morgan rode into Cheyenne about four the following afternoon, tired, out of food, trail dirty, and ready for a long hot bath and the biggest steak in town. Maybe Lottie could whip up something for him.

As he unsaddled his horse and put the gear away, he tried to figure out if he wanted food or a bath more. His stomach won out and he strode up the street to the cafe. There was only one customer, and when Lottie saw him come in the front door she yelped and motioned to him and led him into her room in back of the kitchen.

"Land sakes, wonder you ain't been shot! You been gone for some days, I'd guess."

"Five days," he said.

She stared at him, hands on plump hips. "Yep, sure as the dickens! You do look like him, like that Slade Johnson. He paid the town a visit two days ago and robbed two stores, shot a deputy sheriff, and rode out of town laughing. The deputy died. The general store and a jewelry store got robbed. Jeweler claims he lost fifty thousand dollars worth of diamonds and rubies, but nobody don't believe him."

"Food first," Morgan said. "I'm half starved. Two steaks and some fixings, and a pot of coffee."

"I'll get it going," she said. She pushed up against him, mashing her breasts into his chest, and kissed his lips. When she eased back she grinned. "Yeah, it's just as good. I feed you and then you stay all night. Ain't safe you being on the street until you change your look."

She left then. He dropped on the bed, and a moment later she came in with a pot of coffee and a big cup. She poured it full, then hurried out.

Morgan sipped the coffee and wondered about the outlaw. The likes of him couldn't last long. Now that he was wanted for murder there would be a reward and some bounty hunter would bring him in. Maybe.

Morgan couldn't figure the man. He evidently had something of a reputation. Why was he robbing stores when there were two banks and a Railway Express car coming through town twice a day? Maybe he was a stupid bandit. Thinking about Slade made him remember Shirley, the tall, shapely blonde with the sexy ways in bed. Just how did she tie in with the bandit? She must be traveling with him, only by train. How did he and his gang travel, by horse? He'd have to investigate that question, and the sexy lady one of these nights.

He had dozed off when Lottie came back. She

had a serving tray with two inch-thick steaks, medium, and another plate loaded with vegetables, mashed potatoes, and brown gravy and two pieces of cherry pie with a cross-hatched-stripe crust.

She set them down in front of him. He reached out and kissed her, then grabbed his knife and fork and began eating.

"I love to watch a man eat."

He looked up. "I love to watch a woman strip off her clothes."

Lottie giggled. "Later, darling. I close up at eight. By eight-oh-three I'm gonna be bare and bouncing and ready to fuck you silly."

"That's a date," Morgan said, then forked another piece of tender steak into his mouth.

Morgan ate with purpose, and soon the steak plate and the second plate were empty. He was on his second cup of coffee when he started the pie.

Lottie came in in a moment. She had a line of sweat around her forehead from the stove, but grinned when she saw him.

"You done damn good. Want some more pie?"

He shook his head.

"Another steak?"

"Enough. I'll finish on coffee. Lot of business tonight?"

"Yeah. Lots of my regulars from the railroad shops."

"Don't you need some help?"

"Had a girl once. She stole everything she could reach. I make do by myself. If the guys don't want to wait a few minutes, I tell them to go somewhere else. I'll be back."

She hurried out to the kitchen. When the door

opened, he could hear a dozen different people talking out front.

A copy of the *Cheyenne Sun* lay on a small table. He picked it up and the headline stretched across all seven columns.

SECOND WOMAN MURDERED IN CHEYENNE.

He read the story that led down the right-hand column.

"A second woman has been murdered in Cheyenne, just two days after the first one, according to Sheriff Verne Goranson. Mrs. Faye Henderson, 54, widow of Jessie Henderson, was found dead in her home on Central Street Wednesday morning when a friend called to take her to a quilting party. The sheriff reports there was no sign of forced entry.

"Sheriff Goranson said he could not release any details of the crime, but said it was murder most foul. The sheriff has asked anyone who might have seen a man entering or leaving the Henderson home anytime Tuesday evening or early Wednesday morning, to give a report to his office.

"Jessie Henderson is remembered in Cheyenne as a pioneer merchant, who sold out his business five years ago. He passed away three years ago.

"The first woman found slain was in the alley behind Center Street and was found Monday afternoon. Witnesses report that she had been killed with a knife.

"Sheriff Goranson would not say if he thought there was a connection between the two killings. He did not reveal if he had any suspected perpetrators of the ghastly crimes.

"He did indicate that in a town the size of Cheyenne, there were always a few disreputable people clinging to our civilization. He said drifters and travelers and new settlers came in every day on the train.

"Mrs. Henderson will be long remembered in Cheyenne for her efforts to begin the Cheyenne County Library. She began the first collection of books shortly after she and her husband moved here in 1874."

Morgan looked away. He'd seen the first woman dead in the alley. Someone had enjoyed the work with the knife before that woman had died. He wondered about the other victim. Had she been killed with a knife as well?

The sheriff was right. The killer could be anyone, or any two. Both murderers could have been on the next train out of town and there would be no way in the world of finding them.

Unless there were some clues, some similar circumstances, a method that was the same. For example, if the second woman had been killed by a knife.

The long day, the good food, and the warm room caught up with Morgan. He put down the paper, had one last drink of coffee, and stretched out on the soft bed just behind the kitchen. For a moment he heard Lottie's shrill voice talking to someone. Then it faded and his eyes closed and he felt the signs of sleep slipping up on him.

It was like the rushing sound of a waterfall, the soft breath of a sleeping baby, the flutter of a hummingbird's wings, and then the soft easy glide into the glory of sleep.

Sometime later, Morgan mumbled in his sleep. Something bothered him, but in the murkiness of his slumber he couldn't figure out what it was.

Then the fog cleared and he came awake. He didn't move, didn't even open his eyes.

He knew at once what bothered him. Gentle hands worked at his crotch. His belt was off and his fly opened and hot blood coursed into his genitals.

Morgan slitted open one eye to see who sat on the bed beside him. A naked woman. She turned to look over her shoulder at him. Lottie.

He jolted up his hands and grabbed both her shoulders. Lottie shrieked.

Morgan sat up laughing, then so did Lottie.

"Just wondered if I could seduce a man when he was asleep," Lottie said, jiggling her big breasts. "Almost made it. You're more than ready. I was about ready to straddle you and slide him up inside me until he hit bottom, or top." She giggled. "Or whatever."

Morgan stroked her large breasts, tweaking her nipples, and watched them fill with hot blood and double in size. He bent and kissed both of them and Lottie gurgled with pleasure.

"No sense wasting a fine hard one like that, Morgan. You ready for some serious poking?"

Lee Buckskin Morgan kissed her breasts again and gently pushed her over backwards on the bed.

"Pretty lady, I'm almost always ready. Finding the right woman who is ready sometimes is the problem."

"No fucking problem tonight," Lottie said. She spread her legs and lifted her knees. "Why don't you just come on into my parlor and see me, right now!"

"Why don't you get on top like you was aiming to. Variety adds some spice to anything."

"Even fucking?"

"Especially fucking."

Morgan lay on his back and she rolled over and lifted above him. He grinned at her.

"You been on top before."

"Time or two. I been playing sexy games like this since I was fourteen. I had big boobs even back then. You want to hear about my first time?"

"No, it couldn't be any better than this one is going to be. Now pay attention so you don't break me in half."

She held him upright with one hand and then lowered her bulk downward at exactly the right spot.

"Oh, God!" she shouted when he pierced her and then slid along her canal as she lowered farther and farther. "Damn, don't you ever stop? How long is that thing, about a foot and a half?"

She moaned softly as her belly hit his, stopping the penetration.

"Oh, damn, I think I made a mistake and hit a two-foot broom handle you had under the bed."

"You have to do the work," Morgan told her. He lay there, one hand on each of her big breasts, working them around and round, then making them sway from side to side.

"The work?"

"Ride me like I was a young steer and you're a heifer in heat. You said you'd ridden top-saddle before."

"Oh, damn!" She began to move then, forward and back, as she felt him settle into position, and she faded back a little so she could get a better slant on things.

Soon she was galloping along like a trail herd

boss. The first dozen strokes set her off like a calliope.

It began with a long keening sound that grew stronger and wilder as it progressed. Then she grunted a half dozen times, moaning like she was on fire somewhere. Her orgasm climaxed with a long slow bellow that shaded off into a series of rolling spasms that shook her body for three minutes leaving her breathless, sagging on top of him, and panting like a steam engine newly filled with water.

She was quiet for two minutes, gasping for breath. Morgan punched upward with his hips and she chuckled.

"Oh, damn, are you still there? I thought I killed you. About time for another one." She started moving again, and soon Morgan sensed his own ending coming. Before he got there she climaxed again with the same long keening. Morgan powered upward a dozen times countering her strokes, and soon he let out a bellow of primal domination as he blasted into a climax that shot eight loads of freight upward. Then he evaporated into a spent, huddled mass as Lottie flashed through her second orgasm and collapsed on top of him, driving him deep into her featherbed mattress.

It was ten minutes before either of them moved. At last she lifted up on one elbow and stared down at him. "Why are you so fucking sexy?"

"Just trying to match the wanton woman pussy pounding away on top of me."

She stared at him a minute, then grinned, kissed him quickly, and fell back on top of him.

"Thanks, Morgan. Nobody ever said anything so nice to me before."

An hour, and two encounters later, Morgan begged off and said he had to get some sleep.

"I've been riding for fifteen hours, I'm sore and tired and half-starved—*was* half-starved, that is—and if you don't let me go to sleep I'm liable to drop off halfway through something I'd much rather finish in person."

Lottie laughed and rolled off the bed. "I'm having a bath, want one?"

"In the morning," Morgan said, dropping his head on a pillow. He knew he took up more than half of the bed. He was too tired now, too drained and sleepy to care. She'd know how to push him over. He tried to imagine how she would do it as he took one last deep breath and went to sleep.

Morgan didn't wake up until after daylight. There was a note about Lottie doing breakfast. He decided to wait on the bath. He read the paper again about the death of the two women. Two so close together could have been the same man. A killer like that often was a madman of some kind, like that crazy man in New York who killed six prostitutes.

Grand Island. Morgan washed up and shaved carefully with a straight razor he found on the dresser. He put on his trail clothes, and then found paper and a pencil and wrote out the message he had to send to Mr. Bishop in Grand Island.

"ALONZO BISHOP. GRAND ISLAND, NE-BRASKA. HAVE LOCATED BOY AND YOUR WIFE. YOUR WIFE KILLED BY CAVALRY IN RAID ON CHEYENNE SUMMER CAMP A

WEEK AGO. BOY CLAIMS TO BE A CHEY-
ENNE WARRIOR. DETERMINED TO AVENGE
HIS MOTHER'S DEATH. TALKED TO HIM
ONCE. WILL TRY TO PERSUADE HIM TO RE-
TURN NEXT TIME WE TALK. WHAT CAN YOU
OFFER HIM TO HELP HIM DECIDE TO RE-
TURN? SOMETHING SPECIAL? LEE MOR-
GAN, SENDING."

Morgan carried the message to the telegraph
office in the train station and watched the telegrapher while he sent it. Morgan took the piece of
paper and pushed it back in his pocket. Morgan
stared at the smaller man behind the key.

"If anyone hears anything about this message,
I'll blame you and enjoy making you suffer for
talking," Morgan said, his voice even, level, and
with a deadly ring.

"Never say a word," the clerk said. "One of our
guarantees. We can't even tell the sheriff if bank
robbers are coming."

Morgan nodded and walked out of the station
and directly to his hotel. His room was intact
and everything was in place. He ordered bath-
water from the clerk, found the bathroom on his
floor unoccupied, and waited for the six buckets
of hot water to be carried up the steps.

Morgan luxuriated an hour in the bath until
the water had cooled. Then he dressed and put
on his town disguise so he would not be confused
with Slade Johnson, the outlaw. The glasses were
effective. He used the second hat he'd bought, a
cloth one in the style of a cap with a bill. He
could pull it down lower. It made him look something like a dandy. He found a town shirt and
even put on a string tie.

Then he walked the streets of Cheyenne until

he was sure no one would recognize him as Slade Johnson. He went back to the hotel, strode directly to Room 322, and knocked. This time there was no pause. The door opened quickly and Shirley stared at him wide-eyed for a minute, then sighed and pushed the panel the rest of the way open.

"I shouldn't let you in. You promised me you'd be back to see me and that was a week ago. Only four days, maybe five, I've lost count." She wore a thin silk gown of some sort that was so sheer he could see right through it. She had nothing on under it.

"What do you want?" she asked.

"What do *you* want, Shirley?" He stood with his feet a little apart, facing her, his hands on his hips. She watched him a moment. Then her gaze ran down his chest to his crotch and stayed there. When she looked back up she smiled.

"You know damn well what I want, just like on the train. That was so good. It's the kind of lovemaking a woman dreams about but doesn't get often enough."

"Where is Slade?"

"Still in his camp, I'd guess. He hasn't been in town for three or four days."

"Not since the robberies and the killing?"

"You heard. Folks say it was him. I don't know. He don't tell me what he's planning."

"If he's such a fearless bandit, why doesn't he rob a bank or two? That's where the big money is."

"He's done banks before. He just likes to be sure. Some banks have guards."

"Some don't. Do you always dress that way?"

133

"Only when I'm in my room and I want to. Does it bother you?"

"Not a bit. I know what the whole package looks like, remember? Did Slade kill those two women?"

Shirley laughed. "Slade? Kill a woman? Not a remote chance. He likes women too much. Any woman. He's a cock-hound. But he is good at making love. He's not much of a suspect there. Do you think the same man killed them both?"

"Might have. Not my problem. Slade is my problem. I don't fancy wearing a disguise like this for as long as I'm in a town that Slade is harassing."

"He could be moving on soon. I heard him saying something about two more big jobs and they would ride out. He always tells me which direction he's going and what hotel to stay at. I usually get a job dancing at a saloon to fill in my nights."

"If he tells you when he's going, will you tell me?"

"Depends. If you have me flat on my back making love to me, there's a chance I will. I lose my willpower then about everything."

"Let's hope I catch you on your back on the right day," Morgan said. He moved toward the door.

"You're not staying?"

"Just remembered. I didn't have any breakfast."

"Fine, stay here and I'll send down for two steak dinners."

"Next time, I promise."

"I'll be through early at the saloon tonight. Come see me about eleven."

"Last time I tried that I met a shotgun blast."

"Won't happen again. I live here."

Morgan went out the door, waved, and hurried down a floor to his own room, 228. He stood at the wall side of the doorknob and keyed it unlocked, then unlatched the door and pushed it inward. No shotgun blast went off. He stepped inside and locked the door behind him.

He had to decide what the hell he was going to do about Slade Johnson. The sheriff didn't seem to be doing much. If the bandit had any ambition he'd be back to town for the bank. Maybe he didn't have enough men for the Railway Express car. If Morgan could warn the banks, then catch Slade in a shoot-out at a bank and make sure he didn't get away, that would solve the Slade Johnson problem.

Trouble was, looking something like Slade, how would that allow him to approach the banks? He lay down on the short bed and tried to figure it out. There had to be a way.

Chapter Ten

Slade Johnson counted their money. He had the bills and coins in stacks on the rough table in the farmer's house east of town. This time he had a lookout downstream about a mile to watch for a posse or any curious bastard who might wander that way.

He still hadn't figured out why Morgan had shot out his windows and wounded Chiseler last week. Maybe he was a lunatic, but why would he just start shooting? Slade shook his head and looked at the figures he'd written down.

Not a hell of a lot of loot for two holdups. The diamond rings he could get rid of in St. Louis or maybe Omaha or Denver, but for now they were so many chunks of rock.

He added the numbers, checked his figures, and added them again.

"Four hundred and twenty-three dollars.

Damn, we've done that good robbing a stagecoach."

Slade was tall, well-built, had dark brown hair, and was clean-shaven. He usually wore a buckskin shirt and jeans and boots. A good working outfit. There was a thin scar down his left cheek that showed only when his face turned angry and red.

He began dividing the money into seven parts. Two shares for himself and one each for his five men.

As he clinked the gold coins, his newfound half-breed Cheyenne squaw came up and put her arms around him. She was a breed he'd found in town yesterday. He'd ridden back to town under a big hat and with the start of a beard to see how the town took the robberies. He'd also wanted to look at the banks.

Two of them in town. He wanted to hit one of them on his way out of this territory, but he hadn't decided which one yet. The richest one was by far the best fortified. He'd changed a ten-dollar bill into ones and seen two sawed-off shotguns behind the teller cages and an armed guard at the door who looked like he could use his six-gun and his shotgun.

The other bank didn't have a guard in it. He asked around town and most people said they trusted the smaller of the two banks the most. That was the one without the guard and shotguns.

He pulled the half-squaw around in front of him and grabbed her breasts.

"Yeah, how come a breed like you got such big tits?" Slade asked.

"Big tits, hot cunnie," she said, grinning, showing where three of her front teeth were missing.

Slade pulled up her blouse and looked at her breasts. Best tits he'd seen in a week. Damn near as good as Shirley's. He wished he could see the big blonde more. But it was a risk just going into town, and she wouldn't live in their hideout with them. It had been that way for six months. He should dump her and take this little pootang along with them. That way he could throw it into her twice a day. He'd think on it. His squaw breed had told him a name but he'd forgotten it. Now he just called her Big Tits and she liked it.

He finished dividing the cash and called the men.

"Sixty dollars for each of you," Slade said. "My figures are right if any of you want to do the dividing." The four men there shook their heads. Chiseler was still hobbling around. The stranger's rifle slug had torn through the calf of his right leg and put him down to a crawl.

The lead had gone all the way through and not hit the bone. Muscles would heal, but it would take some time. Slade knew enough about gunshot wounds. He would make sure that Chiseler stayed off that leg for a week. By then they would be ready to ride. Chiseler would have to stay mounted and hold the horses when they hit the bank.

That only left five of them to take down the bank. Should be easy. He'd do it the way he had before. They would get inside the bank as customers just before it closed. When the last regular customer had been let out the locked front door, they would pull down the shades, take over the place without firing a shot. Nobody would know the bank had been robbed maybe until morning.

He'd done two banks that way and got near a day's head start on any posse.

"About decided we'll do the smaller of the two banks. Not so many shotguns to worry about. Chiseler will stay mounted and hold the horses in the alley. We'll do it at closing time."

Two of the men laughed.

"No sense getting shot at unless we got to," Langley said. He was a thin man and short. Sometimes he was mistaken for a boy in his teens. But he was the best revolver shot in the gang. He was always one of the gang members who went over the counter behind the teller cages to clean them out.

"Not sure just when we take down the bank," Slade said. "Long as they don't send out a posse we'll stick here. Kind of like this place, and nobody but that one varmint has been snooping around. When's the food gonna be ready?"

Big Tits came up behind Slade and grabbed his crotch. He turned around and chuckled. "You never get enough, do you, squaw?" He pulled off her blouse and saw the Kid watching the half-naked woman.

"Hey, Kid, I guess it's your turn. Come on over here and show us what a big man you are."

Grits, the cook, laughed. "Yeah, Kid, you kept me awake last night whanging it off in your bunk. Big Tits there is lots better than that smelly old blanket you shot into last night."

The Kid shook his head and ran outside.

"Made the Kid feel bad," Lonesome Harry said. Harry was the last man in the team and had just come in from his lookout spot. It was dusk out. They'd take their chances on a night-time raid. Slade didn't expect one.

"Hell, he's got to try a woman sometime," Slade said.

"His first time should be in the dark without us watching," Lonesome said. "Send him and the squaw outside tonight."

Slade scowled. "Hell, what's the matter with him? I got my first girl when I was fourteen. She was sixteen and her first time too. What a wild time that was. Neither of us knew what we were doing."

"And you put it in her ear," Chiseler said. Everyone roared.

Grits served up supper for them. He'd gotten a roast in town and cooked it to a turn, and served it with potatoes and carrots and big slabs of bread and real butter he'd bought. Coffee finished the meal. They usually didn't eat this well when they were on the run.

Big Tits finished her plate of food and asked for more. Slade squeezed her breasts. "Yeah, I guess you ain't full yet."

As soon as they finished eating, Slade and the half-breed Indian woman retreated to the bedroom Slade used. He'd been poking her once a day, but she seemed to want more.

"Bet you used to be a whore," Slade told her. She bit his nose.

"No whore, just have lots of fucking friends who bring presents."

"Presents, I bet. Like two dollars a poke." She pushed one big breast into his mouth to stop him talking. As Slade chewed on the morsel he nearly decided that Shirley was too expensive to keep in a hotel. He really didn't need her anymore with Big Tits around. She could service the whole gang and come up asking for more. He'd decide before he did the bank. All he had to do was hit the bank and ride out of town without telling Shirley where they were heading. Easy. He'd decide tomorrow.

Thurlow Deeds was back in Cheyenne. He'd taken the train to Laramie, spent two days there making all of his usual calls, and racked up more sales than he expected. These railroad towns were growing so quickly it was amazing.

He hadn't found any woman to his liking in Laramie. Cheyenne was a much larger place with many more possibilities. It was the territorial capital and a big rail center and there was the start of farming and ranching around, as well as some coal mines.

He settled into the hotel and decided that he was hungry. He had tired of hotel dining room food and wanted something different. He took a walk and found several cafes and small restaurants. He picked one at last because he liked the way it looked.

Anyway, he had known a girl back home named Lottie. She had been his first conquest. No, she was the second, but it hardly counted since she wanted to find out about making love and it had been her first time and she'd almost raped him. He grinned thinking about it. So he walked into Lottie's Cafe.

"What can I serve you tonight, sir?" Lottie asked, standing in front of him. She wore the white blouse with the one top button missing and that revealed a deep line of cleavage between her breasts.

141

Thurlow grinned. This was getting better and better. "Let's see, what is the best of the house tonight?"

"I've got some fresh venison steaks that are the best. Course they cost near twice what a beef-steak does. Comes with mashed potatoes, and peas and carrots, and a green salad, and a bread tray with fresh churned butter, and a tray of pre-serves, and of course coffee or tea."

"How much?"

"A dollar."

"A dollar for supper?"

"Not just supper, this is a feast. I only had ten of the steaks and I have just two left. If'n you want one better order now afore I go down to that table of four railroaders. They come all the way from Chicago and are hungry as hell."

"I'll take it, long as you throw in a piece of apple pie."

"Done." Lottie grinned and turned. He watched the way her breasts heaved as they changed direction. What a time he could have with those unencumbered and swinging free!

An hour later, Deeds settled back in his chair and wiped his mouth. It was the best supper he'd had in months. This woman knew how to cook, and the venison was remarkable. He looked up. Lottie stood beside him.

"How was your supper?"

He stood and found himself close to her. She didn't move and there was a glint in her eyes.

"Best damn meal I've had in months. I'll be back for breakfast and then dinner and supper. I'm staying over in town for a couple of days. I've earned a little vacation."

Lottie grinned. A man down the way signaled for more coffee.

"Thanks. I've got to run. See you tomorrow."

Thurlow Deeds left a 50-cent tip on the table when he went up to pay his check. It had been worth it. After eating here three times tomorrow, he'd make a try to get Lottie in bed in her place. He was sure she wasn't married. Oh, what a time that would be!

Morgan had on his heavy disguise as he checked out both banks. One had a guard and he saw shotguns in holders near each of the tellers' windows. He had change made on a twenty-dollar gold piece and went to the next bank.

It was smaller, had only two tellers and two others working in the bank. Both the tellers were men. There was a woman bookkeeper and one person behind a closed door marked "President."

This one, Morgan decided. No bank robber in his right mind would go up against three shotguns at least. And each person probably had a six-gun handy as well. It would be the smaller bank, even though it probably had less cash on hand. Some of these small Western banks didn't carry as much as a thousand dollars in cash. But that would not be true around the time of the railroad payday. He'd heard of banks giving a back room to railroad men to make up pay envelopes for workers so they all got the exact cash they had earned that pay period.

Of the two, the larger bank probably had the railroad's local account.

Morgan went to the first teller available in the smaller bank.

"Yes, sir?"

143

"I'd like to see the president of your bank. Would that be possible?"

"Just a moment, I'll see." The teller left his post and went to the marked door. He came back a moment later.

"Yes, you may see the president. This way."

When Morgan stepped into the room he was surprised to see a young woman sitting behind the only desk in the room. She stood and held out her hand.

"Good afternoon. I'm Sarah Everett, and I'm president of the Cheyenne Territorial Bank. What can I do for you?"

They both sat down. He had been surprised by her manner as well as her round beautiful face and the dark eyes that matched her shoulder-length hair. he looked quickly and saw no rings on her fingers.

"My name is Lee Morgan and I'm new in town. I'm looking for a business to buy or to start a new one, and I'm checking out both banks to see which one I want to use. Can you tell me a little about your bank and your qualifications to be president?"

He saw a muscle in her face tighten and knew he had made a mistake.

"I'm president here because my father died suddenly of a bank robber's bullet and since my mother had already passed away, I became his sole heir. It's my bank with no stockholders. We have a favorable cash-reserve-to-loan ratio, and we have never defaulted on a savings or checking account. We deal with a large bank in Chicago to maintain our cash reserves. We can handle any request for cash within a twenty-four-hour waiting period.

Gunslinger's Scalp

"We now service twenty-seven of the one hundred four merchants in town, not counting the saloons. I'm sure we can be of service to you for checking, for loans, and for day-to-day banking necessities."

Morgan grinned. "Impressive. You even *sound* like a banker."

Her frozen smile melted a little. "That's because I am a banker. I studied everything Papa did. He was grooming me to take over the bank, but he didn't plan that I would do it quite so soon."

"You're about twenty-four years old?"

"Mr. Morgan, that's none of your business. Now, do you have any pertinent questions about our ability to serve you as your bank?"

"You are open ten to five, I see. Good. I dislike those banks that close up at three o'clock. Oh, I notice you don't have any security. Aren't you afraid of being robbed?"

"Not in the slightest. I'm convinced that the reason Papa died is because he fought back. There are no firearms inside the bank. If some desperadoes try to rob the bank they will find a minimum amount of cash on hand. Any loss would not be so great that I couldn't cover it with my personal reserves in Chicago. We even run out of cash sometimes. We prefer it that way to having a large cash supply on hand to tempt robbers. We even have a sign to that effect in our lobby. Did you notice it?"

"I'm afraid I didn't." Morgan watched her. She was beautiful and shapely and unmarried and probably a virgin. He quickly pushed his thoughts in another direction.

"Miss Everett, it's good to meet you and to

145

know about your banking experience and your method of doing business. I like your approach to the robbery issue. The only thing that bothers me is that a lot of desperadoes out there robbing banks don't know how to read."

Her glance shot up at him and frown lines etched into her smooth forehead. "Oh, my, I'd never thought of that."

"I didn't mean to upset you. I'd guess that in most of the robber gangs at least one of the group can read."

She looked up and her face had softened. It was even more beautiful now, a warmer, friendlier look. "Thank you. I might also put a typed notice on the entrance door. That might help."

Morgan stood and held out his hand. "I want to thank you for your frank and honest review of your banking services. I'll decide what to do in a few days and get back to you, Miss Everett. Thanks for your time."

She stood and shook his hand, and held it a little longer than usual. Her smile was warmer now. The touch of a grin slipped around past her eyes and down to her mouth.

"The fact is, Mr. Morgan, I'm twenty-five and single. That was the other question you wanted to ask."

"Caught me," Morgan said. "You must admit, it's unusual to find such a beautiful young lady who is the president of her own bank. A natural curiosity. I'm sorry if I offended you."

"No offense at all, Mr. Morgan."

"But I guess this still wouldn't be a good time to invite you out to dinner tonight."

"Not really a good time for that, Mr. Morgan." She smiled. "But perhaps another day."

He nodded, turned, and left the room.

On his way out of the bank, Morgan saw the notice. A bank was a bank. Any potential robber would laugh at such a sign and clean them out of whatever cash they had. But how could you warn somebody like Sarah Everett, whose father had died in a shoot-out in his own bank. It might be impossible. If he had any way of knowing, he could catch Slade and his gang just as they came out of the bank. It would be worth it to get rid of an outlaw who looked like him.

As he walked back to his hotel, Morgan went over his arrangements with Jim Breed for a report on the Cheyenne band of Gray Owl. If the band moved north and if they stopped in the Medicine Bow Mountains just to the west of Cheyenne, Jim would ride into town and leave a message in Morgan's hotel room key box.

In case they kept moving north across the open stretches toward northern Wyoming, Jim would also ride in and tell Morgan so they could give chase. It was chancy either way.

He went down the boardwalk toward his hotel. It was almost time for supper. It had been a long day but he felt nearly back to normal after his hard ride the day before.

A good night's sleep and maybe he'd have an answer back from Bishop. It had been over eight hours since he'd sent his message. He detoured past the train station, and the telegrapher said he did have a wire for a Lee Morgan.

It came in an envelope now for privacy. Morgan tore open the envelope and read the message:

"LEE MORGAN, CHEYENNE, WYOMING. SHOCKED ABOUT WILLOW. BRING BACK HAROLD AT ALL COSTS. GUARANTEE HIM A

147

TRIP TO ENGLAND, A RACEHORSE OF HIS OWN, HARVARD FOR SURE, AND HIS CHOICE OF CAREERS. I HEREBY DOUBLE YOUR BONUS. A. BISHOP SENDING."

Morgan took the message and went back to his room. He lay on the bed and read it again. Tomorrow he should ride out to the Medicine Bows along the rails and then turn south hoping he could intercept the Cheyenne.

He had dinner in the hotel dining room and went directly back to his room. It looked small after living in the outdoors for a few days and nights.

For a moment he thought about Shirley, and the delightful curve of her breasts, the delicate blond hairs at her crotch. He groaned softly in honest pain and slid into bed. He needed the sleep. He would get back to the ever-hungry Shirley as soon as he could. Maybe tomorrow. No, he was riding west tomorrow. Or should he wait for a message from Jim Breed?

He would figure it out tomorrow.

Chapter Eleven

At breakfast the next morning, Morgan read a special edition of the *Cheyenne Sun*. The headline raced across all seven columns of the front page: TWO WOMEN KILLED BY SAME MAN.

The story went down the right-hand page again, this time set two columns wide in larger type. "Sheriff Goranson said his experts have told him that the same man probably killed both the women murdered in our town in the last few days. Both had been sexually assaulted and both died of knife wounds.

"The sheriff says he has no firm 'suspects' yet, but he is checking out three different men with a history of violent crimes in this area. He has little evidence from the sites of the killings to help him, but he said he has turned up 'certain material' which will be vital in the investigation."

Morgan skimmed the rest of the story. It was a rehash of what had happened and how the women had died and where and who they were. So it was the same man, a knife man. They were harder to find, they were silent, and like that crazy man in New York City, they often appeared to be entirely normal—until they went on their killing rampages.

The idea of digging into the problem and trying to find the killer intrigued Morgan, but he remembered his first job and that was to find Harold Bishop and persuade him to come back to his father's house and care.

Which brought up his duty for the day. Did he ride out blind hoping to find some trace of Jim Breed or the Cheyenne? Or would that be a waste of energy, time, and good horseflesh?

Jim had said he would contact Morgan if the band moved beyond the railroad tracks. That had been only three days ago. The Cheyenne would move about 25 miles a day. It would take them two days to reach the tracks, then another day to get deep into the Medicine Bow Mountains.

The Medicine Bows were beyond Laramie, but there were some mountains between Laramie and Cheyenne. Those were the Laramie Mountains. It would be most logical for the Gray Owl band to strike for them. They would have only to drive straight north and a little east to hit the mountains between the two towns.

To reach the mountains west of Laramie they would have to swing 75 miles to the west from their present location. Morgan knew this was all speculation, but he had nothing else to go on. Say the band left two days after Morgan left. They would now be approaching the Union Pacific tracks and moving into the hills to the west of Cheyenne.

Four days. Two after he departed and two to get up north. With that as the yardstick, the message from Jim could come sometime today. It would not be good planning to ride out on a wild-goose chase and miss the message.

That meant he had to wait through the day and see if Jim arrived with some word on the band.

Which left him a whole day to play detective, or to try to track down Slade Johnson and catch him and turn him over to the sheriff, who would surely see that he was hanged for killing his deputy in that robbery.

Then too, there was the chance that Slade would rob one or both of the banks. Morgan had about decided that Slade didn't have enough men to take on the Union Pacific. They had been riding with a shotgun guard inside the Railway Express cars on some runs. It had to be the bank. Why else would he stay around here? Morgan figured that as long as Shirley was in town, Slade would be nearby.

Morgan put down the newspaper and finished his coffee. So it would be the double killing. He went for a walk and found the alley where the woman had been murdered. He walked to where he had seen her before. There were a half-dozen cardboard boxes still there. He saw that most of them had been moved, probably when the sheriff made his search.

One more look wouldn't hurt. Morgan studied the dark stain on the dirt. It was the woman's blood. She had died about there. The rape had probably happened behind the boxes, not so much for privacy as for safety for the rapist.

Morgan moved some of the boxes. He found one that had been sliced in half. Could that have been done by the killer? It could have provided more privacy. He looked under more of the old boxes. Behind one, near the wall of the store, he saw something glitter.

He frowned and bent to examine it. He picked up a small pin, the kind that some lodgemen and women's club members wear. This one looked like a bird with a big bill, and two small stones which could be diamonds were set on its body. The pin itself was no more than an inch and a half long. It appeared to be made of gold. There was a simple clasp on the back of it to push through fabric and catch. This bit of jewelry could be important. The woman might have fought with her attacker and stripped the pin off his jacket or shirt.

Morgan dropped the pin in his pants pocket and kept looking. The alley wasn't used much. It was behind a furniture and hardware store, with a saloon on either side. The saloons both had outhouses in the alley, but they were well to either side of the death scene.

He remembered what the newspaper had said about the woman. Priscilla Lang, 34, an unmarried seamstress and dressmaker who worked in a dress shop and lived upstairs behind it. Her place was on the other side of the street and a block down. What was she doing in the alley?

Morgan picked the closest end of the alley and walked out to the street. He moved the way the killer might have. Nothing made any sense. The store had been left open. There had been money in the cash box, a dress being worked on and spread out on a cutting table.

So the woman had not left the shop of her own free will. But how could the killer abduct her in broad daylight? Most likely out the back door into the alley there, which was a street and an alley over from where she was found.

Since the door was left open and there was money in the cash drawer, it must not have been a random kill. The knife-man had picked out his victim, probably because she had big breasts. So he was a breast man? Or did he just like to carve up big-breasted women?

Morgan knew he had a lot more questions than he did answers. Knives, a knife. No weapon had been found at either killing. Which could mean the man liked his knives too well to leave them behind.

Murderous passion, but tempered with the reality of taking the offending weapon away with him to help him avoid detection.

It was a puzzle.

Yet when the second killing was layered on over the first, there were few facts that meshed or duplicated. Both victims had been women. Both had been sexually used and then killed with a knife. The first tortured and cut so she would bleed profusely.

But the second dead woman had had only a small knife wound in her back that had severed her spinal column. No slashing. No blood. No torture. At least that was what the newspaper had said.

He fingered the gold pin with the two diamonds. Someone around town might have seen it. First he took it to a jeweler whose sign said he had diamonds for sale. He was the same man who had been robbed by Slade Johnson.

"Yes, sir, how may I help you?" a medium-sized man said from behind a counter that had a glass top. The jeweler had a "glass" in his eye and dropped it out as he smiled at Morgan.

"Just wondered if these are real diamonds and if it's made of gold."

Morgan put the pin on a velvet cloth on the countertop. The jeweler put the glass back in his eye and examined the diamonds.

"Yes, yes, they are diamonds. Blue white we call them. Of course they are small, and of little value. It indeed is gold, a high percentage. See how it's been nicked here and there. Might be even fifty-percent gold. Doesn't wear well and can be bent with little pressure. Worth? Twenty dollars at the most. And that's almost all for the gold. You found it or was it a gift? I see the clasp has been broken here on the back."

"Yes, a gift. Have you ever seen anything like this before?"

The jeweler studied it a moment. "I craft jewelry myself, so I would notice that pin. It's different enough. What kind of a bird is that?"

"I'm not sure." Morgan thanked the jeweler and went outside and down the boardwalk. He moved along the street slowly, trying to jiggle something into place that had been bothering him. The knife. What kind of a knife was strong enough to cut through a backbone?

He turned and went to the general store and found the display of knives. There were a dozen different kinds, from meat cleavers to potato peelers. These were mostly kitchen and butchering knives. Most ranchers and farmers butchered their own animals so there was always a need for knives in the West.

He picked up a sturdy blade that was six inches long, with a tapered point that was slightly curved.

A clerk came up beside him.

"Going to do some butchering?" the clerk asked.

"Maybe," Morgan said.

"That's one of our best skinning knives. The curve of the blade on the end is preferred by some men so they can slice along and do the skinning quick and easy. Some guys hate the curve."

Morgan picked up another knife. It was slender, no more than a half-inch wide and so thin and with such a wide cutting edge it reminded him more of a razor. It was a full eight inches of blade.

"Now what's this one for?" Morgan asked.

"Filleting knife," the clerk said. "Use it mostly on fish. Make the first cut below the head and the gills. Go right in to the backbone, then turn toward the tail and slice right next to the bone all the way to the tail. You leave about a half inch of fish and flip out the part you just cut off. Then run the knife under the skin and all the way back to the front of the fillet and you have it done.

"Seen some guys who can fillet a good-sized bass in fifteen seconds."

"I was really looking for a good penknife, lost mine."

The clerk nodded. "We need to go over to the next display. We have some fine penknives made in Maine. Did you know that the penknife was designed for use in trimming quills that were used not too long ago for pens? That was before the steel nibs we have these modern days. Here we are."

He showed Morgan a selection of penknives and other pocket knives.

"The penknife always has just one blade," the clerk went on. "Since it only had one use, it had one blade. We have some fine pocket knives that have three folding blades."

Morgan chose one of the three-bladed types, paying the high price of 80 cents for it. But the blades were good and sharp. Now he would never be without some kind of a knife, even if he had to leave his belt blade in his hotel room.

Outside on the boardwalk, he looked across the way at the Cheyenne Territorial Bank. Morgan wore his town disguise again, including the bill cap and spectacles. He walked across the street, careful to miss the horse droppings and cow pies left by a pair of oxen that had just pulled a heavy wagon down Eddy Street.

Morgan decided it was worth taking a chance with Miss Everett. She had to be warned, even though he figured it would do no good. He walked into the bank and found her door open.

Morgan went up to it and knocked on the door casing. No one else was in her office. She looked up, frowned a moment, then smiled.

"Oh, yes, Mr. Morgan. I have a question to ask you. Why do you wear that silly cap and those spectacles? It seems unnatural for a man of your young years. The first time I saw you, you had on a proper Stetson. You looked much more at home dressed that way. I bet you've spent a lot of time in the saddle."

Morgan grinned as he walked in. He took off

the cap and then the glasses and looked down at her.

"Do I remind you of anyone, Miss Everett?"

She frowned for a moment, then reached in her drawer and took out a piece of folded paper. She opened it and compared the two. Her eyes went wide and she gasped.

"That is why I wear the glasses and cap, usually pulled low over my eyes."

She looked up and then back at the paper, which he knew had to be a wanted poster on Slade Johnson.

"But . . . you're not the same. I can easily see the difference around your eyes. Your nose isn't quite as big as Slade Johnson's and your face is a little leaner."

"The man on the street who tried to shoot me didn't see those differences, Miss Everett. That's why I wear this silly hat and the spectacles and no more buckskins."

"I don't blame you. I just wanted to know. Now, did you have a banking question for me?"

"Yes. You know about Slade Johnson. I've got a hunch he's not through with our town. I think before he moves on he'll rob one of the two banks."

She frowned and watched him. "You know this for sure?"

"No, just a hunch. That's his business. He might not have found much cash in those two stores he robbed. He'll come back for a bank and then ride on west."

"You think he'll rob mine and not the other bank?"

"Yes. He's seen the shotguns they have, and the guard. He'll take the lower risk for less money. Gold is hard to spend if you're dead."

"My father taught me that, which is exactly why I won't hire a shotgun guard or give guns to my tellers."

"So you'll just let them rob you?"

"If it comes to that, yes."

"Miss Everett, it's almost time for dinner. They call it lunch in San Francisco now. Why don't I take you out to lunch at one of the cafes and we can discuss this strictly banking problem in more detail."

"I have no..." She stopped and lifted her brows. "Yes, I'd love to go to...lunch with you. But don't try and persuade me. My mind is made up about guns in my bank."

They walked to a new restaurant just across from the Union Pacific station. A train swept in with steam spewing and cinders flying. It screeched to a stop with steel wheels sliding on steel rails the last three feet. Sarah Everett stopped and watched it, then gave a small cheer.

"That railroad is this town, do you know that? The Union Pacific decided they needed a town every fifty miles or so along the tracks when they were building through here back in 1867. We were set up as a supply point for the construction crews, and the town remained when the rail-laying crews moved on west and established Laramie fifty miles down the line. I love the railroad. Twice now I've taken the train all the way to New York City. It's so exciting."

They went into the restaurant. It had white tablecloths and silverware and china already set on the table.

"I heard it was elegant, but I've never been here," Sarah said.

They sat down and ordered, and then the deep brown eyes of the woman looked up at Morgan.

"Do you have any idea just when this assault on my bank might happen?"

"No. Soon, the next week or so."

"Not much help. I could send most of my cash on to Chicago, or dig a hole a bury it in the ground. This is so terrible I just don't know what to do."

"How much cash do you usually have in the bank, in the safe and in the tellers' drawers?"

Sarah looked at him hard for a moment, then took a deep breath. "I don't believe that I'm telling you this. I met you yesterday, and now I'm telling you the details of my banking business." She lifted her brows and then frowned. "Usually about twelve to fifteen hundred dollars."

"That would be quite a loss for you. It's also the average pay for a workingman for four years. More important, your depositors might not think their money was safe."

He had a bite of a sandwich they had ordered and she sipped at the coffee. "What can I do?"

"For a week or two, you could hire three shotgun guards. Put one outside the front door, put one in the lobby behind a thick oak door with a small window in it, and put the third guard at the back door."

"But who would take such a job?"

"Lots of men would jump at it. Pay two dollars a day and you'll have twenty men wanting the jobs. Six dollars a day for two weeks would be only seventy-two dollars. That seventy-two dollars could persuade Slade and his five men to try the next town for their bank robbing."

159

"But I've always promised myself I'd never hire an armed guard for my bank."

"Now you have the safety of your depositors' money to consider as well. It was just an idea."

"Starting when?"

"Tomorrow morning. You write out the offer and I'll tack it up in the three biggest saloons in town. Men to report to you at five this afternoon in front of the bank. Oh, they'll have to furnish their own weapons and ammunition."

Sarah watched him over her coffee cup. She put down the cup and held out her hand. "Done," she said. "But you pick out the three men to be the guards. I wouldn't know a drunk from a sharpshooter."

"Done," he said. "Now, we can enjoy what's left of our lunch. So far you haven't even known what you were eating."

Sarah laughed and it scrunched up her eyes and made her face even more attractive. Morgan caught himself liking this small girl more than he should.

"What are you grinning about, Morgan?"

"Me? I just decided that you're about the prettiest and most charming banker I've ever known."

Less than an hour later, Morgan tacked the notices up on the doors of three big saloons and watched the reactions. Two dollars a day was more than twice the normal workingman's pay and he figured there would be a lot of interest.

At five o'clock, 40 men waited outside the bank. Morgan stared at the group and got the men's attention.

"How many of you gents have ever killed a man?" he asked. Ten held up their hands. Morgan had them move to one side. He looked them over. "You men may leave. This isn't a killing job." He looked back at those left.

"How many of you were ever in the Army?"

Six held up their hands. He moved them to one side and looked them over. He talked a minute with each man, picking the three he figured were the steadiest.

He thanked the rest of the men and gave them each a quarter he had talked Sarah out of.

"Have a couple of beers on the Cheyenne Territorial Bank." There were some grumblings, but most of the men walked away happy.

Morgan talked to the three winners. "Be here at the bank in clean clothes, hats, and with a double-barreled shotgun and a pocket full of shells tomorrow morning at nine o'clock. You'll be standing up all the time so wear some comfortable boots."

Inside the bank, Sarah had found an old door that had a foot-square window in it. Morgan broke out the window, and anchored the door between chairs at the far side of the bank. He left it three feet from the wall. The inside guard would be behind the door, safe from any sudden attack and able to fire around the door or through the small window.

"You're all set," he told Sarah. "Tomorrow morning put the men where we talked about, and go about your business as if they aren't there. Let's hope Slade spots your guards before he tries to hold up your bank."

"Thanks, Morgan. I'm not good at saying that. Would you come to supper tomorrow night at my house? Stop by for me here about five o'clock."

Morgan smiled. "A home-cooked meal! Music to my tired old ears. If I'm in town I'll be here. A good chance I'll have to ride out west in the morning. If I'm not here at five, I hope you'll understand."

"Work?"

"Work."

"I didn't think you were going to open a business here. You're just not the merchant type."

"I'll take that as a compliment. You be careful walking home. Our town killer is still around."

"Oh, dear."

"Hey, I was just joshing you. I'll escort you home."

Morgan waited a minute until she was through closing up the bank. Then he walked with her the three blocks to her big white-painted house on 4th Street.

Five minutes later he stopped at the desk at the hotel. There was a message in his box. The clerk gave it to Morgan, who ripped it open.

Chapter Twelve

Mighty Dawn had not seen them coming. He should have. He was one of the trailing warriors on the march north. It was the fourth day of their trek and he was tired. He'd never ridden a pony so far or for so long.

The Pony Soldiers had come at them from out of the sun, blazing into the middle of their long line of march, killing three horses and a woman and a child before the warriors rallied and drove them off.

Now Mighty Dawn crouched behind a large boulder and watched the Pony Soldiers. There had been no more than ten of them at the start. Why they had challenged a larger party, he could not figure. They had, and now the mighty Cheyenne warriors had chased them and punished them and cut them down one at a time until now there were only six left.

They had dropped off their horses and bellied down behind rocks on a small rise. It was a good spot. No warrior could race toward them without exposing himself to fire from the Spencer carbines these Pony Soldiers had.

The warriors had already captured six of the repeating rifles and revolvers and caught five horses. Now it was the final phase of the battle.

Mighty Dawn saw Walks Alone raise up from where he crouched behind a boulder and make a dash for another rock closer to the top of the rise.

Four rifles fired at him. Mighty Dawn leaned around his protective granite and fired twice at where the Pony Soldiers had shown blue smoke, but didn't know if he'd hit any of them. He looked back at Walks Alone and saw him sprawled halfway to the cover of the rock. He lay still for a while, then rolled and tried to get to the rock.

The Pony Soldiers fired again, and this time Mighty Dawn could see the warrior's body jolt as the slugs ripped into him. The young quarter-breed looked away and he blinked tears out of his eyes. He had known the warrior. Walks Alone had helped teach Mighty Dawn how to use a bow and arrow.

Suddenly Mighty Dawn wanted to leap up and charge up the hill, firing as fast as he could. He wanted to surge over the top and shoot the rest of the Pony Soldiers and stop them from killing his friends. He raised up slightly, then dropped down, his good sense beating down his charge of emotion. It would only get him killed if he stormed the hill, and that wouldn't help a bit.

A gentle breeze caressed his cheeks. He turned into the wind and let it calm him. The air blew toward him and up the slope toward the Pony Soldiers. The idea of what to do came as easily as if he had been trying to think of it for hours. He fished in his travel bag over his shoulder and found what he wanted. A small box with white-eyes matches in it. His mother had insisted that they bring them when they came to the band. He had been too embarrassed to use them.

Now he checked the heavy dry grass in front of him. More of the dry spring grass swept to the top of the rise.

He took out a match, scratched it, and let it start to burn well, then caught a handful of the dry grass and lit it. He reached it around the side of the boulder and let the torch catch more of the grass afire.

He heard a shout of approval from a warrior 20 feet away. The wind caught the flames and quickly they spread and then began to race up the hill, catching the tops of the dry grass and moving with the speed of the wind.

The grass burned out quickly and gave off a heavy smoke that also blew up the hill toward the soldiers. It made a perfect screen for the warriors as they rose up from behind their rocks and moved upward behind it.

Mighty Dawn jumped up, and ran through the still-smoking stubble of grasses toward the top of the small hill. There were six warriors on this side of the slope. Even before they got to the top, the warriors could hear firing from above. The white-eyes Pony Soldiers had been forced off the top of the hill by the flames and pushed down the other side into the sights of the Cheyenne.

Only two of the other Cheyenne had rifles, but they were close enough to use their deadly bows

165

and arrows. Soon they would have more rifles.

Mighty Dawn ran up the hill to get in on the rest of the battle. By the time he got there and the smoke had blown away, the fight was over.

All but two of the Pony Soldiers were dead. One had serious wounds from a battle axe and two arrows in him. The second man was not wounded. He had been knocked unconscious by a slanting blow of a tomahawk and sat dazed and shaken, staring around him at the hooting and screeching Cheyenne.

Mighty Dawn walked up in front of the soldier and lifted his rifle to kill him. Gray Owl knocked down the rifle. He shook his head and spoke slowly so the new warrior could understand.

"We keep him for ceremony later," Gray Owl said. "You started the fire, you get credit for the great victory. We will have dance and ceremony tonight. First we must travel many miles so more Pony Soldiers can't find us."

The wounded man looked at the Indians and screamed at them. He grabbed a rock and tried to hit one of the warriors. The Cheyenne snorted in disdain at the pathetic soldier and crashed his war axe down, splitting the trooper's skull.

Minutes later the bodies had been stripped of clothing and equipment. The two dead Cheyenne warriors had been tied to their war ponies. There were ten new rifles for the band. Mighty Dawn found out where the troopers carried their ammunition and he went from body to body digging out every round he could find to fit his Spencer.

They captured five more horses from the Pony Soldiers and left to return to the band on the move. From the scene of the battle the 18 warriors rode in 18 directions. They would meet at the valley just ahead that had the broken pine tree that had been hit by lightning.

An hour later at the meeting place, Gray Owl gave his orders. There would be Pony Soldiers trying to find them. They must split up and go in three directions. They would meet again at the headwaters of this small river they had found. It meant turning back toward the railroad, but the mountains were better there for hiding.

The captured horses were trailed on ropes behind the warriors who caught the animals, and the prisoner was bound with rawhide and tied on one of the horses. There was no time now for a traditional Cheyenne burial ceremony. They would do that after they set up a temporary camp.

It took them most of the day to ride a circle route they hoped would throw off any trackers. The problem was that now many of the Pony Soldier units had Indian trackers who knew all the tricks. Gray Owl's band would try and hope.

In the meantime, there was a great victory to celebrate. There would be tales of valor and bravery, and a feast would be prepared by the women.

Much had to be done before the celebration could start. They found a small valley that was covered with trees and contained the start of the tiny stream and set up a traveling camp. No tipis were erected. The cooking ware and food had been packed on the travois in such a way that it could be reached on the run.

Now the women built fires and began preparing food for the celebration. The warriors groomed their war ponies and worked out exactly how they would describe their own exploits.

The telling of the battle and of each individual warrior's bravery would have a bearing on who was awarded any contested coups.

Mighty Dawn did not think what he would say. He had no thought of making any speech. He would watch and learn. He drifted over to where Knows a Lot sat working on yet another arrow. He knew that over a hundred arrows had been lost today. After every battle when it was possible, the warriors scavangered the battle site to find unbroken arrows that they could use again.

Even so, Knows a Lot would be working hard for a month to replace the arrows that had been lost. He was getting short on cured sticks for the shafts.

"Have you seen any good willow trees nearby?" he asked Mighty Dawn. The young warrior shook his head. "If you find any, and cut me fifty straight willow shoots as long as your arm, I'll make six more arrows for you."

It was an offer Mighty Dawn couldn't turn down. He walked upstream for a quarter of a mile and found a stand of willow. He decided which size would be about right for arrows, then using his belt knife, he cut 60 of them, wrapped them with a piece of leather strip from his waist, and took them back to the old arrow maker.

By then the food was nearly ready, and the warriors had built a fire, ringed it with rocks, and prepared a special place for the council to sit. They would determine who won coups and who did not.

Just before dark, they ate a variety of meats and dishes set out on the grass near the stream. It was a banquet for the usually light-eating Indians.

Gunslinger's Scalp

As it grew dark, a small drum began to beat. It went faster and faster until at the very top speed a warrior bellowed out a Cheyenne war cry, and a dozen warriors rode their war ponies around and around the fire, calling everyone to the council fire for the celebration.

Every woman and child settled down near the council fire, but left a path through to the very edge of the fire and the council itself.

Near the council, a worn buffalo robe had been pegged to the ground. It had dozens of slashes and cuts in it. Mighty Dawn wondered what it was for.

Then another Cheyenne war cry pierced the night air and a warrior rode his mount out of the darkness and down the narrow path between the onlookers, and raised his lance and threw it into the ground so the point pierced the buffalo robe.

At once the warrior jumped up and stood on the back of his mount as the war pony remained rigid. The warrior spelled out what he had done in the attack and the great victory over the Pony Soldiers. This warrior, Walking Wing, claimed two coups for touching a hard-riding Pony Soldier before he knocked him off his horse with his war axe and then killed him with two swift blows.

Half of the deed was in the telling, and this warrior was adept at making his story as impressive as possible. When he finished, he dropped down to straddle his war pony and without using his hands, turned the animal around and charged out of the council area.

Immediately the next-ranking warrior rode into the celebration and recounted his exploits in the recent battle. He had captured one horse and a shoots-many-times carbine, and had made coup twice on the unwounded Pony Soldier before he was captured.

One after another the exploits of the warriors were spelled out until all were through.

The council would decide later which warrior would win the coups that were contested.

Now the leader of the band stood and everyone quieted. He told them they had come far, but they had still farther to go. He had heard of a Cheyenne band in these hills and he would send out scouts in the morning looking for them. Perhaps then they could join the others and be stronger to fight off the Pony Soldiers.

Then the warrior who had put aside his lance and shield for the healing herbs and for communication with the Great Spirit, becoming their medicine man, came forward and scattered smoke to the four winds and then asked blessings of the mighty spirits. On his signal the prisoner, naked, was marched into the light of the council fire.

Three warriors ran out each with a tipi pole. They quickly tied them together and set them up forming a peak. At the top of the poles, they tied a strong rawhide rope and let both ends dangle almost to the ground.

Another warrior hurried up with a fire brand and started a small fire where the ropes touched the ground. The rope was lifted then and the prisoner forced into the scene. He screamed and bellowed his rage.

Mighty Dawn had frowned when he saw the white man marched in naked. Surely they would give him a chance to defend himself. Then

Gunslinger's Scalp

Mighty Dawn saw that the man's hands were tied behind his back.

One end of the rope was tied around the man's ankles and before he could protest, he was up-ended so he hung by his feet from the top of the three poles.

Mighty Dawn frowned. He had never heard of anything such as this before. He wasn't sure what they planned, but slowly a cold chill crept into him as he realized there could be only one end to such an arrangement.

The prisoner was four feet off the ground, his head pointing directly at the small fire that flickered below him. A woman slipped into place by the fire. She had a bundle of sticks, and she fed the branches and sticks into the fire so it maintained a nearly even level of flame.

The medicine man wailed and chanted. He let some of the smoke from the small fire waft over him and he closed his eyes and lifted his hands skyward. Then he mumbled some words and backed away from the fire into the darkness.

At once the braided rawhide rope holding the prisoner was loosened and the man lowered slowly toward the fire. He was stopped when his head hung three feet over the fire.

Not a sound came from the assembled Indians. All of the adult Cheyenne's eyes glowed as they watched the ritual.

A chant began by two warriors somewhere in the darkness. They stopped.

The rope lowered the body another foot.

In a sudden burst of flame, the trooper's hair burned off, leaving his skull blackened. With the flaming hair came a shrill cry from every throat in the assembly except Mighty Dawn's.

The trooper bellowed in fear and anger and pain. For another minute the chanting that had begun with the burning hair continued. Then the chanting stopped again.

The warrior tending the rope lowered the trooper another half foot. The chanting began. Now the victim's head was black from the soot in the smoke that rose past his head. His face was coated and when he blinked, the whites of his eyes could be seen even from far back in the crowd. The trooper brayed in pain and fury. He kept up a continuing scream and cry of agonizing pain.

Mighty Dawn turned away.

A sudden roar went up from the crowd.

Mighty Dawn turned and stared at the white man. A gout of blood came from his nose and dripped into the fire. The trooper bellowed again, but this time there was less force behind it. His cries were growing weaker.

The chanting stopped.

The body dropped another half foot toward the fire.

The continuing wail and scream of pain from the Pony Soldier faded and then stopped. He had lost his voice.

For a moment nothing happened.

Then blood seeped from his ears and dripped into the fire bringing another gush of screaming and yelling from the crowd.

A war cry pierced the darkness and the rope let the body down another foot until the trooper's head was less than 18 inches from the ground, barely a foot over the steady flames.

The chanting stopped.

The woman who managed the fire added one

last pair of small branches to the blaze, then backed away and sat in a spot ten feet away that had been reserved for her.

The crowd was waiting for something.

Mighty Dawn took one more look at the hanging body. Surely the man must be dead by now. Blood boiled from his nose and both ears. He must be dead. His agony was over. How much more humane a single shot to his head would have been.

A high thin wail began somewhere in the crowd. It was joined by another and then another as the volume built gradually. Soon almost every person in the group was adding a voice to the keening high wail of some strange unfinished melody.

The sound grew and grew.

Then there was a sound Mighty Dawn had never heard before. It was not an explosion, more like the sound when he dropped the big watermelon and it broke into a dozen pieces.

This time the sound came when the trooper's head exploded, and rained brains and hot blood and bits of skull on those seated closest.

The high keening sound stopped at once and the whole clan went into spasms of loud cheering and clapping and singing. A drum pounded out a cadence and men and women began dancing around the small fire and its gruesome trophy.

Now the victory was complete.

Mighty Dawn turned and rushed into the darkness of the woods. There he knelt down, braced himself with both hands, and threw up everything he had eaten.

When he finished, he hurried to the creek and washed out his mouth again and again to rid it of the taste of bile and outrage. How could they do something like this?

He thought of what his mother had said. "It is the way of the People." She let that solve all problems of trust and honesty and caring and justice. The way of the People. But were these really his people? Was this *his way*?

The way of savages, he decided. These people could be warm and wonderful, but then at times like this, their action and morals and way of life were enough to make him cry out in alarm and anger.

Still, the Pony Soldiers had murdered his mother. He was not anywhere close to killing ten Pony Soldiers to avenge her. With all of the fighting today, he could not account for one clean death.

Still, was the basic idea any different? In Omaha he had seen a man die in the rail yards. A brakeman had been crushed to death between two cars when the brakes failed. Was that so different? Somewhere a rich man made a profit from the brakeman's labor and his death. If one man died, another would be hired to take his place. Were the white-eyes so different after all?

That night, Mighty Dawn slept little. He now had a Pony Soldier's pack to carry his goods in. There was the treasured package of U.S. banknotes that he had carefully wrapped and hidden in his other gear. He had his bow and 12 arrows, but no lance or shield. No new shields could be made since they had not seen a buffalo in a year.

One warrior could never pick up a fallen man's shield and use it. It was bad medicine. Every warrior needed all of the good medicine he could get when he went into battle. Good medicine helped deflect the Pony Soldier's bullets, helped the warrior to fight bravely and emerge without a drop of his own blood being lost.

Mighty Dawn was starting to wonder about "his people." Was this the life he wanted to live for the rest of his days? Did he want to learn more and more how to kill Pony Soldiers? They seemed to be the band's only enemies now. To hunt and to fight and to raid and to kill. Was that what he wanted out of his life?

He moved his pallet so he could see through the leaves and find some friendly stars in the great heavens. He still wondered about them. What were they? How far away were they? What were they made of? Where did they come from?

The moon edged into his small plot of the universe and he marveled at the shadows and marks on it. What made them? How far across were the dark parts? Did the moon have rivers and soil and trees? Were there other men living on the moon looking down at them?

That night he tossed and sat up and rolled over and found little sleep.

He could only think that in a few days Morgan would be back to talk to him about going to live in Omaha. What was he going to tell the man? What could he say that he hadn't said? How could he decide what to tell his father? There was no one to talk to, to ask questions of. Only one thing was certain. In a few days he would have to make a decision that would make a tremendous difference in how he lived the rest of his life.

The day before, he had reached his fourteenth birthday. Mighty Dawn wondered how many boys of 14 had killed a man, watched their mothers die, been hunted like animals by the U.S. Army's Cavalry, and been living like a savage for four months.

His eyes were heavy when dawn came over the treetops. He hurried to the creek to bathe, then slipped on his grimy breechclout. No matter what he decided, today he was a Cheyenne, and he would live like a Cheyenne, and fight and die like a Cheyenne warrior if he had to.

He didn't know what would come tomorrow. All he could do was live his life one day at a time—at least until Morgan came back and he had to make a decision.

Chapter Thirteen

Morgan unfolded the note he had just received from the hotel clerk and read it.

"Jim back. We need talk. They moved. Jim in shack." It was signed, "Jim."

Morgan reversed his direction and left the hotel. Less than five minutes later he called softly, then pushed aside the blanket that served as the door to Jim Breed's new home, a shack behind a saloon.

"Jim? Jim? You there?"

"Yeah."

Morgan stepped into the faintly lit shack and saw Jim on his pallet. He had been sleeping. An empty bottle lay beside him. He rubbed his eyes and sat up.

"Where are they, Jim? Have we lost them?"

Jim picked up the bottle and threw it across the shack. It hit a wooden post and shattered.

"You drunk, Jim?"

"More drunk soon."

"Where is Mighty Dawn and the Gray Owl band?"

"Medicine Bows." Jim stopped and looked around. "Got whiskey?"

"No, Jim. Not until you tell me what happened."

Jim scowled, shrugged, and rubbed his face with one hand. "Left days after you. Go west, far into Medicine Bows. Ride two days. North more. Seventy miles. Last day ten Pony Soldiers attack. Jim come here. Two long day ride."

"How far from town?"

"Eighty miles."

"We best get back out there. Don't get drunk, Jim. We're going to ride tonight. Can you make it? I'll get some sandwiches and a jug of coffee. You get some sleep. I'll be back in an hour. Jim!" The sharp command brought Jim up straight.

"Jim, make damn sure you don't get any drunker. You've got to ride tonight. If we lose that band of Cheyenne now, my job here is over, and so is your payday."

It took Morgan two hours to get what he wanted. The sandwiches and coffee from the hotel dining room, a change into trail clothes, and a pair of rented horses from the livery. He put the copy of Bishop's telegram in his pocket. He then picked up the cooking gear and the trail food and rode back to the alley shack.

Jim wasn't there. Morgan swore for two minutes, then charged into the nearest saloon. Jim sat at the end of the bar watching the drinkers. Morgan grabbed him by the arm and powered him out the back door.

Jim was no drunker than he had been. He could ride.

They moved west along the shining steel rails. For the first five miles, there was a track of a road leading to two small farms and a ranch or two. Then the trail petered out and they worked across country, always in sight of the tracks in the moonlight.

It was dark and after nine o'clock when a train came through heading west. A combination freight and passenger train as most of them were these days, it slammed along at 35 miles an hour, and Morgan wished he were on board instead of on horseback.

They rode until midnight and Morgan decided they would catch some sleep. Another few hours wouldn't make or break his mission. They tied up their horses in a small grove and Jim dropped to the grass and went to sleep before Morgan got the blankets off his mount.

They left the animals saddled for a quick getaway if they needed it. Morgan expected no trouble but out here you could never tell.

He awoke the next morning at six when the sun slanted through the trees and warmed his face. Morgan roused the Indian. They had a quick breakfast of coffee, and the last of the sandwiches and rode. He figured they'd made 20 miles last night. There were 60 to go.

Jim was fully sober now. He kept hitting the side of his head with his hand as if to make a headache go away. Morgan grinned.

They rode hard all day, pushing their mounts to their limits, backing off when the animals tired. By six that evening, Morgan figured they had covered 50 miles. They must be close. Jim pointed to the right.

"Cheyenne trail from the south."

They turned following the sign. A half hour later they found where the Cheyenne tracks were smothered with those of shod Army hooves and the chase had begun.

A half mile down the trail of hoofprints, they came on the battle site. One Cavalryman lay dead on the ground near his bloated horse. A Cheyenne warrior curled in death a dozen feet away and an Indian woman and a small girl sprawled a short distance further on. They saw a dozen broken arrows, a ruined six-gun, and more evidence of a fight.

Jim rode a circle around the battle and soon signaled with a nighthawk call. Morgan rode up to him.

"Trail go west. Now Cheyenne travois go north, but Cheyenne ponies ride west, chase Army soldiers."

"Ten against twenty, I can see why. Whoever attacked the band made a mistake."

They rode faster now. The broad trail of the 20 Indian ponies and eight or nine Army trooper mounts was easy to follow.

Two miles later on a small hill, they discovered the burned remains of a second fight. Here they found the mutilated remains of eight troopers. A small grass fire had burned up one side of a hill and over the top. The bodies lay just beyond the fire. They had been stripped, slashed, scalped, and broken. The Cheyenne, like most Indians, believed that an enemy who was cut up in death would not be able to fight again in the afterlife.

"Everything that could have been salvaged has

been," Morgan said, looking at the corpses. An Army patrol would find them soon enough.

"Which way?"

The trail turned back south and to the west. The country got rougher and steeper, and soon they were in a patch of heavy timber and jagged hills and mountains.

"Cheyenne hide. Take many trail. All go same place."

They found a small creek and the trail of a dozen Cheyenne ponies that worked upstream. Now they saw the trail of the other ponies and the travois. Jim stopped and stared ahead.

"Cheyenne have plenty scouts out. Watch for Pony Soldiers. Jim go look."

Morgan dismounted and Jim rode into the growing dusk. Morgan settled down on some grass after watering the horses. Now his one big hope was that the Indians weren't so on edge that they kept running all the way to Canada.

He spent the time sharpening his belt knife, then cleaned his six-gun and did some pacing back and forth. At last he lay down on a patch of grass and took a nap.

It was near midnight before Jim came out of the brush without a sound.

"Fire okay," Jim said and began gathering sticks, grass, and small branches to build a cooking fire.

"Coffee," Jim said.

Morgan knew that Jim would tell him what he found in his own time. When the coffee was ready and they sat sipping the brew and chewing on jerky from the food sack, Jim motioned to the west.

"Five miles, Cheyenne half camp. Lookouts

181

watch stream. Bury bodies on hill. Not see boy."

"With first light we'll both watch again, Jim. He has to be there and you have to get him out of the camp so I can talk to him."

"Hard," Jim said. "Try."

They let the fire die down and slept.

An hour before daylight Morgan awoke. His movement woke up Jim, who was quickly ready to go. It took them an hour to move the five miles west. It was dawn when they rode along a ridge near the stream and left their horses in a protected little valley one ridge over. Then they worked their way silently past the sleepy young warrior who stood guard, and moved down to the creek.

It was about eight o'clock in the morning when they edged up to the last ridge line and looked down on the Cheyenne. The half camp was just that. For every tipi set up, another was still packed and loaded on the travois ready to ravel.

"Fast camp," Jim explained. "Move quick. Two women work on tipi take down."

Morgan wished that he had brought the good pair of binoculars he had. They were back in town. Next time he would have them. The two men moved down the slope to get close enough to distinguish individuals.

"Must find Mighty Dawn and talk to him," Morgan said again.

Jim nodded and took off his shirt and hat, then kicked out of his trousers. He had on under them a traditional Cheyenne breechclout. He took off his boots and socks and grinned.

"Real Cheyenne. Get in camp not be seen."

"You can't just walk in?"

Gunslinger's Scalp

"No reason be here. Gray Owl smart. I follow just to say hello?"

Morgan grinned. Jim Breed knew more English than he sometimes let on.

Two women came out of some brush 30 yards from the men and picked berries off some bushes. The berries were blue and small.

When Jim saw them he made a bad face. "No damn good," he whispered. The women cleaned the bush and wandered off in the other direction looking for more berries.

Morgan concentrated on the camp. He found some young boys playing, but Mighty Dawn was not with them. He was larger than the others. Once a group of warriors assembled and talked.

Morgan looked for Jim Breed. For five minutes, Morgan could see Jim walking through the camp. He talked to no one and made himself as unobtrusive as possible.

Morgan hoped the Cheyenne could find the boy. Now all he could do was wait for Jim to come back with some kind of news.

Morgan knew he couldn't start a fire there. It was too close and the Cheyenne would pick up on the smoke and track it down within a half hour. He chewed on jerky and filled a canteen at the stream and waited.

He kept watching the camp. A hunter passed by 20 yards away but didn't see Morgan. Twice more Morgan saw Jim in the camp. After what he figured must be three hours, he heard a cry of a turtledove. It was Jim. Morgan gave his wounded-dove version of the same call and moments later, Jim stepped from the brush into a patch of grass ten feet from Morgan.

"Found boy," Jim said. "Back to horses."

Again Morgan had to wait for the half-breed to say what had happened. The trait of extreme patience in this Indian drove Morgan mad, but there was nothing he could do about it.

When they got to the horses, Jim lifted a rabbit from his belt and started a fire. While the fire burned down to hot embers, he skinned out and cleaned the rabbit, then cut it into sections and started them roasting over the glowing coals.

At last Jim looked up. "Found boy. He will talk. Go hunting upstream today at sunset. We find him."

"How did he sound? Is he eager to talk? Has he had enough of the Cheyenne way of life?"

"Don't know. Spoke quick. Scouts hunt other Cheyenne bands in area."

"If they find another band, that would be bad news. Also, I expect that the Army will be coming out from Fort Russell with a company-sized attack force to find their patrol and then to chase down this band. They don't like to lose a ten-man patrol."

"Pony Soldiers soon come."

"This little band will be wiped out if they can find them."

"Gray Owl band go soon. Quick stop, then Montana maybe."

"Now that would be bad news. I've got to get the boy away from them before they leave the Medicine Bows and before the Army finds them."

Jim handed Morgan a quarter of the rabbit roasted to a delicious-looking brown by the hot coals. Grease dropped into the coals and flared up, but there was no other flame. Most meat Morgan roasted over a fire was burned black on the outside.

Morgan took a bite, let it cool, and then had a larger one.

"Damn good," Morgan said.

Jim grinned.

An hour before dusk, the two moved in a wide circle around the small camp and back to the stream above the village. They moved a quarter of a mile above the last tipi and settled in to wait.

With the fading light they saw the camp settle down. Smoke began to rise, then men entered the tipis or went to cooking fires. The horses were in a simple rope enclosure at the middle of the camp. Morgan figured that was another "quick camp" procedure, so the men could claim their mounts in a hurry if they had to ride and fight.

Morgan settled in to wait. He had grown better at waiting on this assignment.

Two hunters started upstream, found a quarry, and turned off into the slopes.

It was a half hour after dusk when they saw a lone hunter armed with a bow and arrow move upstream. He wore the traditional breechclout and carried no food sack, so he was not a long-range hunter.

He came on steadily, and it wasn't until the youth was within 50 feet of them along the creek that Morgan recognized the young man as Mighty Dawn. He looked older now, somehow. The chase, the fights, the Indian way of life had matured him beyond his years.

Jim Breed stepped into the open and met the youth. Then they crossed the stream and worked back into the thick brush where Morgan waited.

Up close the boy had changed more than Morgan had expected. There was no boyish smile. This Cheyenne warrior was grim, his eyes

185

showed small lines around them, there were creases in his forehead, and his hands never stopped moving.

"I'm glad we could talk again. It must have been terrible with the Cavalry chasing your band."

"It was terrible for them. We killed all ten of them, and lost only two of our warriors."

"At that rate you have ten more battles before your warriors will all be dead and the U.S. Army will still have thirty thousand troops against you."

"I know that, Mr. Morgan. I know. I'm still trying to figure out what to do. I saw ... I saw a white man roasted over a fire, head down, until his skull exploded. It was terrible. I threw up. I don't ever want to see anything like that again."

"Then come with us, right now. I have sent wires to your father. He has offered you several guarantees if you will come back home."

"What, money? He's always offered me money. I have money of my own now."

"Oh, what from?"

"Not your concern. What did my father say to tell me?"

"He said he would take you on a trip to England. Evidently that is something you want to do. He said you could go to Harvard if you wished and study anything you fancied. He said he would buy you a racehorse so you could race him. He also said you didn't have to go into his company and could have any career that you wanted to."

"He is smart, my father. He's offered me everything that I ever asked him for. Now what should I do?"

"Throw away your bow and arrows and come with us back to Cheyenne. We'll have you dressed in some regular clothes, fed up, and put on the next train for Omaha. You'll be home in two days, and all of this terror and savagery will be behind you."

The boy stood, walked to the creek, threw stones in the water, and came back. "I can't just leave without thanking Gray Owl for taking care of me these past several months. It would not be right to run away. I'm a warrior. If I decide to go with you, I have that right. I'll explain it to him. He'll understand. But I haven't made up my mind what to do yet."

Morgan shook his head. "It wouldn't be a tough decision for me to make. A trip to England, the best education this country has to offer a young man at Harvard, your choice of careers, and even a racehorse to run at the Omaha fairgrounds. What more could a young man want?

"No more worry about the Pony Soldiers sweeping down on you with five hundred troopers. No more living on the edge of starvation and freezing your nose off this winter in some windy tipi. It would be easy for me. But I respect your consideration for Gray Owl."

"Does my father know about Mother?"

"Yes. He said he was sorry about what happened."

Mighty Dawn looked away. He took a deep breath and rubbed his face. "I hope he is. He and Mother never got along together the way parents should. Even I knew it."

"Will you come back with us today?"

"No, I'll have to talk to Gray Owl, then say my

good-byes. If I decide to go back with you. I still have to decide."

"I can wait two days. How do you like the way the Cheyenne treat their women?"

"What do you mean?"

"The women do all the work, the men hunt and sit around and watch the women work."

"That's the way of the People."

"What about the way the soldier died head down over the fire? Was that the way of the People?"

"Yes, he was a mortal enemy."

"What do the Cheyenne warriors do with captives, Harold?"

"Whatever they want to. The women can become wives. The children are raised as Cheyenne."

"Some of the captive women are slaves?"

"Yes." He looked away. "Or are killed. I saw one warrior kill a woman prisoner because she was crazy. He simply slit her throat, like you'd kill a fly or a mosquito.

"Is that the way of the People?"

"I know what you're doing, Mr. Morgan. In some way the Cheyenne are savages, uneducated, violent, warlike, unkempt, and sometimes little more than animals. But they took me in as one of them when my mother died."

"You'll have to make the choice, Harold. I can give you the rest of today and tomorrow. Let's meet this same place tomorrow at dusk. By then I'll need to know one way or the other."

"Not much time to decide."

"The decision can be made in a half second. It's the reasoning and evaluating that take the time. We'll be here tomorrow at dusk. Come and tell us either way what you decide. If you're going with us, bring your Indian pony. Then you won't have to ride double."

Mighty Dawn stood from where he had been sitting on the grass and stared at them both. Morgan held out his hand. The youth ignored it, merely nodded, and then turned and ran down stream toward the settlement, his bow and arrows firmly in his right hand.

"Will he come with us?" Morgan asked Jim.

"Maybe yes, maybe no. Jim can't say."

It took them an hour of quiet movement through the woods to get back to where they had left the horses and where a fire was possible. They boiled coffee and then some jerky, and ate the last of the hard biscuits they had brought along.

"You know where there are any more jackrabbits around here?" Morgan asked. "If you do, you're on the hunting detail tomorrow. Otherwise we won't be eating much for the next two days or for our trip back to Cheyenne."

Chapter Fourteen

The next morning, Mighty Dawn went to Gray Owl's tipi and sat outside near the entrance flap where the leader could see him. It was the way of the People. Once Mighty Dawn had sat there for two hours before Gray Owl asked him to come in and talk.

This time he had barely lowered to the ground and arranged himself for a wait when one of Gray Owl's wives came out and said he should come into the leader's tipi.

Mighty Dawn went around the inside of the tipi to the right as was proper. Gray Owl sat before a small fire watching it—reading the coals, Mighty Dawn decided. The older man raised one hand and motioned for Mighty Dawn to be seated.

Ever since the fight on the fire hill, Mighty Dawn had been considered a warrior and something of a celebrated one. He had won the day for the Cheyenne. That was why he was received so quickly today by Gray Owl.

The young warrior sat down and stared at the fire. He could read nothing in the coals.

"You wish to speak, Mighty Dawn?"

"Yes, Chief Gray Owl. My heart is troubled. Sometimes I am not sure that I am a true Cheyenne."

"You proved yourself in the fight on fire hill, Mighty Dawn. You earned the right to be called a Cheyenne warrior."

"Still, I am troubled." He took a small stick and stirred the coals. "Is it true that you can read the future in the coals of your fire, Gray Owl?"

"Some say I can."

"Do the coals tell you anything of my future?"

"Stir the fire again, young warrior."

He did so, then dropped the slender stick on the fire, and it flamed up at once burning into a long ash that slowly disintegrated into a fluffy line, and then even that was gone.

Gray Owl looked at the boy quickly. "The coals say that you may not be with the Cheyenne people forever."

"Great Chief, only one quarter of my blood is true Cheyenne blood."

"But your heart is that of a great Cheyenne warrior."

"Why then do I have so many doubts? When the warrior killed the woman captive on our raid on the stagecoach, I was shocked and saddened. I know it is the way of the People. But it did not seem to be my way."

"The young warrior has much to learn. The woman was weak, she could not work. A woman

191

who can't do her share of the work is cast aside like a broken bow. She is useless. That woman was also out of her mind. It was a favor to her to kill her quickly rather than leave her there where she was alone and would starve to death or be attacked by wild animals."

"It still is not my way." Mighty Dawn looked at the fire again and then at the tipi.

"Will the Pony Soldiers find us here?"

"If they have the renegade Cheyenne scouts, they can find us if they work at it hard enough. One day they will come again. We must be ready to fight them well away from our camp. We need every warrior we have. That is why I hope to find another Cheyenne band to join in these mountains."

"We have scouts out, lookouts to watch for the Pony Soldiers?"

"Yes, Warriors, not young boys."

"The soldier who was hung upside down over the fire. I don't understand that. It was a ceremony?"

Gray Owl looked up sharply, his face showing a trace of anger he seldom let anyone see.

"It is one of the Cheyenne's most revered ceremonies. It was the sacrifice of a brave warrior of the Pony Soldiers to the Great Spirit. A gesture of oneness with the Great Spirit and the Cheyenne people. The ceremony has become one of the greatest of the Cheyenne. It brings our people together, makes us whole, rededicates our lives to the band and to the Cheyenne tribe."

"Great Warrior Gray Owl, I still don't understand. It can only mean that I'm not worthy to be a Cheyenne warrior. It is something I must think on a great deal today and tomorrow. If I am not worthy to be a Cheyenne warrior, then I'll have to leave your camp and make my way back to the white-eyes town and live there with them."

"No!" The word came sharply and Mighty Dawn looked up at the old warrior. "You are a Cheyenne warrior. You are needed here to help defend the camp. Soon you will take as wife one of the widows from our camp and make her husband. You are Cheyenne!"

"I'm not sure, Gray Owl. So many things are confusing. My mother is not here to explain them. Often we say one thing and do another. The ceremonies are not real to me since I can't understand them or the reason for them. I must think on all of these things."

Mighty Dawn stood and nodded at the older man. "I must leave now and think. Thank you, Great Chief, for your wise advice and counsel."

Gray Owl nodded, releasing him, and he left the tipi. His pallet was under a tree only a few yards away. Mighty Dawn lay down and stared through the branches at the sky above. He had a lot of thinking to do. He wasn't sure he could make up his mind by tomorrow afternoon.

When the young warrior left his tipi, Gray Owl stood and walked around the enclosure three times. The young man was wavering. Right now the band needed every man who could pull a bow or fire one of the new rifles. He must do something.

He called in two of his older warriors who he counseled with and together they worked out the plans.

They would send out more scouts. There was a Pony Soldier fort near the railroad town of Laramie, a day's ride from their camp. The Pony

193

Soldiers would soon be searching for their patrol and then for the Cheyenne.

They would take two more days here to rest and prepare for the long trip. Then they would be moving to the far north. The only other choice was if they found another Cheyenne band they could join. Their scouts had gone out the first day to the west, searching into the higher Medicine Bows the other side of the white-eyes village of Laramie. There must be more Cheyenne in that area.

With the plans made, Gray Owl sent for Mighty Dawn. The young warrior came in and watched, but Gray Owl did not motion for him to sit down.

"You and Walks With a Limp will go out at once on a scouting mission toward the rails of steel to the rising sun. You will watch there all day. If you see any Pony Soldiers heading this way, you must follow them. If they find our trail, you will ride back at once and warn us."

"But I must decide what to do," Mighty Warrior said. "I must decide if I am a true Cheyenne warrior."

"You will have plenty of time to think and talk with Walks With a Limp on your watch. Leave as soon as you prepare a food tube for two days."

Mighty Warrior left the tipi. What should he do? If he defied the leadership of Gray Owl he would be in trouble. He had been ordered to go protect the band. He could do nothing else. Walks With a Limp waited for him. His woman had prepared a food tube for both of them and they went to get their horses.

Mighty Warrior brought along his rifle and 40 rounds of ammunition. He put the shells in the saddlebags. He had two now, both with "U.S.

Army" stamped on them. He tied one over the back of his war pony and they rode away to the east. The older warrior had instructions how far to go. There were other scouts out as well. This time the band would not be surprised.

Mighty Dawn knew he would not be able to contact Morgan the next evening. There was nothing he could do about it. They would probably be so far away he couldn't get back for the meeting no matter what kind of an excuse he gave to Walks With a Limp.

They had been riding about three hours when they turned sharply and climbed a hill. At the top they could see for ten miles across a wide plateau to the east.

"Here," Walks With a Limp said. "Here we watch during the day, we listen at night. Pony Soldiers make many smokes when they ride. See smoke or dust trails first."

They made a small camp there, cutting pine boughs to make a lean-to, then more boughs for their beds. One of them always sat or stood on the highest point concealed by a pine tree.

Nothing on the wide plain moved as Mighty Dawn watched.

"Why are we here?" he asked Walks With a Limp.

"You know. We watch for the Pony Soldiers, and any other band of Cheyenne we see."

"Then there are other Cheyenne in this area?"

"We do not know. Here or farther to the west in the higher peaks of the Medicine Bows."

"So we watch and we wait," Mighty Dawn said.

"For one day. Tomorrow night when it is so

195

dark we can't see our war pony at a long arrow's flight, we go back to the camp."

Mighty Dawn gave an inward groan of pain and anger. By then it would be too late to see Morgan. It didn't really matter what he decided. Morgan would be gone and so would his chance to get back to his father.

If he wanted to go back. When it grew too dark to watch, they listened and watched for fires. They expected to see no fires and hear no troopers. All was quiet.

It gave Mighty Dawn time to sort out his reasons for staying. The first reason was to avenge his mother's murder. He had killed one trooper, wounded one, and perhaps killed another. He had made it possible for the Cheyenne warriors to kill the five other troopers at the hill of fire. He could count them. That would be seven.

Revenge, it was played out. Yes, there was no more reason to stay for revenge. He had seen enough killing.

Why else stay? To be with his mother's people. But were they his people? Could he accept all of the "way of the People," the way of living and killing? He didn't know.

Was he truly a real Cheyenne warrior or did he just happen to do some things that made him appear to be a warrior? He had a strong feeling the latter was true. He was only 14 years old! He should be in school and playing games and chasing other kids and having fun.

In Grand Island? He sighed. He didn't know. He never had been close to his father. His father had always been away at his business. Was it worth another try?

But the Cheyenne had taken him in. He was of

Cheyenne blood and any Cheyenne could join any band he wished to. But the people had accepted him and helped him.

Twice during the night he sat up from his blanket, sweat beading his forehead. But it had only been a dream. The Pony Soldiers were not attacking the village with 500 troopers and cannon that fired shells that exploded with they hit.

He lay down. It was the Pony Soldiers he feared the most. In the end they would kill every Cheyenne not on a reservation. That meant they would kill him too.

At last he went back to sleep, his mind not made up yet. He would have to decide soon. Sometime before the band moved again. He knew where he was. He could find the great bands of steel that formed the transcontinental railroad. Once he found the rails he would turn east and ride or walk until he found the railroad towns of Laramie or Cheyenne. Then all he would need to do was send a telegram to his father, or find Mr. Morgan. Now with the alternatives more firmly in mind, he went to sleep.

The day of waiting was hardest for Morgan. That morning he carved a whistle from some willow shoots. He made a carved hook for their cooking fire, and found some especially hard and tough branches to use for holding their small pots over the fire.

Jim Breed had killed a rabbit the night before and they roasted the second half of it the next morning. They would have meat for the rest of the day. Morgan burped. He could easily go without food for two days if he had water. They were less than a day and a half from Laramie.

What would Harold Bishop say when they met just at dusk at the end of that day? Would he leave the people of his mother and return to civilization?

A chill crept over Morgan as he wondered what would happen if they arrived at the campsite only to find it gone again. He figured this was a temporary camp. The band needed to find allies or move deeper into the Medicine Bows. The peaks rose to more than 12,000 feet. Some of the little settlements were resting at over 8,000 feet. Up in there it would be much harder to track down the wily Cheyenne.

Morgan whittled. Jim turned on his side and snored contentedly.

Two more hours before they needed to start for the Cheyenne camp. Morgan tried to figure the odds. The kid wanted to avenge his mother's death. For a boy of 14 he had already killed his first man, a trooper at that, and he wanted nine more. That kind of hatred/anger would wear off. But was he ready to give up what he had become accustomed to these past six or seven months and go back to Grand Island? Omaha, maybe, but Grand Island?

Morgan flipped the knife, making it land point-first and stick into the ground. Nothing dulled a knife so much as stabbing it in the ground.

He wiped the dirt off, took out his whetstone, and sharpened the blade again.

Mighty Dawn would not be ready to return to civilization yet, Morgan predicted to himself. He roused Jim. They could leave a little early, then move down to the meeting place when it started to get dark. Where were they to meet? Upstream from the camp. There would be less security there.

An hour later, they bellied into the grass and looked out to find the camp still in place. They had seen smoke from half a mile away, but now Morgan was glad to determine that the smoke came from Cheyenne cooking fires and not from burned-out tipis with 100 Pony Soldiers scavengering the site of a massacre.

"Now I feel better," Morgan growled at Jim. "At least they haven't taken off on a run again."

"Soon," Jim said. "More tipis down. Maybe leave tomorrow."

"That will give Harold more reason to come back with us. It might be working out for us just fine."

They were 200 yards from the creek and that far upstream from the last tipi. They could see increased activity in the camp, but Morgan couldn't say exactly what was going on.

Morgan looked at Jim. "What's happening down there?"

"Scouts, lookouts coming in. Women getting ready to move. Maybe sunup."

"How far will they go? Any idea if they are preparing a lot of trail food? Will they live off the land? Any idea where they are going?"

Jim just grinned and shook his head. "Find out tomorrow."

In an hour it was nearing dusk. They burrowed deeper into their concealment and waited. Two boys ran up the creek playing water tag, but they soon got cold in the evening air now that the sun's rays did not hit the creek. They splashed some more, then played tag back toward camp.

No hunters came from upstream.

No women came that way searching for berries.

A warrior started up the stream, but went only a short way beyond the last tipi and stared ahead a moment, then turned and went back. He was too stocky and grim-looking to be Mighty Dawn.

Slowly dusk settled over the valley. Then suddenly it was dark.

"He didn't come," Morgan said.

"Wait," Jim suggested.

They waited another half hour by Morgan's estimation.

"He isn't coming. What does that mean?"

Jim shook his head. "Maybe mean nothing, maybe mean trouble you."

"We'll stay here until morning. He still might come. Are we out of the way in case there's a sudden move?"

Jim nodded. "You want me go into camp?"

"You don't have a why."

"No need. All run around, mix up. Move always crazy time."

"You could get in and find out what happened to Mighty Dawn without being in any danger?"

"Me Cheyenne. Come and go as please."

"Give it a try. Yes."

The slender Indian rose to his feet and moved without a word. Morgan tried to hear him leaving but didn't detect sound, not even walking through the brush and trees.

Now all Morgan could do was wait.

Mighty Dawn eyed the dark sky. It would be after ten o'clock before they got back to the camp. He and Walks With a Limp had stayed at their post until they couldn't see 50 yards ahead. Then they rode for the camp. They had seen no sign of Pony Soldiers or anyone else coming into this side of the Medicine Bows.

Morgan had probably gone back to Cheyenne. He might have waited an hour, then decided that Mighty Dawn would always be an Indian and he would tell his father that in Grand Island.

Mighty Dawn had argued with himself for most of the two days. He was still not sure just what to do. In some ways the Indian life was brave and free, wild and wonderful. In other ways he missed the benefits of his father's money; nice things to eat, to wear, riding in a fancy carriage.

He hated to admit it, but he also missed school. He had been a good student, and he liked to study and learn new things. Especially about the stars and the planets. When he got back he would go talk to Gray Owl again. By then he had to have his mind made up one way or the other.

He rode automatically without thinking about it. At least he had become an excellent horseman while he was here. He was surprised when they rounded a bend in a small stream and were back in their short-term camp. He still hadn't decided what to do.

They went to Gray Owl at once. Walks With a Limp gave his report. Nothing to fear right away from the east.

"Gray Owl, may I talk a moment with you?" Mighty Dawn asked.

The leader looked irritated, but nodded. The other warrior left at once.

They were in the open with only a good-sized fire near the front of the tipi to give light to those taking down the camp.

"Great Chief Gray Owl, I am mixed-up and troubled. I am still not sure if I am a true warrior. I'm thinking of returning to the white-eyes world."

"That is a difficult decision to make, Mighty Dawn. Your grandfather named you with the idea in mind that you would lead your people to a new dawn, a mighty dawn of new power and respect throughout all of our old hunting grounds."

"I know. My mother has told me the story often."

A commotion to the left caused both men to look that way. A warrior ran out of a tipi. He caught a woman ahead of him and held her fast by an arm.

"You did not do as I ordered!" a warrior Mighty Dawn recognized as Long Knife bellowed. He struck the woman, and she sprawled in the dirt near the fire. Mighty Dawn saw she was the big white woman who had been captured on the stagecoach raid. She started to get up, but had made it only to her hands and knees when Long Knife rushed up and kicked her in the stomach, dumping her sideways into the dirt on her back.

Long Knife dropped on her, held his knife poised over her, and lifted her ragged woman's shirt and slit it down the front, pulling it off her, leaving her naked to the waist.

"Don't!" she shouted in English. Long Knife lowered his knife and slashed her across the cheek. Blood gushed. The white woman screeched in pain.

"A mere woman does not tell Long Knife what to do!" the warrior screeched, this time at the top of his voice. His knife slashed again and a blood line three inches long opened across her right breast.

The white woman screamed at the new pain and then sobbed in agony. She sat on the ground, her arms folded now over her breasts to protect them.

Long Knife used his blade again and again on her arms until she screamed in terror and fear of her life and dropped her bleeding arms to her side.

"No woman tells Long Knife what to do!" the warrior snarled. This time the blade came out and traced a scratch across her throat. The woman's eyes went wide in the firelight. Then she gasped and tried to control her sobbing.

Survive, Mighty Dawn thought. He had urged her to do as her warrior told her so she could survive. Rescue was impossible if she didn't *survive*!

"Please," she said in English. "Please. I'll do exactly as you say."

"Quiet!" Long Knife thundered in a language she didn't understand.

She was on her knees now in front of him. Her bleeding hands clasped as she begged him.

"I'll do what you say. Please. Please don't hurt me any more."

Long Knife had no idea what she had said. His face clouded and he roared in anger and fury, and with one short stroke slashed the sharp blade across the white woman's throat.

She looked at him in a moment of terror. One hand thrust toward her throat as blood spurted from her severed arteries. Blood splashed on the warrior twice, then three times, spurting with each heartbeat.

The woman's brain quickly registered a lack of blood and its life-sustaining oxygen. She crumpled to the side, her hands fell before her, and her face skidded in the dirt. The light in her eyes faded to a dying ember and then to black. One last rush of air came from her lungs, and the captive white woman belonging to Long Knife was dead.

Long Knife grunted. He swiped at the still-hot blood on his chest and turned and strode back toward his tipi. Already his other two wives had the buffalo hide cover off the structure and were pulling down the poles. He nodded and went to see about his ponies.

The white woman captive lay where she had died.

Mighty Dawn had shrunk back a step or two from the savagery. Now he realized that the white woman would lay right where she was as the band completed its move. She would stay there unless Long Knife moved her. She was his *property*!

Mighty Dawn turned back to Gray Owl.

"Shouldn't Long Knife be punished? Is he going to get away with doing this?"

Gray Owl shrugged. "She was his property. He can do with her as he likes. It is nobody else's business. It is the way of the People."

Mighty Dawn swung around and faced the older man. Without knowing it he dropped into English as he ranted.

"Well, it shouldn't be the way of the people. It should be illegal. No one has the right to kill anyone else. No matter what. There should be tribal laws about that. The only way to describe it is savage. That warrior is a savage and he should be taught the importance of human life!"

Mighty Dawn shook his head walking around the small fire.

"I don't see why it took me so long to decide what to do. This is no life for me. I'm wasting my time here. I've missed a half a year of school. It will make me late entering Harvard. I'm going to get out of here tonight."

For the first time Mighty Dawn realized that he had been shouting in English. A dozen of the people around had stopped work and stared at him. He motioned Gray Owl out of the firelight and went back to speaking Cheyenne.

"Gray Owl. I am not worthy to be a Cheyenne Warrior. I could never do what Long Knife just did. I am too much white-eyes. I thank you for your comfort and for taking me in when my mother died.

"Now I must return to the white-eyes world. I will get my horse and ride out now, and you will not have to worry about my telling anyone where you went since I won't know."

He nodded at the old Indian, and looked up with surprise when two warriors as large as he was jumped up beside him and caught his arms.

"I'm sorry, Mighty Dawn. We can't let you go. The council decided while you were away that you have been good medicine for us. You will stay with us for our move. We have found a band of over sixty warriors in the Medicine Bows beyond the next peak.

"We will go there in the morning, far from the angry Pony Soldiers. You will stay with us and you will bring us much good medicine."

The two warriors held Mighty Dawn so he couldn't move. One of them took the knife from his belt and they walked him away toward one tipi which was still standing. Inside they threw him down on a pallet, and one picked up an Army Spencer carbine and chambered a round.

"I can use this well," the warrior said to Mighty Dawn. "If you try to leave, I will shoot you in the leg. I will enjoy shooting you in the leg. I might miss and hit you in the head. Now sleep. You will be guarded until dawn."

Chapter Fifteen

Despite his best efforts, Morgan dropped off to sleep sometime before midnight. He awoke when someone spoke his name close beside him two hours later.

"Morgan, I come back."

Lee Buckskin Morgan snapped awake with the quickness of a steel-jawed trap. His .45 Colt came up in a fraction of a second. Then he recognized the speaker and relaxed.

"Jim, what happened to Mighty Dawn?"

Jim told him what he had learned in the hectic scene below as the Gray Owl band packed getting ready to leave at dawn.

"Boy come back from long-day lookout after dark. Talk to Gray Owl, then led off to tipi with two guards."

"Guards? Are you sure? So even if he wanted to come back with us, the Cheyenne are keeping him a prisoner. What can they hope to accomplish by that?"

"One more warrior to shoot rifle."

Morgan eased the six-gun back into hip leather. "So what the hell should we do now?" He asked himself, not expecting an answer.

Morgan walked around the cleared spot a minute, then looked back at Jim. "Is there anyway we can know where they will be going?"

"Sent scouts to west, found Cheyenne band in west side Medicine Bow Mountains."

"That's twenty miles farther over."

"They move west, join larger band."

"Then why take the quarter-breed warrior?"

"Warriors and women say Mighty Dawn brings much good medicine to band. He big hero. Keep him for much more and better good medicine."

"Won't he run away?"

"Outrun Cheyenne? Out-sneak Cheyenne?"

"I guess not. Jim, is there any way you and I can get into that tipi tonight and get away with Mighty Dawn? He must want to come out now, or they wouldn't keep him under guard. How can we get in there and out . . . alive?"

"Sneak up on two Cheyenne standing guard in tipi?"

"Yeah, I see what you mean. Damnit! He must have told Gray Owl he wanted to leave, so they kept him a prisoner."

"Council decide," Jim said.

"That makes it worse." He stared into the night. These things never were simple. Damn, this one had gone as sour as any he'd ever tried. He made the decision quickly.

"All right, Jim. Here's what we'll do. I need to

report back to the boy's father. Tell him what's happening. You hang behind the band but keep them in sight and trail them to their new camp. I'll leave soon and hope to get up there to Laramie by daylight. As soon as I make my report by wire to Bishop, I'll get a new horse and try and catch you and the Cheyenne."

"Medicine Bow Mountains damn big place. Where meet?"

"I should be able to follow a trail of eighty people and travois and a herd of ponies. If I lose you, let's meet at the train station in Laramie in three days. At noon. This noon coming up will be the first. Then two more and we meet the third noontime."

Jim nodded.

"By the time I start from Laramie, you and Gray Owl's band will be almost to the other Cheyenne group. Can you live off the land for three days?"

"Jim Cheyenne."

"Right. Let's get out of here and find the horses. I've got a long ride ahead of me."

"First few days they guard Mighty Dawn tight," Jim said. "More days, less guard. Week, maybe no guard."

"No rush getting back to him then," Morgan said. "I agree. All we have to do is get there before he decides to take off on his own and they hunt him down and kill him. My worry will be finding you."

"Three noons at Laramie," Jim said.

They faded uphill and around the still-active Cheyenne camp. Some of the preparations to move would take all night in the dark.

It was almost an hour later when the two men

209

walked into their makeshift camp near the horses. Morgan threw the saddle on his bay, cinched it up, and got the rest of his gear together and stowed behind his saddle.

"I'll leave what you want," Morgan said. "The cooking gear, the rest of the food."

Jim nodded. "Good, not much time for hunt."

Morgan stepped on board the bay and looked down at Jim.

"Watch them. Laramie in three days. At the train station. Good luck." He turned the horse downstream and rode for Laramie north and to the east.

When Morgan walked the bay into Laramie, he was still chilled by the night air, sore, and so tired he was cranky. He put his horse in the livery, walked directly to the train station, and sent his wire to Bishop detailing the developments so far and the hope that Harold had changed his mind and wanted to come home.

He saw a Cheyenne paper on the counter. A black headline told the story. "THIRD WOMAN KILLED HERE." He read on. "Lottie Fuiten, owner of Lottie's Cafe, was found dead this morning by early risers looking for their usual breakfast. Sheriff Goranson said it looked like the same man killed her who had murdered two other Cheyenne women recently."

Morgan ran out to the station. The eastbound train was just pulling out. He ran and grabbed the last car and swung on board. He had two days. He had to see what happened to Lottie. He owed her that much.

Two hours later he stepped off the train in Cheyenne and hurried to the sheriff's office. Goranson frowned when he came in.

Gunslinger's Scalp

It took a few minutes, but Morgan finally convinced the sheriff he wasn't Slade Johnson. Then he got right to the point. "Lottie was a friend of mine. What happened?"

"Six men found her when she didn't open for breakfast. She was killed in that back room at the cafe. The bastard cut off her head and set it on her stomach."

Morgan dropped into a chair. "Any clues, any ideas? Any witnesses?"

"Nothing. Not a damn thing."

"Mind if I look around?"

The sheriff shook his head. "Just for my records, where you last night, Morgan?"

"I was in the Medicine Bow Mountains until this morning. I just got off the eastbound train from Laramie."

"Anybody talk with you in the mountains?"

"Yes, Jim Breed."

"Jim?"

"Yes, he's working for me. I'm on a missing-persons case."

"Who?"

"Harold Bishop of Grand Island, Nebraska. He's one-quarter Cheyenne. Fourteen years old and is with the Gray Owl band now headed for the western Medicine Bows."

"Hard to prove. How do I know you're really looking for this kid?"

"Two telegrams from Alonzo Bishop of Grand Island should do it."

"It might, Morgan. Dr. Wilberforce looked over the body. Said whoever cut these women knows what he's doing. Could even be a surgeon."

"Sheriff, I've done some investigation work. I'd like to lend you a hand on this one, if you don't mind. I was partial to Miss Lottie's cooking as well."

The sheriff grunted. "Just don't dress so I think you're that damn Slade."

"He's still around?"

"Near as I can tell."

"He hasn't robbed a bank yet?"

"Not around here. You expect him to?"

"That's his profession. Who's killing the women in this town?"

Sheriff Goranson shook his head. "I've got damn little to go on. Doc didn't help me out much. Said the killer was strong, he had sexual intercourse with each woman before he killed her, and the woman never knew what was coming. He said with Lottie she must have been dead before the killer cut off her head. Almost no blood at the scene.

"I asked Doc what kind of a knife the killer used. Doc said more than one. There was a definite incision around the throat and the back of the neck, almost like a scalpel but not the same. For the deeper cut the blade was wider, heavier. Then at the vertebrae there was some slight jog to find the soft matter connecting the bones that could be cut through.

"Doc said he'd want at least four or five different sizes and weights of knives to do the same thing on a cadaver."

"Any men in town who used to be doctors and got bounced out of the profession or quit and moved West?" Morgan asked.

The sheriff shook his head. "Don't know of any. Three doctors in town now, and I'm sure none of them would do something like this. They see enough blood during the day. Here's a report the doctor made for me." The sheriff handed Morgan a handwritten paper. Morgan read it.

"The knife used went through between the first and second cervical vertebrae. If the woman wasn't dead before, the knife would cut the cortex that goes up through the hollow vertebrae directly to the brain. That would have killed her instantly.

"Then he cut the sternocleidomastoid muscles on both sides of the neck. These hold the head up and let you turn it from side to side. I'd guess he started at the back, went through the vertebrae, and then on to the front under the chin. A neat, professional job.

"The killer could be a crazy doctor, but more likely he's someone who quit medical school or surgeon's school or failed and couldn't complete it, but after this particular area of the body was studied and the surgical skills needed to do this work were learned."

Morgan handed back the paper. "So our killer could be anyone," Morgan said. He turned to the lawman. "Have you searched the room? Maybe the killer left something or dropped something. I've heard of cases where a madman left a clue at every killing hoping the authorities would catch him and make him stop the murders."

Sheriff Goranson snorted. "Fancy chance our killer would do that. He seems to enjoy himself too much with the women first. Why couldn't he just pay them two dollars and leave?" He shrugged. "Sure, I did a search. The room is locked. If you want to take a look at it, help yourself."

Morgan spent the next hour going over and over the room. He went on his hands and knees to check the floor and under the bed. He had just about given up hope of finding anything when he noticed a small square of paper that had been pasted to the copper bedpost. It was an inch square and at first looked like some kind of postage stamp. But it wasn't.

The square of paper had printed on it the picture of a strange-looking bird that had two diamondlike gems painted on its body. It was amazingly like the gold and diamond pin that Morgan had found after the alley killing.

Morgan used his new penknife and gently lifted up one side, then peeled the square of paper off the post. He put it in the notebook from his shirt pocket for safekeeping.

Morgan guessed that the sheriff had been talking to men who used knives in town. That would include the half-dozen butchers in town. Knives seemed to be the tie to all of these deaths.

Morgan closed the side door to the cafe and locked it with the key the sheriff had given him, then walked down to the Underwood Groceries and Provisions store and asked the manager who in town was the local expert on birds.

"That's an easy one, Mr. Morgan. Ida. Ida Nelson, our county librarian. Library opens at ten."

Morgan thanked the merchant and left. He still wanted some breakfast. Lottie! God, what a way to die. She was a great cook who enjoyed sex as much as any woman he had known. That might have been what cost her her life. He ate down the street at Ed Knapp's Saloon and Restaurant. Then, at the stroke of ten, he opened the Laramie County Library door and went inside.

Ida Nelson turned out to be prim, precise, about 35, he figured, and definitely a librarian.

Her dress was plain brown, barely showing any breasts, her harsh brown hair was tied up in a bun at the back of her neck, and gray eyes hid behind spectacles.

She looked at the small picture, then went for a magnifying glass and studied it again.

"Oh, dear, I'm afraid I'm not familiar with that species. It's certainly not from around here. Let me consult my reference books. It could take me an hour or more."

"If you have the time, Miss Nelson."

"Certainly, Mr. Morgan. That's what we're here for, to serve and to inform and educate. If you stop back about eleven-thirty I should have an answer for you."

He left quietly. Outside he asked a passerby where the office of the newspaper was, and was directed over a block and down half a block.

The *Cheyenne Sun* had been out with another issue since the third killing. He read the story on the front page about the three murdered women, but learned nothing new. The sheriff was still "obtaining leads and questioning suspects." Which meant the sheriff didn't have a clue.

Morgan went outside and sat in one of the chairs that could lean back against the Underwood Groceries and Provisions store. The chairs were the domain of the old men in town, but there was room for him in an unused one. The old men chattered and argued, and two played a precarious game of checkers.

Morgan leaned back in his chair until the back hit the wall and he sat there on the rear two legs. The bird had something to do with all three killings, but what? He rocked on the back legs of the chair a moment, then got up and went into the

215

store where he had bought the penknife a few days before. He found the same clerk and motioned to the knives.

"Anybody in town buy several knives lately?"

"Sure. Larch Younger. He uses them all the time. He's the best butcher in town. Sharpens his knives so fast he uses up the blades. One of my best customers."

"Anybody else?"

"You trying to figure out who's been carving up the women, right? Rapes them, then chops them up with his knives. Been thinking of that some myself. Sheriff and I worried it some yesterday, but didn't do no good."

Morgan thanked him and left. He realized he still had his trail clothes on. He was due for a good soak in one of the hotel's new lay-down tubs.

The shock of hearing about Lottie dead and decapitated was slowly sinking into his mind. She had been so enthusiastic, so hard-working, and so damn good in bed. He shook his head and walked faster to the hotel. He'd be late getting back to the library, but Ida would wait. She would be there all day.

He stopped by at the desk, paid for the six buckets of hot water to be brought to the second-floor bathroom, and went up to wait. This hotel had a bathroom on each floor. They consisted of a modern lay-down enameled steel bathtub, two chairs, a rack to hang clothes on, a supply of large white towels, and a small couch to use while changing.

He carried fresh clothes into the bathroom and waited while a boy brought up the water. He brought a bucket of cold water as well and stood at the door watching.

"Is everything all right?" the boy asked.

Morgan reached in his pants pocket, found a quarter, and tossed it to the boy.

"Wow! Thanks a lot, Mr. Morgan!"

The boy closed the door and Morgan reached over and turned the key in the lock.

He needed the cold water. The hot water must have been scalding. He undressed and eased one foot into the water, then jerked it out. He poured in half the bucket of cold water, then the rest of it.

Slowly and with great caution he lowered himself into the 18 inches of hot water. When he was submerged except for his head, he let out a long sigh.

He lay there for ten minutes without moving, letting the glorious hot water soak away the aches of the long horseback ride. When he headed for Laramie he'd take the train. One left every morning and would use up less than two hours to get there.

His back was to the bathroom door, but he had it locked and his six-gun was on a chair he had pulled up close to the tub. He found the soap and a cloth and scrubbed himself from top to toe, washing his hair as well.

Then he rinsed off and lowered himself full length in the tub again, folding his legs so he'd fit. He wanted to lay there until the water turned cold.

He tried to reason out the rape-killings in town. Now he was concerned about them because Lottie had been a victim. It was much more personal now. The two birds had something to do with it, but he couldn't put his finger on what it might be.

He had listened when he was on the street and it seemed that half the people were talking about the killings. He was sure Lottie's death would be the main topic of conversation in town. Cheyenne, even for having almost two thousand people, was like a small town, and gossip and news raced from one house and mouth to the next. It would be impossible to keep a secret here.

He heard a soft laugh behind him and snapped his head around, his right hand darting for the six-gun.

He couldn't believe what he saw. Shirley stood beside the tub, his six-gun in her hand. Shirley stood there in her glorious blond beauty wearing absolutely nothing. He saw a pile of clothes at her feet.

"I usually get eight buckets of water for my bath. But six will have to do. Mind if I join you?"

Chapter Sixteen

Morgan sat in the bathtub there on the second floor of the hotel, unable to move as he stared at the beautifully naked girl. He did manage a grin. Shirley knelt beside the tub and leaned in and kissed him. It was warm and lasting and her tongue probed at his lips until he opened them.

She caught one of his wet hands and brought it up to her bare breasts, and moaned in delight when he started stroking them.

Her lips left his a moment.

"You didn't answer my question. Mind if I join you in your tub?"

Morgan leaned out and kissed her breasts, nibbled on one, and chuckled.

"Shirley, marvelous little lady. I just hope you locked the door after you unlocked it to get in here."

"Sure did," she said, stepping into the tub and

facing him. She lowered into the tub putting one leg on each side of him, and he saw her delightful muff and gently parted nether lips at her crotch just before the water flowed over them and she sat where his feet had been.

"This is cozy," Shirley said. "Want to wash me—all over?"

"Just the important parts," Morgan said. By then his manhood had lifted above the water, and Shirley giggled and reached for it. She stroked it and then leaned forward, but she couldn't reach it with her mouth.

"Later for that," she said.

Morgan soaped a clean cloth and began to wash her chest.

"That feels wonderful, Morgan. It's been so long for me. Where have you been? You promised to come back and you didn't. I've been to your room every night for three or four days."

"Been busy, working. Sometimes men have to work, you know. I wasn't sure you were still in town. Slade hasn't robbed a bank yet. What's he waiting for?"

"I haven't seen that bastard for a week. I don't know where he is and I don't care. I might never see him again."

Morgan scrubbed a little harder. "Then you're not sure he's still out at that farm? What if he's gone on and not told you where he's going?"

"Tough for him. I ain't married to him or nothing."

Shirley pushed forward and lay on top of Morgan. Only a thin layer of water separated them.

"There, that's lots better. I love it on top."

"In the water?"

"Why not, Morgan? Haven't you ever fucked in the water?"

"Once I had a sexual experience underwater, but everyone says that didn't count."

She turned her pretty face into a frown. "Why wouldn't it count?"

"I was alone at the time."

She laughed and hit him in the shoulder. Then she reached between them, found his hardness, and lifted her hips until she could position herself. She lowered her body onto his lance an inch at a time, transforming her face into a vision of ecstasy and fulfillment.

"Oh, yes! Morgan! More of him, more!" She lowered further until their pelvic bones jolted together.

"Oh, damn! I'm coming already!" She shrilled a high soft tone and her face writhed in passion and pain, and then she began to move her hips in a series of spasms that rattled through her body and coursed into his.

Her voice went low and demanding and then cooing, and she eased off the end of the series of climaxes with a soft growl.

"Right after a good one like that I always want to eat my young. Is that natural?"

"Do you have a litter of young anywhere?"

She giggled through her exhaustion. "Not that I know of."

"The feeling should pass before you have your first child, so don't worry about it. I have something else you do need to worry about."

"Oh, poor baby. In my rush I forgot all about him. Poor big boy." She gently lifted away and lowered on him. She made the same movement in perfect rhythm and the buildup of waves in the bathtub slopped water onto the floor.

"Don't stop," Morgan growled. He matched her movements, then countered them, and the splashing continued and Morgan didn't give a damn.

He had been so close for so long he could hardly hold back. He did for a while, enjoying her ministrations from on top. The water cushioned her body so he hardly felt her weight. The combination of the water and having the lovely Shirley over him soon pushed Morgan over the top.

He thrust upward as hard as he could, and heard the water splash over the side of the tub. He also felt his tiny trapdoor open and the fluid rush down tubes toward freedom.

Just as they reached their point of release, he drove as deep as he could into her, and then again and again and again as the powerful surges tightened every muscle in his body and he exploded into the woman driving his seed into the rich reception area.

He thrust half a dozen times more, and then gave a big sigh and settled back on the bottom of the tub. She floated down on him and her face nestled on his shoulder, which was just out of the water. He could see that her long blond hair was soaked. Her brown eyes watched him.

"Bet you never had a woman like that before, Mr. Morgan."

"You're right. Now shut up and let me die in peace."

"You can't die. I want you in my bed. Nothing for good fucking like in bed and us all naked and warm and both of us just loving it."

"Agreed, but who cleans up the bathroom?"

"They do. That's why we pay the fifty cents for

the water. We don't say that it's going to stay in the tub."

He laughed and pushed her away. She stood and stepped out of the tub, picked up a towel, and began drying herself.

He watched her lying where he was. "Have you ever danced ballet?" he asked her.

"No. Just ballroom dancing and some square dances."

"You look like a ballet dancer I saw in Chicago once. All the grace and flowing beauty of the human body."

"I'll try to do that." She picked up a towel. "Come on, I want you dry the next time and before you cool off."

They left the bathroom with half an inch of water on the floor and hurried with their towels and clothes down to her room.

It was nearly three that afternoon before he remembered the librarian. Morgan pushed away from the naked loveliness of Shirley, reached down and kissed both hanging breasts, then reached for his clean clothes.

"Work to do," he said when she looked at him.

"You'll be back for tonight?"

"What's tonight?"

"You promised to show me how to fuck standing up, remember?"

"If there's time. I may be working. I might be here and I might not. Best I can do right now."

When he finished dressing, he kissed her on the cheek. "I'll see you tonight or tomorrow."

Morgan grabbed his trail clothes, checked the hallway, then slipped out her door and down to his own room.

Five minutes later he walked into the Laramie

County Library and found Ida Nelson checking out a book. He waited. When she saw him she nodded and led him to a table where two books were opened.

"It could be this bird, the dotterel, but I don't think so. It has a different style about it. I'd guess that it's a much larger bird than the dotterel.

"That's why I looked at more books. My best match is this one."

She showed him a half page picture of a long-legged bird that had a large bill and what looked like heavy wings. The bill wasn't long enough.

"Do you think this is the one?" he asked.

"Not really. That's the scarlet ibis, but it looks something like the picture. None of them within three thousand miles of us."

He took the gold pin from his pocket and showed it to her.

"Doesn't help me any. It's not a local bird, I'm sure of that. I know every bird in the county."

He thanked her and left the building. The triple murders had him at a dead end. No suspects. Almost no clues, except the damn bird picture and the pin. For just a moment he was glad no one was paying him to solve the sex killings. He wouldn't be earning his money.

There was nothing he could do about Harold Bishop. Day after tomorrow he'd take the morning train and meet Jim Breed in Laramie at noon.

That was when he remembered his dinner engagement with Sarah Everett, the banker. The home-cooked meal he had missed when he and Jim took off for the mountains. He turned and headed for the bank. He'd take her out to dinner tonight. That might make up for his not showing up at her house before.

He walked in the bank and saw Sarah behind her desk in her office. Morgan knocked on the door. When she looked up her stern face gave way to a bright smile.

"Lee Morgan! I'm glad that you found your way back from whatever work-problem you had."

"Miss Everett, I'm sorry about missing our dinner. I was somewhere out in the hills at the time."

"I'm not worried about it at all. Fact is I ate up the roast and it lasted me three days. Your business all finished?"

"No, especially not making it up to you. Could I take you to dinner at the best eatery in town tonight?"

She hesitated just a moment.

He grinned. "I can prove that I was out of town when the last murder happened so it couldn't have been me."

She laughed softly. "I wasn't even considering that. Yes, I have a meeting, but I don't really have to go. They'll get along well without me. An early dinner, about five-thirty? Then I won't have to go home and you can pick me up here."

"Fine. I see you still have your three shotgun guards out. No problems?"

"Not a one. Even the regular customers have told me that they like seeing their money protected a little better. I think it was a good move. But after a week more, I'm just going to have the man inside. I've made my point."

"Still should be enough. I have some business, I'll be back about five-thirty."

"The front door will be locked. Just rattle the knob or knock and I'll come right out."

He watched her a moment. Her soft reddish

brown hair shifted around her face. Her brown eyes looked at him intently and she had a fascinating way of smiling at him.

"Miss Everett, I'll be back for dinner at five-thirty unless I have a broken leg or get shot."

He grinned at her flare of alarm and walked out of the office and to the street.

That had been an easy fence to mend. It was going to be a lot harder to deal with the Cheyenne. If they wouldn't let Harold go, he'd have a straight job of trying to out-Indian the Cheyenne and get Harold away from the much larger band. There would be about 80 warriors. That was a good-sized band for the Cheyenne.

He still owed Slade for that shotgun blast that almost killed him. Morgan would get to Slade, but right now he was low man on the contact list. For now Morgan had a day and a half to try to piece together something on the lunatic who killed Lottie. Morgan figured he owed it to the girl. The sheriff wasn't going to get much done, that was obvious by now.

What new tack could he take? He walked into a saloon and ordered a beer. Near the back, two men were having a knife-throwing contest. They had set up two pine logs and stood 20 feet back and aimed at a V marked on the log. The one who came closest to hitting the log in the bottom of the V won. Morgan watched them throw, wishing he had his own belt knife.

One man missed the log and the blade glanced off and fell harmlessly at Morgan's feet. He picked up the knife and handed it to the man handle-first. The thrower thanked him and went back to the contest.

For a moment, Morgan thought he saw something familiar on the blade of the knife down near the steel hand-guard, but he didn't quite recognize what it was.

He took his beer to a table and sat down sipping at the brew as he marshaled all of the facts in the three killings and tried to find common ground. As before, there just wasn't enough. All three victims were women. All three had large breasts. All three had been raped before they were killed with a knife. Not enough.

Thurlow Deeds sat at a small table 15 feet from Morgan. Deeds had just finished a beer and considered joining a small-stakes poker game. He deserved it. This was his vacation. He had sold well in Laramie. That was the last town in his territory. Now he would work back toward Chicago, picking up the stores that he had missed. Someone was always away for the day or on vacation or their sister had taken ill.

He had done better on this trip than ever before. He was looser, more relaxed. He smiled and fingered the money clip in his pocket. It all was because he was more at ease with his customers.

That was due to his release of tensions as he called it. Three times he had experienced the ultimate climax. Reaching an orgasm at the exact time that the woman under him exploded in her orgasm and then died. There could be no greater thrill, no better high for his emotions than that.

The authorities had become more efficient back in his home town, so he had moved his "activity" westward. Most of these small towns had little in the way of police, and no detectives and no up-to-date or scientific methods for studying a crime.

Kit Dalton

Three women in one town was the most he had ever tried. He should be moving on. He'd taken his two days of rest. Then last night he'd had supper, a late supper with Lottie, and she'd invited him to come see her back room.

It was simple. She locked the front door. There were no other customers in the cafe. They slipped into the back room, and he took his sample case with him. She knew he was a salesman.

He touched Lottie and put his arms around her and then kissed her hard. After a dozen kisses, Lottie was not hard to convince to show him her big breasts. He played with them for five minutes, and then she was as eager as he was to get undressed and on the bed. She was good, soft like a pillow and wild when she was worked up to a passion.

He had her on top and he used the depression between the first and second vertebrae for the initial thrust of the slender knife. He was in the middle of his own climax and she exploded over him, and he found the point and rammed the blade into her spine cutting the cortex, and the glory time came. He finished his own climax and felt her gasp and then go limp and die, even as his life-giving semen spurted into her wasteland.

The thrill, the high was so great that he passed out. That had never happened before. The ultimate! For such a performance there had to be something different. He chose the decapitation at last. It took him a half hour, and he was as precise and sure-handed as his teachers had taught him in the medical college in Chicago.

He had been within two months of graduating when the girl came to him, and he performed a simple scraping on her to rid her of an unwanted two-month-old pregnancy. Somehow things went wrong and the girl went into shock, and then hemorrhaged, and she died a day later.

The medical school board found out. They didn't tell the police but demanded that Deeds resign from the school and never tell anyone he'd trained there. He would never be a doctor.

That had been ten years ago. He knew little of the West back then. With the training he had, he could have moved to Arizona or Colorado or here in Wyoming and set up practice and printed his own diploma and no one would have questioned him.

Instead he had surrendered to the threats and taken a job with his wife's father's firm. Selling knives. They were products he knew how to use. Lately he had been discovering just how well he could still use them.

The placement of Lottie's head on her stomach was significant to him. It represented Lottie's appetites and how they had eventually caused her own end. Sad in a way. What great tits she had. She'd enjoyed sex more than any woman Deeds had ever been with.

He fingered the money in his pocket. It had come from Lottie's money drawer in the cafe, and from a coffee can she'd used as her safe in the small living room behind the kitchen. Lottie had had little imagination in hiding $200 in gold coins. He had found the can after five minutes of searching.

Deeds rose from the chair in the saloon, went to a four-man poker game, and asked if he could join them. The men looked at him, sensed some new money, and nodded. Deeds settled down to a hand or two. Maybe he would stay the rest of the afternoon and then have dinner at the best eatery in town. He'd think tomorrow about going back on his route.

Lee Buckskin Morgan watched the men in the saloon. Anyone of them might be the killer. He had 800 suspects in town. How could he narrow it down?

A decoy? He had shot a few ducks in his time. A decoy might be used to entice the killer to try again. But what if Morgan was too late arriving or missed it altogether? The real live woman decoy could die.

Besides, he knew no woman in town who would qualify. Certainly he wasn't going to ask Sarah Everett to play a sexy big-busted woman prancing around town. If the man were local, he would know at once it was a trap. Morgan would never ask Sarah to do anything so dangerous.

He chuckled when he thought of Ida Nelson being his decoy. The only thing she would catch would be an out-of-work cowhand with poor eyesight and not even two dollars in his pocket for a whang over in one of the whorehouses.

Morgan checked his pocket watch. It was almost five-thirty. He pushed back and stood. No one even noticed when he left the saloon. It was time to go pick up Sarah Everett and take her to dinner. Sarah was not a woman of easy virtue like Lottie. This would be a formal meeting and he would consider himself lucky if she held his arm as he walked her home after supper. She was a prim and proper lady, and Morgan knew she would stay that way. It was interesting to take such a woman to dinner now and then, Morgan decided. It kept his perspective on track.

Chapter Seventeen

Slade Johnson rode down 15th Street in Cheyenne near the tracks. He enjoyed the trains. One wasn't coming right then, but there would be one along later. Slade did not wear his traditional buckskins. He had on town pants and a brown shirt and a low-crowned cowboy hat pulled down low over his eyes. He passed several businesses on the right of the street and turned up Hill Street toward the center of town.

Slade paused with the mare as he saw the shotgun guard standing in front of the Cheyenne Territorial Bank. That was the smaller one, the one that a week ago had had no guard inside and no shotguns behind the counters. What had happened?

He rode on down the street and tied up his horse across from the bank. With a 20-dollar gold piece in hand, Slade walked across the street and went into the bank. He eased his well-worn hat lower over his face. He acted as if he belonged there. Nobody would recognize him, he was sure.

Inside the bank he spotted the guard behind the shield and lifted his brows. At the window he asked for change for the double eagle, took the offered paper money, and left. He had seen what he needed to. It was his second check on the smaller of the two banks.

He still could see no sign of weapons behind the teller cages. The two guards were more than he had counted on. He circled the block on his horse and went up the alley. There was no sign advertising the back door to the bank, but he knew which one it was.

Again, Slade was surprised to see a shotgun-toting guard pacing back and forth in the restricted area near the bank's back door.

Three guards!

He pondered that a moment as he rode toward the Pride of Wyoming Hotel. He was in no mood to argue with Shirley, but he sure would welcome her special ministrations. Instead he just checked at the desk to find out if she was still registered. She was. He nodded and left by the side door. He didn't want to run into her. He was doing nicely with Big Tits, his half-breed squaw out at the ranch east of town.

She did their washing, helped Grits cook, and cleaned up around the place. He was better off with her than the blond gal.

Slade figured he'd seen enough of town. He turned back down Hill Street and rode to the tracks, then headed back to the cabin on the river. He was getting restless. Another few days and they'd be ready to take out that small bank.

Not a lot of trouble. They'd time it out right.

Cut down the guard on the outside by riding by on a horse and using a pistol. At the same time one of them would drop the back door guard with a rifle shot. Then they'd move in the front and back doors at the same time and blow up the inside guard with one of the shotguns and take over the place.

No chance they could rob the bank the way he liked, just at closing time. This one would be a shoot-in and shoot-out, but they still should get $2,000. Last them all the way to Salt Lake City. He'd heard there were piles of Mormon money out there just waiting to be taken. He'd see.

Slade changed his mind and swung around and trotted the mare back to the hotel. He tied her in the alley behind the hotel and went in the deliveryman's entrance, through a short hall to the stairs, and up to the second floor. He knew exactly where he was going. He knocked on Room 230. He knew she had moved down from the third floor. The panel opened a crack, then swung wide.

"Sweetheart! What a wonderful surprise. Come in, come in. I've been wishing you were here. We have time, don't we?"

"Not right now. But save it for me. I'm building up a big need. Soon we'll be heading out for Salt Lake City. We'll ride to Laramie, sell the horses, and get on the train. We'll meet you there."

"You can't get on the train here?"

Slade grinned, reached over, and fondled her breasts. She purred.

"It would be tough to get on the train here right after we've cleaned out that bank down there. The smaller of the two. That comes Thursday.

About two-thirty. So you see why we can't walk down to the station and wait for the fucking train."

"Yes, I see." Shirley had unbuttoned her blouse, and opened it to show him she had on nothing under it.

"So I'll take the train Friday and get off in Laramie and wait for you."

"Better. It's a fifty-mile ride." He bent and kissed her big breasts, then sucked one in his mouth and chewed on it.

"Yes, yes, yes! Slade, do that all afternoon!"

"Can't, sweet-tit. Me and the boys need to make a few get-readies." He put one hand down between her legs and rubbed her crotch. "You save it for me, woman. I'll have a big head of steam up for you in Laramie. Maybe we'll get one of them compartments and we can train-fuck across the country!"

He kissed her quickly and hurried to the door. "You wait, woman. I'll see you in Laramie."

He ran to the stairs, went down them and outside. No one had recognized him. He didn't need to have the sheriff chasing him. Not for a measly store robbery. Slade took one more look at the town, shrugged, and rode to the east toward his camp.

Lee Morgan met Sarah Everett at the bank precisely at five-thirty. She was waiting for him, and stepped outside just before he could knock on the door.

"You're punctual," she said. "At least when you show up at all." She laughed. "I didn't mean that to sound cross. Actually I'm delighted that you asked me out. There aren't a lot of interesting men in this town."

She took his arm as they moved down the boardwalk. Partly she held his arm to be sociable and partly to be practical. The boardwalks were rough and uneven. In some places there were broken boards and in others the merchant had failed to put a boardwalk in front of his establishment. Often the walks were at different heights from one store to the next.

Two blocks down on Sixteenth and Hill Streets, they stopped at the S. S. Ramsey Restaurant.

"I've only been here once before," she said. "It's quite elegant, with white tablecloths and all."

They were seated by a waiter, who brought them cool water, then waited for their order.

"Let me choose for you," Sarah said. "If you don't like it you can change it." He nodded. For him she asked for the rancher's steak dinner with all the sides. She had calf's liver with bacon and onions, and ordered dessert for both of them, a fancy chocolate pudding with whipped cream.

He grinned. "You've fed men before."

She smiled. "I like to think that I observe carefully and take all factors into consideration."

Morgan nodded. "Understood. I think I do the same thing. Which in this case means I can buy you supper and walk you home, but I shouldn't expect a kiss on the cheek, and definitely will not be invited inside to light the lamp in your living room when we get to your house."

To his surprise, Sarah blushed. She smiled weakly and looked away from his stare.

"We'll see," was all she would say.

Kit Dalton

The dinner was delightful, filling and satisfying. They talked about politics, when the Territory could hope to reach the needed 60,000 population to apply for statehood, and who was going to run for President in the next election. She thought that James A. Garfield would run. Morgan wasn't so sure.

"If Winfield Hancock runs, he's going to lose to whoever the Republicans put up," Morgan said. "Hancock is a loser, has been, always will be."

Their dinner lasted nearly an hour and a half, and they walked home slowly. A traveling opera troupe was in town, but Morgan hadn't thought to get tickets. They passed the show hall and continued to her home, just off Dodge Street and 16th.

At the door, he smiled. "It was a pleasant and filling evening, Miss Everett. I thank you."

"I enjoyed it too. Perhaps we can have another outing soon?"

"I hope so. Right now my business is getting in the way of my social life. You can be sure I'll be in touch. You see, I know how to find you anytime during the day."

She smiled and with a quick step came forward and kissed his cheek.

"Good night, Mr. Morgan."

He grinned. "And a good night to you too, Miss Everett."

That evening Morgan played nickel-limit poker. The game took his mind off his problems, and sometimes an answer he couldn't come up with would magically surface during a game. Tonight nothing happened. No new ways to dig out the sex killer. Not even a hint. Besides that, he lost six dollars.

About eight o'clock he walked over to Lottie's Cafe. He figured someone might not have heard about the death and the closing. He wondered if anyone who had been at the cafe late the previous night had seen anyone hanging around who they might remember. It was a slim chance, but that was what he was down to.

He waited 15 minutes. He remembered that Lottie said sometimes she closed at eight, sometimes at nine, depending on how much business she had.

It was nearly eight-thirty when a man came toward the cafe at a brisk walk. He was a railroader by his appearance, and frowned when he didn't see any lights on inside. He rattled the locked door and looked at Morgan.

"Did she close up early again? Damn. I'm hungry."

"Were you here last night about this time?" Morgan asked.

"Why, yes, no business of yours, but it happens that I was here."

"Do you remember anyone else in the place, say just before Lottie closed?"

"See here, what's going on? I demand to know."

Morgan told him about Lottie's killing and the man staggered against the door.

"Lottie murdered! I can't believe it. She was so charming last night. Of course she didn't pay me much mind. Some new guy was at the far table and he took up most of her time."

"What can you remember about the man?" Morgan asked sharply.

The railroader bobbed his head. "I see. You think that man she was talking with might have stayed after closing time and killed poor Lottie."

"Exactly what I think. What do you remember about the man?"

"Let's see. I'm a conductor on the Union Pacific so I have to remember faces and who has a ticket and who doesn't. This guy kept to himself and turned away from me most of the time. He wore a business suit, like a store owner would. Vest and all, and seems like he had a little gold knife on a watch fob across his vest.

"Never saw him stand, but he wasn't an overly large man, say average. He didn't have any pot-belly, wore black shoes looked like he shined them every day."

"What color hair did he have?"

"Hair? Let's see. Yes, it was blond and wavy. I remember thinking he probably had someone set the wave for him every week. Wavy blond hair."

"Did he wear spectacles?"

"No. He was not young. I'd say no more than thirty-five. Yes, about thirty-five. Not young, but not old either."

"Did you hear him talk? Could you tell if he was from around here?"

"Too far away to hear. Figured he was a merchant or maybe a clerk at some fancy men's wear store. Dressed nice."

"He was still here when you left last night?"

"Sure was. Now that I think of it, I was the only other customer. Once I seen him put his hand . . . you know, on her leg, up high. She just stood there and grinned at him."

"How was she dressed? Did her big breasts

show any? You know, usually she showed a little just to get men to look at her."

The railroad man chuckled. "Yeah, that was Lottie. I never did her. Got me a wife back in Omaha, but she was there for the taking, that was for damn sure. A man would have to work at it a little, but yeah, Lottie did like to make love. I liked Lottie. She was doing fine here. Hope you can catch the guy." The man looked up with a frown. "You one of them detective guys I hear about?"

"Something like that. Would you mind giving me your name and where I can contact you?"

"Sure, name is Brent Rubiah. I'm a conductor with the Union Pacific. I'm usually on a six-hour layover here out of Omaha, then take the midnight out of here on the return run. Lousy schedule but I don't have much seniority."

"You best go talk to the sheriff about what you saw here last night. First good lead we've had about the killer. You will do that, won't you, Mr. Rubiah?"

"Yes, sir, right away. That is, soon as I get some supper. I'm damn near starved."

"Some other eateries up the street there," Morgan said.

The conductor hurried off. Morgan turned up the street watching the men. Must be ninety-five percent of them who were wearing hats. Wouldn't help much to find a blond man on the street. But at least he had a description. The man must be the killer. The conductor was a man with a trained eye. He'd even caught the shine on the killer's shoes. Now how did Morgan find the man?

He headed on down the street not paying much

attention to where he was going. He almost bumped into two men, then a moment later heard a shriek in front of him.

He looked up and stopped just in time. Shirley stood there directly in his path.

"Morgan, don't you ever watch where you're walking?"

"'Deed I do, Miss Shirley. I'm thinking on something." He frowned and checked her over. She was dressed well enough, but the blouse she wore over a boardwalk sweeping skirt was far, far too tight. It outlined perfectly her large breasts.

He caught her arm and pulled her gently to the side against a building.

"Shirley, what in the world are you doing, trying to get yourself raped and killed?"

"The first part sounds good, but I'm not excited about the last half."

"Don't make jokes about it. Three women in this town have been murdered. All three had full breasts. Are you still dancing at the saloon?"

"Of course. Until Thursday."

"First you have to live that long. Don't you sense the danger?"

"I like to have men turn and stare at my titties. One time a man came up and stroked them. I slapped him, of course."

"You don't understand. Somebody right here in town is probably looking for his next victim, a woman with big breasts. He doesn't care if she's pretty or not. One woman had her breast cut off."

Shirley heard that. She frowned. "Gawd, he did that? I don't want nothing to do with him."

"Good. Now you get back to the hotel and put on a wrap or something not so revealing for your walk to work. I hope whatever you dance in isn't too skimpy."

"Why, Mr. Morgan, you're talking like my old mama."

"Somebody should. Now you get on back. No, I better walk you back to your room to be sure you make it."

Ten minutes later, Morgan had escorted Shirley to her room, waited for her to change, then walked her to the saloon where she would dance that night. She'd joked about it, but Morgan had felt better knowing she was safe for a while.

What now? Blond men. Not a lot of them around. Like redheads. Most men took off their hats in a restaurant, all did in church, and some did in saloons. He worked the saloons first.

Morgan was surprised how many saloons there were in town. After ten, he got weary and tried a restaurant and had a cup of coffee. No man in the place had blond hair. He didn't even have to look for the wave.

By ten o'clock he was done with the bars, at least a lot of them, and he worked back to his hotel room. Shirley would be dancing tonight until nearly midnight. He checked the room across the hall from his. It hadn't been rented to anybody and his key opened the lock just fine. He moved in for the night with his Colt and the pillow from his room. Sometimes he liked two pillows.

Now if Shirley just didn't figure out where he went, he could get some sleep and decide what to do tomorrow. He had all day tomorrow and tomorrow night. Then he'd have to get out to Laramie and try to find Mighty Dawn Bishop, Harold Bishop. He had to get the kid back.

Morgan was almost sure that Harold wanted to come and the Cheyenne were holding him against his will. Besides, Morgan could use the $10,000 bonus for getting Harold back. That was as much as a workingman earned in 20 years. It was a fortune.

Morgan got his good night's sleep and began early the next morning trying to find the blond man. He worked the whole day, and when the sun went down he realized he knew little more than he had when he'd started all of this. He had a description of the killer and a bird pin. Which meant he had almost nothing.

But the bird was still a clue. He'd shown it to several more people in stores, but no one could tell him what kind of a bird it was or what it might signify.

More and more he was leaning toward the idea of a decoy. He snapped his fingers as he finished his dinner. Shirley! She would be the ideal decoy. Only how did he show her off so everyone in town could see her? And would she agree to do it? He had the idea that she stayed in her room most of the time when she wasn't dancing.

Of course the dancing at the saloon on Eddy Street would show her off. But how could he be sure that the killer would go there, or see her, or care? The more he thought about it, the less it seemed like a good plan. Soon he discarded it altogether. He disliked the very idea of putting a woman in danger that way.

If he had some idea who the killer was and could control things more, it might work. But not with what he knew now.

Back to the starting line. He had nothing.

The next morning, he was on the train for Laramie. Things had to get better. This was the case that counted. This was the race he must win.

Lee Morgan stepped down from the train at the Laramie station and saw Jim Breed leaning against the station wall. At least the Indian was there. So far, so good.

Chapter Eighteen

Mighty Dawn sat in the tipi. They were more than three days' travel from where they had been in the Medicine Bow Mountains when he had decided to return home. The Cheyenne had not let him go and had made him a prisoner. Now they had relaxed a little, but he was still confined to the tipi.

He was not entirely sure where they were, somewhere deeper in the Medicine Bow Mountains. The new band they had joined was led by Red Feather, a chief he had heard of before. He was a war chief and famous for his raids against the Pony Soldiers.

Now they were resting and looking for more bands to join them.

He had heard the talk. Mighty Dawn got the feeling they would rest there for a week or so, then move north into the far reaches of the Wyoming territory and maybe on into Montana, searching for other bands to join into one large fighting force.

He lifted the flap of the tipi and threw it back to get air inside. One of the warrior guards turned and looked at him.

"Stay inside," the warrior said. He was one of the men from the new band. Mighty Dawn moved back inside the tipi.

He sat down on the pallet and beat back tears. He would not cry. A Cheyenne warrior didn't cry! But he wasn't a Cheyenne warrior. He was only 14 years old. He wanted more than anything in the world to get back to civilization and hurry home to Grand Island. He wondered what the members of his class would be studying this fall. Would he be a year behind them? He had missed almost three months of school.

His hand slid under the edge of the pallet and he found what he felt for. The knife was only three inches long and the point had been broken off, but last night he had sharpened the blade on a rock and he had a fine edge to it. Tonight, after everyone slept, he would use the knife and cut a slot a foot long in the back of the tipi covering.

It was thick and old and hard, but he would cut through the tough buffalo leather and form an opening big enough that he could squeeze through. Once out of the tipi, he would work his way to the edge of the camp, find the stars, and begin to hike due south. Somewhere down there he would find the railroad tracks. Once there all he had to do was walk to the east to come to Laramie.

This was the second day they had been in the camp. The guards were easing up on him more and more. He talked with them, joked with them. The language was easy for him now. But tonight about midnight he would be gone.

That afternoon, the guard relented and let him sit in the opening of the tipi so he could watch outside. The warriors were holding a council. He wished he could be there to hear what they were planning.

Slowly he realized it didn't affect him. He was not one of the People anymore. When he saw Long Knife kill the big white woman, he had frozen the Cheyenne people out of his life. That had been the final deciding factor. He was through playing Indian. He did not like the savage side of the Cheyenne. Yes, they could be loving and gentle and kind, but the warrior's whole life was based on his ability to steal and raid and make war and kill. That wasn't the life he wanted for himself.

Anyone who thought the Indians were a kind and gentle people, closely tied to the land and nature, was sorely misled.

He watched the sun set, then ate from the bowl that one of the women brought to him and drank from the pure stream water. He would have no food to take with him tonight when he escaped. He hoped he would be able to find enough berries and roots to last him until he could get to the railroad.

Twice Mighty Dawn dropped off to sleep before midnight. But he had remained sitting up so when he went to sleep he tumbled over and that awoke him. The second time he figured it must be nearly midnight. The tipi flap had been tied shut and a guard sat directly in front of it. Even if the guard went to sleep, he would be roused by someone trying to get past him.

Mighty Dawn stood and walked to the back of the tipi where he had decided the hide was thinner. He felt it, then touched the tough sinew that was used to stitch the hides together.

No, that fiber would be much harder than the leather itself. He picked a spot a foot off the ground and began to slice with the stub of the knife. It was slow work and the inside of the tipi was dark. Twice he cut his finger as he guided the blade into the slice he'd started.

He worked for ten minutes before he broke through the leather. Then it was simpler to cut down through the leather. Another five minutes and he had the slit large enough to crawl through. He spread it apart and looked outside. There was another tipi within 20 feet of his, but it faced the other direction.

He extended the slice another two inches, then pushed his arms through and ducked his head into the hole.

His head came through and then he worked at getting his shoulders outside. A small tree grew nearby, and he caught hold of it with one hand and pulled. His shoulders stuck in the hole a moment. Then he surged forward and pushed with his feet and pulled and he slipped outside.

He lifted his legs through trying not to shake the structure.

A moment later he stood in the open. He wore only the soft moccasins of the People and his breechclout. He had put his treasured saddlebag near the hole. They'd let him keep it since there were no weapons in it and nothing of value. Only the stacks of paper that he said he used to play a game with were in one side of the bag. The papers were bundles of $20 bills.

He lifted the saddlebag out and put it over his shoulder, then holding the stub of a knife in his right hand, he moved cautiously past the next tipi and saw the dark woods less than 50 feet away.

He heard a dog bark somewhere downstream. The creek was to the front of the tipi. He moved 20 feet and stopped and listened. He heard nothing. He went another 20 feet and saw a tipi flap open and a warrior come out. He relieved himself against a tree and returned to the tipi.

Mighty Dawn moved again, running this time into the woods. He peered out at the sky and quickly found the Big Dipper and the North Star. What was it doing there? That couldn't be north, that was south.

He frowned and looked again. The North Star never lied. He wanted to go south. He put his back to the North Star, and began to hike through the woods. He climbed over a ridge and down the other side. Every few minutes he checked the North Star. It stayed in the same place in back of him.

He hiked for what he guessed was an hour, then took a quick break. Mighty Dawn had found another small valley that led generally south, so he had moved along the stream bank. It was much easier than hiking up and down ridges.

Twice more he walked to the south and twice stopped for short breaks. He would hide during the day and the Cheyenne would never find him. He would find a patch of thorns and cut a tunnel into them and the warriors would not think of looking in there.

The sky began to show a faint lightness in the east. He sat down for the last time. He would rest for five minutes, then find his hideout. He was so tired! The excitement of breaking out and running away, of tricking the Cheyenne, had worn him out.

Mighty Dawn's head dropped and he eased over on his back and slept soundly.

The next thing Mighty Dawn knew about was a sharp slap on his face. His eyes flew open and he tried to stand, but a foot on his leg held him in place. He saw it was daylight.

"Did you think you could outwit a Cheyenne warrior?" a stern voice asked. Mighty Dawn looked up and groaned. It was Walks With a Limp. His eyes were angry.

"Why did you try to run away? You are our good medicine charm. We need you. Now, get up and march. You will walk and I will ride and we can be back to camp within three hours. Move or my knife will draw your blood!"

He stood feeling a lot more like Harold Bishop than he did Mighty Dawn. That's how he would call himself now. He had pulled a dumb-kid stunt. Gone to sleep like a baby before he found a spot to hide. Even a six-year-old kid could do better than that. Guess that just proved once and for all he was Harold Bishop and didn't belong out here in the wilderness.

He walked along behind one horse and in front of two more. Now they would watch him night and day. He'd never have another chance to get away. Damn!

It took them three hours to get back to the camp. At least he had walked almost directly due south the way he wanted to. He was proud of that. Even if he'd gone in circles the warriors would have tracked him. He kicked at a rock. What a dumb-kid thing to do.

When they reached the village, the rest of the Gray Owl band warriors were there to welcome him. They picked him up and carried him on their shoulders to the tipi. Gray Owl stood there waiting for him.

"Why did you try to run away?" Gray Owl asked.

"I am not good medicine for the Cheyenne. I am a quarter-breed and I am bad medicine. Did not my mother die at the hands of the Pony Soldiers? Didn't they kill six of our warriors and then two more? When I came to the band there were thirty warriors. Now there are only twenty-two. Is that good medicine?"

"You defeated the last Pony Soldiers that came after us. We killed all ten of them. You made it possible. We captured eight good horses and ten short guns and ten rifles. Since you have been made a Cheyenne warrior, we have defeated the Pony Soldiers."

"One time, only once."

"It is the start of a great series of victories. I have talked with Chief Red Feather. He agrees that you must stay with us. We are fifty miles from any white-eyes. You have no chance to run away. We will always come and find you. To show you that we want you to stay, we are giving you a tipi of your own with a woman to serve you.

"She will cook for you and do her woman things. You will stay with us and be a warrior and talk at council. This is your tipi. Enter."

Harold wanted to scream and yell at him, but

a warrior didn't do that. At last he turned and bent to go into the tipi. It was darker inside, and for a moment he could see little. Then his pupils opened more and he could see.

Standing in front of him was a woman, a girl. She wore a white-fringed doeskin dress. She seemed to be no older than he was and three inches shorter. Long black hair tumbled over her shoulders and reached her waist.

She smiled. "I am Morning Blossom. I am your woman."

He simply stared at her. She was prettier than most of the Indian girls, and her breasts thrust out under the doeskin. She smiled. "Am I pleasing to you, Mighty Dawn?"

"Uh . . . yes, I'm surprised."

"I am fifteen summers. I am woman." Slowly she lifted the soft doeskin dress and took it off over her head. She wore nothing under it. Her hand-sized breasts lifted and bounced as she removed the dress. Then she lowered her arms and watched him.

"Now am I pleasing?" She reached for his hand and led him back to the pallet. It was now wider and had more robes on it. She sank down on it and tugged at his hand until he sat down beside her.

Slowly she reached out and nuzzled her cheek against his. She caught his hand and put it over one breast and smiled at him.

Harold Bishop was like most 14-year-old boys. He'd never seen a naked woman before, never touched a soft bare breast.

She reached down and unfastened his breechclout and lifted it away. His manhood was stiff and lifted tall.

She smiled at him, "Yes, Morning Blossom does please Mighty Dawn!"

Harold knew there were things he should be doing first, but he'd never talked much with the other boys about girls.

"Mighty Dawn, do you want to lay with me?"

"Yes, I guess. I don't know if I know how."

She smiled. "It is not hard. I did ... one time before. I can show you."

He rubbed her breast and bent and kissed the other one and she gasped, then smiled.

"Morning Blossom will show you."

He felt an overpowering urge. She eased backward on the pallet and pulled him with her. She moved him over her and helped, and a moment later he surged into her and he grinned. He was doing it!

His hips seemed to know what to do. They thrust forward and he held himself up by his hands, and after only three hard strokes he felt the whole world explode. His hips jolted again and again and again as he spewed his seed into her.

Every muscle in his body tightened and then spasmed and his breathing sounded like a whirlwind, and at last he dropped on top of her, spent and sweating and his breath coming in huge gasps.

Morning Blossom's arms locked around him and her legs came up and twined over his back. She began a gentle thrusting with her hips against his softening member.

A few moments later she crooned and shivered and then her whole body shook like a railroad train had passed by. Soon it was over and she opened her eyes and reached up and pressed her lips to his.

They lay that way, locked in each other for ten minutes. Then he moaned in rapture and eased up from her and lay beside her.

He leaned up on one elbow and watched her. "Morning Blossom," he said softly. She looked at him, smiling. "That . . . that was my very first time, you know that? Oh, I whanged off a few times looking at a naked picture, but never before . . ."

She hugged him. "Good, much good. Now Mighty Dawn stay with Cheyenne and marry Morning Blossom and we raise six sons and they all be fine chiefs of the Cheyenne!"

Slowly he realized what Gray Owl had done to him. The wise old chief had caught his good luck charm running away, so he'd brought him back, given him a hero's reception, then given him something he had never had before—a naked girl. The crafty old man!

But it wasn't going to work. He'd stay a few more days. He would pretend to be happy and pleased. He'd take advantage of Morning Blossom and make love to her most of the time. But he would find out exactly where they were. He'd find out at council what they were going to do and where they planned to go.

Then when he had the chance, he would slip out of his tipi, take his war pony, and ride like the wind for the closest bit of civilization. His pony was as fast as any of them, and with a six-hour head start they would never catch him!

Morning Blossom stirred beside him. She reached down to his crotch and began fondling him.

253

"Again," she said softly, rubbing her cheek against his.

"Don't think I'm ready yet."

"Plenty ready," she said. This time she rolled on top of him and Harold found out that he was ready.

Four times they made love before they left the pallet. Then she jumped up, built a small fire in the cooking area in the center of the tipi's fire pit, and began boiling half a rabbit in a metal pot.

He pulled on his breechclout and fastened it and watched her.

"Morning Blossom, do you think I'm good medicine for the Cheyenne?"

She smiled. "You are good medicine for the Cheyenne. You are wonderful medicine for Morning Blossom. Today you make Morning Blossom with child. I know, I know!"

Harold looked at her in wonder. He wasn't exactly sure how a man and woman made a baby, but it took more than this. He was sure it did. He'd heard six times. Anyway, she couldn't know so soon. Could she?

He sat up, his eyes watching her breasts. She smiled as she watched him.

"You couldn't know so soon that you might have a baby, Morning Blossom. Now make lots of food. I'm hungry."

She nodded. "Warrior hungry after, good sign. You make baby, wonderful son for Blossom and Mighty Dawn. He will be great chief."

Mighty Dawn put his moccasins back on. He had to relieve himself. He growled at Morning Blossom and hurried out the flap of the tipi. Twenty women from the two bands had gathered around just outside the tipi flap waiting.

When they saw him they cheered and shouted bawdy statements at him as he hurried through them and into the brush where he could urinate.

They had been waiting for him. It was like it had been a marriage or something. Everyone in camp knew that they had been in the tipi making love! For a moment he was angry, then he grinned. At least he had done that part of it right. Now all he had to do was wait for the right chance to get his horse and escape. He'd have to start riding near camp. He would tell them he needed to train his war pony more.

What about Morgan, the man who came from his father? There wasn't a chance that a white-eyes could follow them, track them. The Cheyenne had ways. Morgan was a lost cause. Now Harold Bishop had to rely on himself. Two or three days, maybe four. He'd set up his chance and hope it was in the dark of the moon.

At the Laramie train station, Morgan had just spotted Jim Breed when the Indian left his perch against the station house and walked around to the street side.

Morgan followed him and found him 50 feet ahead waiting. Morgan fell into step beside the half-breed.

"Anything happening?"

"The sheriff here don't like me, so I figure not to get you painted with my brush."

"You find the Cheyenne?"

"Follow them all way. They a day-and-a-half ride. Meet band of sixty warriors. Now give Pony Soldiers good fight."

"Is Harold still with them?"

"Yes. Watch one day. He still kept in tipi."

"Jim, you know we're going to have to go in and break him out of there. Shoot our way out if we have to. Can you do that to these Cheyenne people?"

"For a dollar a day, Jim shoot out anybody."

"Except me."

Jim looked up and grinned. "That cost three dollar a day, but Cheyenne don't got money."

They both laughed.

"When do you think we should go in and make our try to get Harold out of there?"

"Three more days. Then they trust him more, he come out of tipi. He warrior."

"Will they try to change his mind and get him to stay?"

"Yes. Many ways. Honor him. Give him woman."

"A woman, a girl? He's only fourteen."

Jim looked up at Morgan and grinned. "You have woman when you fourteen."

Morgan laughed. "Right. Maybe they will tempt him with a pretty little girl. I don't think it will work. He wants to get out of there."

"Jim think so too."

"You have a place to stay here?"

"Find place behind store. Hotel won't let Jim in."

"Damn them. I'll rent a room and you use it. They can't tell me who can sleep in my room."

"Maybe no. But you not here. Cut Jim's balls off they catch him. Hate breeds here."

Morgan gave Jim five dollars. "Eat something, don't drink it up. Meet me at the station again in three days from now. Tomorrow, next day, next day at noon."

Morgan heard a train whistling for the station. He looked up and saw a freight coming.

"I'm going to get that freight and go back to Cheyenne. Few loose ends there to tie up."

Jim nodded. "Three noons . . ."

Morgan ran for the freight. It was a mixed train, mostly freight cars but with one passenger car. He caught up with it just as it began moving out of the station.

He had two days and two nights to take care of his "business" in Cheyenne. He hoped it would be time enough. It had to be enough. He couldn't risk being a day late here and blow his chance to get Harold out.

Chapter Nineteen

Morgan walked away from the train depot in Cheyenne slightly after two in the afternoon. He had a thought and stopped by at his hotel room. He picked up the picture and the pin of the bird and went to see Sarah the banker.

He checked on his way in, and the two shotgun guards were in place. Morgan looked in the president's office. The door was open and she had no company. He knocked on the door casing.

Sarah Everett looked up and mild interest turned into a big smile.

"Morgan, I was hoping you'd come in today. That home-cooked supper is still available. Would tonight be too short a notice?"

Lee Morgan frowned. "I'll have to check with my appointment secretary and see for certain." When she looked puzzled he laughed.

"Miss Everett, tonight would be just great. I'll

look forward to it with all my taste buds ready and waiting. Now, I have some business for you."

"Oh?"

He went to her desk and put down both the pin and the small picture.

"Identification. Any idea what kind of bird this is, and any idea what they could signify, mean, represent, or who might wear such a pin?"

"You don't want much." She picked up the pin and turned it one way, then the other.

When she looked at the small picture she smiled.

"Yes, I know what kind of bird it is. We lived on the coast of Maine for some years when I was growing up. These are my favorite birds of all time. It's some kind of a pelican. I'm not sure if it's the white-headed pelican or the gray pelican or maybe the Florida pelican."

"Pelican. Those are sea birds. None of them around here so Ida Nelson is certainly correct. So, we've identified the creature. Have you ever seen it before as a representation of a product or on a product, or the pin being worn by anyone here in town?"

Sarah picked up the pin again. "The clasp is broken. I imagine that you know that."

"Yes. I'd guess that's why it was lost."

"Sorry, but I can't remember seeing anyone wearing such a pin. It's not a woman's pin. More like it could be worn by a man. Why the two diamonds?

"No idea. Maybe perfect attendance at Sunday School for two years."

"Where did you find it?"

"The picture was pasted to the bedpost in Lottie's back room."

"Oh, dear. And the pin?"

"I found it in the alley where the first lady was murdered."

"So there is a connection between the two killings, probably all three." Sarah closed her eyes and shook her head. "Mr. Morgan, I'm just not good at this sort of thing. Figures and interest and market value are more my field."

"But you see a lot of people. Maybe your tellers could take a look at it."

She stood. "Let me ask them. Then you won't have to stand in line." Morgan liked the way her hips worked under the tight skirt she wore as she walked past him.

The very puzzle that he was facing made it all the more appealing. He wanted to solve the thing before he had to go back to Laramie. A pelican. A strange bird for a product or a service. Must be something else.

What came from the East Coast that they used? Why did he keep coming back to a product?

Sarah returned then and he enjoyed her passing him. Her breasts swayed just enough to attract attention but not to be blatant.

"No luck with the tellers. One thought he'd seen the pin once but couldn't remember where or when."

"So, I'm back to canvassing the whole town."

"You think the killer is a local resident?"

"Either that or he comes through here often. I met a trainman the other night who comes in six days a week, lays over six hours, and takes the train back to Omaha. Could be a trainman doing his killing out of town."

"Dreadful business. Now why don't you run along so I can plan supper. I need to go to Mr.

Underwood's Groceries and Provisioner store. Go now and look for pins."

Morgan smiled and stood. He liked this little lady. It was a good thing she didn't know how much he enjoyed being with her.

"Yes, ma'am, I can certainly do that. Shall I pick you up here at five or come to your house?"

"Oh, the house, at seven. That should give me time. I'm still not certain what to fix, but you'll find out what I decide."

He said good-bye and waved as he left. One final look and he grinned all the way to the street. He was surprised such a beautiful little lady with a bank wasn't married. Maybe she was particular.

Morgan walked down the street to the Craig and Gardner Furniture store, and leaned up against the wall in one of the chairs set there for that purpose. Few were occupied today. He let the brim of his hat come down over his eyes and tried to put together the case.

Nothing came together. He walked down to the courthouse and checked with the sheriff.

"Hell, no, I haven't made any progress. Some galoot came in saying he might have seen the killer, but we get them all the time."

"Was his name Brent Rubiah, a conductor for the UP?"

The sheriff looked up quickly. "You mean you talked to him too? There might be something to what he said?"

"I think there is. A blond man, medium height, wearing a suit and vest with a watch fob and shiny shoes. Should be worth a look by your deputies."

"Yeah, yeah, I got it all down. I don't know

what else to do. We don't have one of those scientific criminal departments here that we can find all the outlaws."

Morgan said he had nothing new either and left. He should have told him about the pin and the picture and the pelican, but somehow he didn't want to reveal that yet.

He still hoped that he had a chance to catch this guy. He walked down the street, and noticed that there was a picture of Shirley outside the saloon where she danced. It showed a surprising amount of leg and the slightest hint of cleavage. He was sure the picture alone would pull in half the sex-starved men in town.

He should ask her to take down the picture until after they caught the killer. Yes, good idea. And at the same time he could check to see if she knew anything about Slade Johnson's plans.

He walked to the hotel and up the steps. Shortly he knocked on her door and it opened almost at once. She waved him inside. Shirley was dressed and looking ready to go out.

"I saw you come across the street and hoped you'd come up. You have time?"

"No, I want you to take down that picture in front of the saloon. It could bring the killer right into your room."

"Not a chance, silly. That picture helps bring men into the saloon and that's what I get paid for. Forget it. Not a chance. Now, if you'd rather talk about something else..." Shirley began to unbutton her blouse.

Morgan stopped her. "What about Slade? He picked a day yet to rob the bank?"

"Might have. You want me to tell you?"

"If he has, you better, otherwise too many people are going to die."

"He was in town, but I don't know if I should tell you."

"Why not?"

"Then you might kill Slade. He's asked me to meet him in Laramie at the train station after it's over."

"Then he *has* picked a day. Tell me when."

Shirley flounced across the room. She unbuttoned her blouse and pulled it off and threw it on the bed. She glared at him as she unfastened the wrapper over her breasts, undid it, and discarded it as well, leaving her breasts free and swinging and bouncing from the effort.

"Damn you, Morgan. You're worse than Slade is. He expects to get me anytime he wants me. Lay down and spread your legs, he's always saying to me. He's a real romantic.

"You I want and you never tell me to lay down. Morgan, we're good together. I'm better for you than any other girl. Try and tell me it isn't so. Let me travel with you, Morgan. By train or coach or horseback and we can make love every night."

"I'm not going anywhere, Shirley, not for a while."

"Then move in here with me. The bed's plenty big enough for two, especially with one of us on top of the other one."

"When, pretty lady? When is Slade going to hit the bank?"

"Oh, shit! You make me so mad."

"Tell me." Morgan pulled her close and kissed her.

Shirley sighed and shook her head. "Can't tell you."

He moved his mouth down to her breasts and sucked on each one and kissed them, then bit her nipples. "When, Shirley?"

"He'd kill me."

He knelt and ran his kisses down her skirt-covered leg, found her crotch, and breathed his hot breath into her heartland.

"Oh, God! Don't do that!"

He did it twice more and she climaxed, jolting and whimpering and falling on the bed, her hips bucking upward against some imagined man.

She quieted and Morgan lay down over her crushing her into the mattress.

"When, sweet Shirley? When is Slade hitting the Cheyenne Territorial Bank?"

"Thursday. God, he's going to be there Thursday at two-thirty."

Morgan bent and kissed her lips. She clung to him. He eased upward and away from her and stood.

"Thanks, Shirley. If this works out, you and I will have a long hot time tomorrow night. Promise."

She sat up and blinked. "You wouldn't lie to a hot woman?"

"No, Shirley. Tomorrow night after you dance."

"I quit dancing after tonight. Thought I better tell you."

"Good. See you later on."

Morgan went directly back to the bank. It was closed. He knocked on the door until Sarah came.

When she saw him she opened the door and he stepped inside.

He told her what he knew about Slade and his plan to rob her bank. "Do you want me to tell the sheriff?"

She watched him from deep brown eyes. "I'll take all of the cash and bonds home at noon except what I need for the afternoon. I'll be sure that both tellers are gone at two, so I'll handle the windows myself. I often do that. Which means neither of them will be in danger."

She paced back and forth in the bank planning.

"Sarah, shall I tell the sheriff? He could plant a man inside and have two or three outside."

"No, I don't want anyone killed. You men, you always want to use your guns!"

He caught her hand and turned her around. "Slade will bring five men with guns. That means if we don't have any, he kills everyone and takes your money. If we have guns we might be able to stop him. I'm going to go tell the sheriff. It's the only responsible thing to do. Keep your three guards. We'll tell them to be especially careful at two-thirty. They can hide behind wooden boxes or something for protection. Slade knows your guards are here, so he'll figure out how to kill them first."

"Oh, dear. I thought I could handle this."

"You can. Let me go talk to the sheriff and see what he wants to do."

Slowly she nodded.

"Sarah, it will be all right."

Tears came to her eyes. Her face fell apart into crying. He held out his arms and she went to him and nestled her head against his shoulder. His arms came around her and she felt good there.

For two minutes she cried, and then pushed back from him.

"Thank you for your help, Morgan. I thought I could handle this better. Yes, go see what the sheriff suggests. He can put men inside if he wants to."

Morgan gave her a small hug, let her go, and hurried out the front door.

Sheriff Verne Goranson listened to what Morgan had to say about the possible bank robbery. He grunted and lit a cigar.

"Morgan, all you've got is some loose woman's blathering about what a wanted man might do."

"He told her he would do it, then ride to Laramie and get the train there."

Goranson stood and walked to the window, then back toward the cells, and when he came back he nodded. "All right, let's give it a try. If it doesn't happen, we won't have lost much. I'd say we put two men inside the bank. They can be behind the counter and out of sight. A third man can be a customer trying to get a deposit written up at the stand-up desk. I'll have another man cover the alley from the roof so he can see the back door.

"Anybody try to get in the back way will face my man with his shotgun. I'll have Andy with his sniper rifle across the street on the roof covering the front of the bank. If the bastards get inside and then try to come out, Andy can pick them off like grapes from a bunch."

Morgan nodded. "Sounds good to me. I'll be inside behind the counter as well."

"Why, Morgan? You ain't no lawman."

"Friend of the family."

"Suit yourself. Be in place by two o'clock, no later."

Morgan left the sheriff's office and went back to the bank. Sarah was waiting for him at the door. He told her what the sheriff had suggested.

"Oh, I can't have those men in the bank."

Morgan looked at her. "Why not?"

"Banking laws and rules, and..." She shrugged. "I guess it will be all right if you're there."

"At two o'clock you will go out the front door and down two doors and stay at a store until it's all over."

"Oh, I couldn't do that, Morgan." Her face pinched into a frown and she shook her head.

"You can and you will, or we simply close up the bank at noon and forget about the robbery."

She scowled. "But Slade will still come."

"Yes, and take whatever is there. He'll smash the window and walk in."

She sighed. "All right, Morgan, you win. I'll leave before the robbers come. Now, the bank is closed, the tellers are gone, I'm ready to go to the market. Looks like you'll have to come with me to carry home all the food."

Over a half hour later they had been to the market and were now in Sarah's kitchen. It was bright and cheery, with a big window opening on a garden, a good wood-burning kitchen stove, and a counter for preparing food.

He sat at the kitchen table, a sturdy pine plank surface varnished to a high gloss.

"Are you a good cook too?"

She turned. A smile beginning. "Too? What else am I good at, Mr. Morgan."

"You cry well, and I like the way you hug. Then

there's always arm-holding and kissing a man's cheek."

She blushed a moment, then looked up. "Yes, I'm a good cook too."

An hour later he found out. They had steak because it was quicker than a roast, and potatoes and gravy and a fruit salad and slabs of fresh baked bread and strawberry jam. She had cooked carrots and pan-fired sliced parsnips with just a touch of butter.

"Better than the meal last night at the fancy cafe," Morgan said, easing back from the table.

"Thank you, kind sir. The cook appreciates it. Someday I want to stay home all day cooking and baking and tending to a house. To me that sounds wonderful."

"First you need someone to tend the house for ...or with."

Sarah lifted her brows. "I know. I know exceedingly well. I admit that I've had two proposals during the past year. One was an outrageous fortune hunter. He admitted it. The second man was in an advanced state of insobriety. I'd say that one didn't count since just after he proposed to me, he went outside and proposed to his horse."

"Right man hasn't come—"

She looked up at him sharply. "My aunt from Omaha constantly says that, Mr. Morgan. Spare me the sound of it again. I just may not wait for the right man. I could marry the wrong ones two or three times just for practice."

Sarah looked up at him and closed her eyes. "Oh, dear. That's one of my major faults, my temper. Forgive me."

"Nothing to forgive and the dinner was delicious. Now, do you want to wash or wipe the dishes?"

She laughed. "I don't believe it. You're offering to help me with the dishes?"

"Of course. I helped get them dirty."

They did the dishes. Then he started a fire in the fireplace to take a chill off the house and they sat in front of it. Her hand crept into his.

"I'm worried about tomorrow. Will it be bad?"

"I hope not. We should surprise him and he should give up. If not, there'll be a lot of shooting."

"Don't let anyone shoot you, Morgan. I'll be just mad as I can be if you wind up dead."

"I won't be so happy about that myself," he said, and they both laughed.

She leaned toward him. "Mr. Morgan, I know a lady isn't supposed to do this, but if I don't you won't and I want you to, so would you please kiss me just once, then leave quickly and let me sit here and dream a moment?"

Morgan watched her face, saw the desire in her eyes, and bent and kissed her trembling lips. She responded for a moment, then relaxed. He came away from her.

"Sorry, that wasn't quite right," he said. "We better try that again." They kissed again, and this time she relaxed and pressed against him with her breasts, her lips quivered again, and a soft sigh escaped from her. He held the kiss, and then let her go and stood quickly.

"What an interesting evening, Miss Everett. I hope to see you tomorrow. I'll be there about noon. Now try not to worry." He bent and kissed her lips again so softly that she barely felt him, then turned and walked quickly out the front door.

The next morning, Morgan went to half the stores in town but found no one who recognized the pin he showed them. He didn't use the name of the bird, thinking that might confuse some people.

He had a quick bowl of soup for lunch and walked into the Cheyenne Territorial Bank shortly after twelve noon. There was only one customer there.

He talked to Sarah, who paced in her office behind the door.

"Did you tell the guards?"

She shook her head. "I can't believe it's happening."

"It is. I saw the sheriff this morning. His men will be here at one-thirty. I want to talk to the guards."

He went to the man in front and told him what could be happening at two-thirty.

"You need a shield, so they can't pick you off from across the street or ride by and blast you." The hardware store next door had 50-gallon water barrels in a stack out front. They were four feet high and made of hickory.

"Take a good rifle slug to go through both sides of those," Morgan said. They rolled two of the barrels down from the hardware and stacked one on the other. They positioned them just to the left of the bank door and two feet from the wall. The guard could stand there and slip behind the barrels if any trouble showed up.

The back guard was easier. The hardware had discarded two wooden boxes six feet long and three feet wide. They were only a foot deep. Morgan and the guard stood one of them against the bank wall and firmed it in place. The box blocked any view from down the alley. The guard stood behind it and was out of sight of anyone coming into the mouth of the alley 50 feet away.

Inside the bank, he told the guard what might happen.

"Figured something should be coming soon," the man said. "I used to be a lawman down in Arizona. Seen my share of bank jobs."

"If they get inside and the shooting starts, go for anyone with a shotgun first," Morgan said. He told them about the three guns they'd have behind the counter.

"Good. Didn't want to be in here alone with five shooters," the guard said. He checked his shotgun and the six-gun on his hip.

It was almost one o'clock. Two men drifted in the front door and Morgan tensed. Both wore handguns. He checked and saw that each had a deputy sheriff's badge. They went and talked to Sarah, then found spots behind the counter.

Morgan escorted Sarah out of the bank and two doors down. Then he went back and settled down behind the counter. He had decided the clerks had to be in the bank to make it look normal.

He talked with each one. At the first sign of any trouble they were to drop to the floor and stay there.

"Anybody tries to come over the counter is a dead duck," Morgan said. The tellers, both men, grinned nervously.

A customer came in. He looked around, then took a deputy sheriff's badge off and put it in his pocket. He went to the stand-up desk and began making out a deposit slip. Morgan checked his watch and eased back to the floor to wait. Two-thirty would be there before they knew it.

Chapter Twenty

On the roof of the Cheyenne Territorial Bank, Deputy Sheriff Dillion waited patiently. He was near the gutter, down where he could see along the length of the alley and the entrance to the bank. He had been on the force for five years and knew what he was doing. He checked the alley again.

Nothing moved.

It was almost two-thirty. That was the time the robbers were supposed to come. He sighed. Maybe another false alarm. He hoped so. Martha was making roast turkey for supper. She made the best roast turkey in town.

A few seconds later a long-bladed knife drove into Deputy Sheriff Dillion's back, slashed through his lung, and penetrated two inches into his heart.

He gasped only once before he slumped down on the roof dead.

Chad Langley grinned. It had been easier than he thought. The boss had been right about them knowing something was up. Langley peered over the edge of the bank roof at the back door. The guard was there with a shotgun and behind the wooden shield. No damn problem.

Langley was the knife man in the bunch. He selected a throwing knife from the lining of his jacket. He hefted it for a moment, then leaned out and threw. The blade turned over once, then the knife drove into the guard's throat, slashing his windpipe, continuing on to sever his spinal column.

The guard sprawled on the ground in a spewing shower of blood and died before he could cry out. Langley stood and motioned with both hands over his head. He saw the same signal at the end of the alley. He tied a rope to a ventilation pipe on the roof and lowered himself over the side to the ground in the alley 20 feet below.

By then Slade Johnson and his four other men had slipped into the alley and stood beside the back door.

"Remember, get the guard behind the shield. Chiseler, you run to the front door and lock it and we've got the bastards." He put his hand on the doorknob and opened it silently.

"Let's go," he said, and they slipped into the short hallway without a sound, then came to the door and burst into the bank.

"Nobody move!" Slade shouted. He triggered his sawed-off shotgun at the guard behind the shield. Some of the slugs from the double-aught buck should bounce behind it and nail him.

Gunslinger's Scalp

Chiseler ran for the front door.

Then all hell broke loose. A shotgun roared from behind the teller's cage and two handguns blasted from the same area.

Lonesome Harry took half the shotgun blast and his face disintegrated and showered on the far wall in a tattoo of blood, bone, and brain fragments.

Slade caught a .45 slug in the shoulder and spun around. He got off a shot at the teller's cage, but then a customer produced a six-gun and killed the Kid with a shot to the side of the head.

"Out!" Slade roared.

The second shotgun blast wiped out his scream and chopped up Chiseler's chest so badly that he slammed six feet to the rear and sprawled in death on top of a tipped-over chair.

Slade began backing toward the door, firing his shotgun once more, then fisting his six-gun and blasting at the far end of the teller's cage where the scattergun must be.

He stormed around the corner into the safety of the short hallway. Langley dove between his legs and got up holding his right leg. Grits got off one round from his sawed-off scattergun and leaped to safety beside Slade.

"Out the back!" Slade whispered. The other two took off on a run, Langley limping as he went. Slade pushed the muzzle of his shotgun around the corner of the hall and fired once, then again. He reloaded and ran for the back door.

Half way down the 20-foot hall, he turned and fired the shotgun again, then kicked open the door just as a six-gun blasted behind him hitting him in the leg.

Back in the bank all quieted.

"Anybody hurt?" Morgan called.

The deputy in the main part of the bank bleated in pain. Morgan and the two other deputies vaulted the teller's counter and ran for the back hall. Before they got there two shotgun blasts slammed through the opening but missed all of them.

Morgan waited a moment, then dove to the floor and peered around the corner of the wall down the hall from the floor level. Slade turned at that moment and pointed the scattergun to the rear. Morgan jerked his head back just before the blast came. As soon as the slugs stormed past him, Morgan kicked his right fist around the wall and fired at the door.

He heard a yelp of pain, then the door slammed shut. Morgan ran down the hall and kicked the door open, but remained next to the heavy wall beside the doorway.

Two revolver shots snarled from outside and whispered through the air beside Morgan. He chanced a look then and saw three men racing down the alley.

He stopped a moment by the deputy outside, but saw he was dead. The sheriff raced out the back door and stood beside Morgan.

"We got three of them, but how did they get in? I had two men back here." Then he saw the dead man beyond the door and the rope coming down from the roof.

"After them!" the sheriff shouted. "They killed two of ours! We'll get horses on the street and chase them." The two deputies ran back into the bank with the sheriff.

Morgan sprinted for the end of the alley. Slade had come with six men and six horses. That left three unused ones. He was breathing hard at the end of his 40-yard run, but saw what he hoped he would. Three horses stood tied to a small fence just beyond the alley mouth. He grabbed one, untied it, and listened, but could hear no hoofbeats.

He looked at the dirt of the street and found the three sets of hoofprints leading straight down Ransom Street. He kicked the sides of the sorrel and rode that way. Twice he lost the tracks in the movement of other riders and rigs, but he found them again. They went straight out Ransom heading for the edge of town.

Morgan raced three blocks ahead and then slowed and checked for tracks. The trio was still moving north. Their hideout was to the east. No, they would have closed up the place and taken everything they wanted to travel with. He checked the saddlebags on the horse he rode. They were packed with trail food. A pair of blankets had been rolled and tied behind the saddle. They were ready for the trail.

Only they didn't have the extra weight of gold coins or a gunnysack full of banknotes to slow them down.

The street was flat and straight, but he couldn't see any riders galloping ahead of him. He slowed and checked the tracks again. They were still there. Were Slade and his two men that far ahead?

He watched the tracks more closely, and almost missed them when the trio swerved sharply to the right down 21st Street. Now they were going east. He surged ahead past a house with a small barn and a windmill.

Three shots blazed at him from 50 feet away.

One grazed the horse, but the distance was too great for accuracy. Morgan drew his six-gun and charged the trio, who still sat on their horses behind the barn. They scattered, going in three different directions.

Morgan picked out Slade to follow. He was by far the tallest of the three on a pinto pony. He spurred to the east and Morgan trailed him. He was just out of handgun range. Morgan wished the man who'd owned this horse had carried a rifle.

They both charged forward, staying out of good range. Morgan couldn't gain on the outlaw. Both were still galloping their mounts, and Morgan knew neither would last much longer at this pace. There were few houses here on 21st Street, and while there were street signs and a semblance of a graded street, it was mostly a trail that would one day be a street.

Slade's mount slowed and Morgan gained on him. Slade took one look behind him and angled off the street toward a house. It was a two-story residence with a buggy in the front yard. Morgan tried one more shot with his six-gun, but missed.

Slade jolted off his mount and rushed up to the front door, jerked it open, and stepped inside.

Morgan knew he had trouble. There must be someone living there. The buggy indicated callers might be on hand as well. He turned at the last moment and came up on the side of the house without any windows. He jumped off the horse and stepped to the clapboard siding.

He listened but could hear nothing. He ran to the corner of the structure and looked around. There were three windows and the front door. He waited.

A moment later he heard a woman scream from inside the house, then more silence.

A window squeaked as it was raised.

"Morgan?" a voice boomed from the window. "Must be you, Morgan. You've got trouble. Right now you get out here in front of the house where I can see you. You don't and some women are gonna start dying in here. I've got four women at a quilting bee. Gonna be woman blood all over that quilt if you don't move fast. Do it now, Morgan."

Morgan knew he was trapped. Nothing else he could do. He holstered his six-gun and ran 30 yards to the side, then swung around front well out of pistol range.

"Good, Morgan. Good. You even stayed out of range. Now get on your shank's mare and hike back to town. Turn around now or this sweet little thing gets her head blown to bits. You hear me, Morgan?"

"I hear. I still owe you, Slade."

"Don't count on getting even anytime soon. Now move!"

Morgan walked away from the house. With his horse around back, he had no way to give chase. Slade would take both horses with him, Morgan was sure. When he was a hundred yards out, he turned around and walked backwards. By that time, he had passed Evans Street and was over two blocks away. He stopped. That was when he saw a figure come out of the house. Then he saw that it was two people.

Both horses were brought up and the second person mounted. Then Slade led the horse to his, where he mounted. He rode away to the east, trailing the second mount behind him.

As soon as the horses began moving, Morgan ran back to the house. He knocked on the door.

"Ma'am, I'm trying to help. That was the bank robber Slade Johnson. Did he take a hostage with him?"

The door opened a crack and a shotgun muzzle showed. Morgan didn't move.

"Yes, he took my girl Mary. Don't let him hurt her."

"Ma'am, you have a saddle horse?"

"No, not a one."

"May I unhitch the buggy horse? I can ride bareback."

"Yes, do it. Just save my little girl."

While Morgan unhitched the buggy horse, he asked the woman to go upstairs and watch what direction Slade took. She did, and called from another upstairs window.

He had the horse unhitched and leaped on her back. He cut some of the reins for a lead and rode the horse to the back of the house.

"Went straight east, then turned south like to go around town," the woman called.

Morgan rode away sensing the direction, watching for their tracks. If they went through too much traffic he would lose them.

A half mile farther on he saw where the tracks turned east again. Now the horses were moving faster. Far ahead on the flat land, he saw two riders. He kicked his mount and bounced on the bare back of the mare as she galloped for the first time.

It was a bumpy ride. He held it for a quarter of a mile, then slowed the animal. He had gained on them. Now he could see Slade slumping in the saddle. He'd been hit once, maybe twice, with bullets. He must be losing blood.

Morgan urged the horse forward again at a trot. The distance closed. He kicked the animal into a gallop and the buggy horse responded. Her ears laid back, she pounded down the track of a trail.

Soon Morgan was within 100 yards. Then he cut it to 50 yards. He saw Slade look back once. Slade lifted his six-gun toward the girl, but she pulled up one leg and jumped off the horse away from him. She hit hard and rolled in the dirt, but soon sat up.

Slade kicked his mount into a gallop. By then Morgan was close enough to hold his Colt with both hands and fire three times. One of the rounds hit Slade in the back, and he slammed off the horse and tumbled to a stop when he hit the ground.

Morgan hurried up and saw that Slade's revolver had crashed out of his hand. The young woman jumped up and brushed the dirt off her dress and stood watching.

Morgan glared at the robber. He could see one of his hands. The other arm was under his body. Morgan held his six-gun covering the man as he came up closer.

"End of the trail, Slade. Sheriff Goranson will have you up for murder faster than you can tie a hangman's knot."

"Won't do no damn good. I'll never hang," Slade said. His face was sallow, his eyes moving slow. He'd lost a lot of blood.

"You want to lay there until I bring a doctor, or you want to ride back to town with your hands tied to the horn?"

"Don't matter."

Morgan figured he had to give Slade a chance.

"I'll send the girl back." He turned toward the hostage, then snapped back around quickly just as Slade jerked his hand from under his leg with a derringer in it. Slade pulled the trigger before he could aim the small weapon.

Morgan fired at the same time. The short-barreled derringer sent the bullet wide. Morgan's longer barrel held the round straight and true. It cut into Slade Johnson's left eye, bored upward into his brain, and exploded out the top of his head taking a three-inch swatch of scalp, skull, brains, and hair with it.

Morgan lowered the six-gun slowly and pushed it back in leather. Then he turned and walked over to the girl. She was near 16 and pretty as a newborn colt.

"Mary, your mother's worried about you. Let's catch you a horse and take you home."

Her eyes were wide, her face white. She trembled. "You killed that man."

"Yes."

"You said you were going to take him to the sheriff."

"Then he tried to kill me with a hideout gun. Didn't you hear two shots?"

She nodded.

"Are you all right?"

"Yes. I want to go home now."

It was nearly an hour later before Morgan got back to the bank. The front window had been shot out. Two carpenters were boarding it up with a temporary wall.

Inside, the two tellers and Sarah worked to clean up the blasted structure. She looked up, saw him, and came off her knees and rushed to him.

Her arms went out and he held her tightly.

"I'm so thankful that you're all right. The sheriff never did find the robbers."

"Looks like you're getting things back in order here. No cash missing, just some incidental damage. You know about your one guard in back who was killed?"

"Yes. I'm terribly upset about that. I'm giving his widow five hundred dollars. She's going to move to Denver and stay with her sister."

"I'm sorry."

"Yes, I am too. But it was better than letting Slade kill all of us and then take the money."

She eased away from him, her blush showing. "Thanks for the hug. I needed it. Seems to be coming a habit for me."

"A good habit I hope you don't break."

She flashed him a smile. "I figure forty dollars for a new window, and another ten for wood putty and varnish stain to cover up the bullet holes. If we work all night we should be ready to open in the morning."

"We?"

"Of course. That's the price of my hugs. Here's a can of the wood gunk and you can start right over here. Oh, I'm hiring the inside guard full-time, but letting the front one go. He understands."

"Do you feed the help dinner?"

"I've arranged for sandwiches, coffee, and watermelon to be brought in. Does the menu satisfy you?"

"Only if I get one more hug when we're done."

"If you earn it," she said sharply, then grinned and went back to picking up wood splinters off the floor.

Morgan dug double-aught buck out of wood-work for an hour, then filled the holes with wood putty and let it dry and sanded it. When it was completely dry he put on varnish stain to match the wood, then varnished over that.

The sandwiches came and Morgan ate three of them. They were done with the cleanup by seven o'clock and he walked the banking lady home.

At her door she hesitated. "Do you want to come in and light the lamp for me?" she asked.

Morgan went in, lit a match, and found the lamp. Another match started the wick on fire and he put on the glass chimney and turned down the wick so it wouldn't smoke.

When he looked for Sarah, she stood close to him. She held out her arms and gave him the tight hug she had promised.

"You earned it," she said, lifting her face from his shoulder. He bent and kissed her lips gently.

"Oh, Morgan! I wish you wouldn't do that. I know you're in town for a short time and then you'll be gone, and I absolutely refuse to fall in love with you so you can break my heart."

"Wouldn't think of it," he said. With that he bent slowly to kiss her. She didn't turn away. In the end she stretched upward to meet him and a soft sigh escaped her as she responded to his embrace.

When the kiss ended she held him tighter.

"Damn you, Morgan. You know what I want to do, and you know I won't and I know I won't, and that makes it frustrating all the way around." She caught his head and pulled it down to her breast.

"Lee Morgan, kiss me just once here and then run out the front door. Please."

He kissed her breast through the cloth, breathed hotly on it, then raised up and kissed her lips once more. Her eyes closed and she moaned. Her body pressed tightly against his all the way from her hot breasts down to her knees.

He broke off the kiss. She nibbled at his lips once more and shook her head. "Damn you, Morgan. You know I love it. Now get out of here before I have to find my shotgun."

Morgan backed up, reached out, and steadied her when she almost fell. Then he turned and walked to the front door. She followed him.

"Come see me tomorrow at the bank."

He nodded.

"Oh, you didn't say what happened to Slade. Will he stand trial?"

"No, Sarah, that won't be necessary."

She lifted her brows. "What?" Then she nodded. "Oh, I see. Dead men never stand trial."

He went out the door and closed it gently behind him.

Morgan stopped at the first saloon he passed and had two beers. He kept his head low. Most of the talk was about the robbery attempt.

"Hear old Slade got his right in the eye," a drinker said. "Blew the top of his damn head off."

"Town's a lot better off without Slade Johnson," a cardplayer said. "Whole damn territory is better off."

Morgan finished his beer and headed for the Pride of Wyoming Hotel. He could do with some sleep.

The first thing he did when he got into his room was to lock the door and put the straight chair under the handle. Anybody trying to come in would have to break the chair to move it.

He sat down on his bed and took apart his Colt .45 and cleaned and oiled it. When he had it put back together, he loaded in five rounds and holstered it.

A knock on the door came as a surprise. He eased to his feet and pulled the weapon from leather.

Morgan stood against the wall next to the door. "Yes, who is it?"

"Oh, good, you're back. Morgan, this is Shirley, I need to talk to you."

Morgan opened the door and the tall blond woman stepped inside. She was dressed conservatively, and she did not smile.

"I hear you killed Slade Johnson. What the hell am I supposed to do now?"

Chapter Twenty-One

Lee Morgan looked at the tall, shapely blonde and nodded. "That's right, Shirley. I gave him the option of coming into town and going to jail. He pulled a derringer and tried to kill me."

"So you murdered him!"

"No, I was defending myself." He took her by the shoulders. "Maybe you should sit down a minute."

"On your bed? Not a chance. I've found a gentleman who appreciates me. He's old-fashioned and hasn't even tried to kiss me yet. He's taken me out to dinner twice."

"Good for him. Then you weren't planning on taking the train to Laramie anyway."

"Oh, yes, I was! Slade was my man. He took care of me."

"And treated you like trash. You're better off without him."

She slapped him sharply and he let go of her. "The door's open, Shirley. Be careful on your way out."

"I will." She glared at him for a minute. "At least I know one man in this town who is decent and honorable. He appreciates me for my mind."

"I can see why. Are you through?"

She snorted and walked to the door. "He tells me I'm pretty but not that pretty. He tells me I have a fine mind and I should go to college. So there. Thurlow says I'm his idea of the perfect woman. Tonight I just might let him kiss me after I do my dances at the show house."

"You're dancing again?"

"Yes, they gave me a raise to fifteen dollars a week. A girl has to make a living."

"This gentleman friend Thurlow hasn't kissed you yet?"

"Of course not. He's very proper. Maybe I'll let him kiss me tonight."

"Kiss you where?"

She slapped him again, but not so hard. He saw the sex-starved look coming into her eyes, and he took her arm and hurried her to the door.

"You go find this Thurlow and play checkers or something. I need a good night's sleep. Goodbye, Shirley."

She stood in the hallway a moment, then flounced away toward her room.

Morgan locked his door, put the chair under it, and wished Thurlow good luck. The first time Thurlow kissed her she'd flip on her back and spread her legs and beg for it.

Morgan undressed and dropped on the bed. Tomorrow would be his last day to find the sex-killer. He'd show the pin to more people. Maybe get lucky.

When he woke up the next morning, it was just past six o'clock. He dressed in his town clothes and a new low-crowned cowboy hat and went to find breakfast.

He wondered about Lottie's Cafe. If no heirs came forward within six months, the property would probably be taken over by the county for taxes and sold. It wasn't a perfect system, but that way a property would be back on the tax roll and somebody could get some use out of it.

After breakfast, he showed the pin to people on the street and in stores. He got some interesting comments but nobody gave him any help. The sheriff was just as vague when Morgan showed the pin to him.

"Just telling me about it now?" Sheriff Goranson thundered. "What if it had been important? Withholding evidence. I could jail you for that, Morgan."

"So far it hasn't been that important," Morgan said. "You don't have anything new on the killings?"

"No, do you?"

"When I catch him, I'll let you know. Oh, did your men did find Slade Johnson?"

"They did. I decided not to prosecute you for murder for killing him. You were kind of deputized."

"Thanks."

"Six bodies for the undertaker in one day," the sheriff said. "He wasn't overly pleased, especially since his grave-digger quit. Funerals this afternoon for my deputies."

Morgan said good-bye and left. He worked at

showing the pin to people on the street, but gave up after an hour. He leaned back in a chair next to the hardware and scowled at everyone. What the hell did the pelican bird mean? How did it fit in with the damn killings?

He took out his new penknife and began to clean his fingernails. He'd never examined the knife much before. It had just one blade, a sturdy one designed to sharpen quills, but now mostly carried by men as a small pocket piece.

He looked at it more closely. It had some sort of trade name on it and he studied it.

Morgan's chair's front legs hit the boardwalk with a thump. He stared at the blade again. Frantically he dug out the pin of the pelican and looked at it, then squinted his eyes and concentrated on the small design stamped into the penknife blade.

They were identical.

Morgan ran for the store where he had bought the knife. He rushed inside and up to the knife display.

"Anybody here?" he called when he saw no clerk. A moment later the same young man who had sold him the knife came out smiling.

"Yes, Mr. Morgan. The man who shot Slade Johnson. Good to have you in our store."

Morgan held out the knife. "I bought this here. It has the picture of a bird on it. Is that a trade name for the brand of knives or what?"

"Yes, sir. The Pelican line is a fine group of cutlery that is made in Maine and is sold through here by a traveling man. Fact is, he was here just a week or so ago."

"A drummer?"

"Yes, quite a nice-appearing young man. He

covers this territory and we placed a good order with him. The knives come in all sorts from skinning knives and special types for butchers to household knives and sporting and hunting knives as well."

"The man, the salesman. What does he look like?"

"Oh, he's about average height, shorter than you, slender, well-dressed. Usually wears a dark suit and a vest."

"Does he have a small knife on a gold chain on his vest?"

The clerk smiled. "Indeed he does."

"Does he have blond hair with a wave in it and are his shoes always shined to a turn?"

"You must know him. His name is Deeds. I'm not sure of his first name. He's always just Mr. Deeds to me. I have his card here in case of special orders."

The clerk reached in the display and took out a card. "Yes, here it is. He's Thurlow Deeds. He usually stays at the Metropolitan Hotel on Fifteenth Street because it's close to the train station. Can I give him a message the next time he comes in?"

"When would that be?" Morgan asked, wanting to run somewhere, but not certain just where.

"Oh, he only comes here once every three months, so he isn't due for almost three months, less a week."

"Do you know if he's still in town?"

"Probably not. He stops here, then goes on to Laramie and comes back through on his way home to Chicago."

"You said his name is Thurlow Deeds. Thurlow is his first name?"

"Yes, that's right."

Morgan made the connection. It was an unusual name. Not a lot of Thurlows around. That was the name that Shirley had used for her new gentleman friend last night. He hadn't even kissed her yet. What was he waiting for? Maybe he did kiss her last night and then cut up her body with his knives!

Morgan turned and ran out of the store. He sprinted down the boardwalk and then the dusty street all the way to the Pride of Wyoming Hotel. He dashed in the front door and took the steps two at a time.

He rushed past his own room and pounded on Shirley's door. There was no response at first. Morgan put his ear to the panel and listened. He thought he could hear whispers.

Morgan knocked again, four short, sharp raps.

"Yes? Yes, who is it?" The voice was Shirley's.

"Morgan. I have to talk to you."

"I'm still in bed."

"I've seen you in bed before. Open the damn door." He let a touch of the panic he felt edge into his voice.

"Just . . . just a minute."

He heard some movement in the room, then steps toward the door. A key rattled in the lock and the door opened a crack. He saw a slice of Shirley's face past the door.

"What do you want, Morgan?" Her voice was angry but controlled. "We have nothing to say to each other."

"Oh, but we do." He put both hands on the door and rammed it open. Shirley jolted backward from the force of the thrust and stood there her mouth open.

Morgan rushed into the room his six-gun out. The bed was mussed and two pillows had been used during the night. He had the terrible feeling that someone was behind him who had hidden in back of the opened door. Before he could turn completely, he saw the blur of something moving, and then it hit his head and he bleated in pain and dove for the floor. Morgan fought against the blackness, but it surrounded him and then blotted out most of the room. For a fleeting second he saw two perfectly polished and shiny shoes coming toward him. Then the darkness was complete.

The blackness wouldn't go away. So deep and heavy, like the inside of a coal mine at midnight. Morgan blinked. His eyes were open and the pain in the back of his head proved that he wasn't dead. Where was he?

Shirley's room? He tried to move and realized that his hands were tied behind him. His feet were tied too. His eyes became accustomed to the blackness, and gradually he saw the outline of a window. The blind was down, but he could see fingers of light around it. His head hammered like a roaring freight train.

Inside. He was inside somewhere. Maybe still in Shirley's room. It had to be Thurlow Deeds who had hit him. Why was he still alive? Maybe Deeds killed only women. If he'd been with Shirley all night why hadn't he killed her too, the way he had the three others?

Too many questions. He wiggled and moved his wrists. Deeds had used too much cord. It was wrapped around and around his wrists and then probably tied. More wrappings left more room for slack.

He wondered if he could still do the old parlor trick. He lay on his side and doubled his legs up toward his chest. Then he pushed over so he rested on his knees and the top of his head. Gingerly he spread his arms and tried to slip them down over his hips.

Most people couldn't do it. He had longer arms than usual, and had made a few dollars on bets when he was a young man performing the trick.

Now it was vital. He strained his arms. Not a chance. Slowly he worked the rounds of rope lower on his crossed wrists. Yes, there was slack enough. After ten minutes he had the rope low enough to provide more room to slip his arms over his hips. He tried again.

This time he put more pressure on his arms and strained and pulled. Almost. He tried again, and this time his forearms slipped past his hips and his bound hands fell to his legs behind his bent knees.

He rolled to his back and lifted his bound wrists up and over his legs and feet. Now he could get to the bindings with his teeth.

It took him another five minutes to untie his hands. His feet came next. His six-gun was gone. He carried no hideout weapon.

Morgan found the door and cracked it open. Yes, it was Shirley's room. Where would he have taken her? An alley, a saloon, his room at the Metropolitan Hotel? Maybe. Deeds had no way of knowing that Morgan knew who he was. Yes, his room might be it.

Morgan rubbed the circulation back into his fingers, then slipped out the door and down to his room. From the bottom of his carpetbag, he took out a Colt .45, twin to the one he had lost. He checked it, loaded five chambers, and slid it into his holster.

The Metropolitan Hotel was down 15th on the corner of Ferguson Street. He trotted all the way, and went inside to see the room clerk.

"I was supposed to meet Mr. Deeds in his room, but he didn't tell me what the number was."

The clerk shook his head. Morgan slid a dollar bill across the counter and the clerk took it quickly.

"That would be in Room 214, sir. Head of the stairs and turn left."

Morgan went up the stairs with great restraint. It wouldn't do for the clerk to see him taking the steps four at a time and his gun out and screaming a Cheyenne war cry. That was what he wanted to do.

At the top of the stairs he turned left and found 214 just three doors down. No one else was in the hall. He put his ear to the door but heard nothing inside. Morgan tried the door now without making any sound. It was locked.

He knocked. No one responded. He knocked again. A sleepy voice answered. "Yes?"

"Telegram for Mr. Deeds."

"Telegram? Slide it under the door."

"You have to sign for it."

"Since when?"

"New rules this week, sorry."

There were mumblings from the other side of the door and Morgan could hear steps coming. A key rattled in the lock, and just as the door started to open inward, Morgan hit it hard with his shoulder and his weight behind it and drove it into the man on the other side.

The lamp was lit in the room and Morgan saw the man slammed backwards, lose his balance, and hit the floor. Morgan had his .45 out and held it covering the man, who lay on the floor where he had fallen. He wore some fancy pajamas and evidently had been in bed, alone.

"Thurlow Deeds?"

"Yes! What's the meaning of this?" He sat up and glared at Morgan.

"Don't move again or you're a dead man, Deeds." Morgan held out the small pin and showed it to Deeds. "Is this yours?"

"Might be. The company gives them out for salesmanship. Supposed to be valuable. Worth about ten dollars. Why?"

"You know damned well why. You lost it when you raped and then butchered the woman in the alley."

"I don't know what you're blathering about. I'm a drummer for the Pelican line of fine knives. Now can I get up?"

"No, sit right there. Where is Shirley?"

"Who are you talking about?"

"Shirley, the girl you've been seeing lately. She told me all about you. I was just too dense to catch on."

"I don't know what you mean. Go ahead and shoot me if you want to. I'm getting up and sitting on the bed. You better have some good explanations for all this."

"I do. The best. Her name is Lottie. She used to run the cafe before you sliced off her head and left it sitting on her chest."

"I do that all the time. Are you crazy? I'm a

respectable businessman. Tops in my business. Most sales of any route man last year. Wire my boss in Chicago."

"We have a witness. Remember the last customer in the cafe that night just before Lottie closed up? He remembers you. He's a railroad conductor, he's used to remembering faces and tickets. He'll identify you as the last man in Lottie's cafe before you raped her and murdered her."

"You, sir, have a vivid imagination. Are you the sheriff in this county?"

"No."

"Then get out of my room. If your sheriff wishes to charge me with a crime, I'll defend myself. Until then, you leave or I'm calling the manager."

Morgan laughed. "Where's your sample case?" As soon as he said it Morgan saw the leather case at the foot of the bed. Morgan lifted it and undid the snaps and extended the fold-out displays of knives of all kinds and descriptions.

"How interesting. Your company even makes surgeons' scalpels. One was used on Lottie. I'm sure one of our microscopes will find fresh blood on several of these knives. You can wash and scrub and scrub again, but the microscope can find those minute particles of blood that the human eye can't even notice."

"I don't believe you. Anyway I did a butcher shop demonstration last week. Got blood on a dozen knives."

"A good chemist can tell the difference between animal blood and human blood. Any more excuses?"

"No excuses, everything I've told you is true."

He sat near the head of the bed. His left hand snaked under the pillow, grabbed, and lifted. He had a one-shot derringer pistol aimed at Morgan.

Morgan had let his six-gun go to his side. Now he was covered.

"I also always go armed in case of riffraff like you. I'll tell the sheriff you tried to rob me."

"Won't work, Deeds. You have one shot. Even if you hit me in the head, I'll get off two shots into your heart before I die. You want to trade queens that way in this chess game?"

Deeds frowned. "You may be right. Drop your weapon or I'll fire."

"Same logic, Deeds. I won't let go of the Colt. What you going to do now?"

"Take the next best choice." He darted to the open window. It had been hot that day and the room was still stuffy. He stepped through the window keeping the weapon trained on Morgan, then dropped out of sight.

Morgan blew out the lamp and ran to the window. A single shot sang through the void missing Morgan. The window opened on a hitch roof that ran down to the ground floor of the hotel. Just as Morgan looked out, he saw the killer in the moonlight turn and look at the window, then drop off the roof to the ground.

Morgan followed him out the window onto the roof. He stopped when he hit the ground and listened. The killer wore only pajamas, tops and bottoms, and held the derringer. Where would he go?

Two doors down the alley he found the answer. It was the back door to a fancy whore house. Morgan took the steps two at a time and burst through the back door. He saw the pajama-clad legs of Deeds vanishing up the open stairs to the second floor.

Morgan raced after him. Upstairs there were six doors and the killer was not in sight. These rooms were not the usual small cribs. The doors were spaced ten feet apart. He opened the first one and found it empty. There was no place to hide.

The second door banged open as he kicked it. A woman screamed. A naked man over her snarled some foul words at Morgan. Morgan didn't bother to close the door. The third door on that side was locked.

Morgan stepped back and planted the sole of his boot against the door beside the door handle, and the lock snapped and the door careened open. A man and a woman lay on the bed. They weren't touching each other. That told Morgan a lot. He saw heavy drapes at the window. Under the curtains he saw bare feet.

Morgan fired one shot knee high and Thurlow Deeds screamed and dove out the window smashing the glass. Morgan rushed to the window and looked down. Deeds had landed on a heavily branched shrub. He bounded off it and sprawled on the ground. Before Morgan could get off a shot, Deeds leaped up and went limping down the alley and into the darkness.

It took Morgan two minutes to get down the steps and out the back door. He studied the alley a moment and hurried in the direction Deeds had run. He couldn't be far.

A block farther west, Morgan heard a woman scream. It came from the back of a small house on the side street. Morgan ran to it, saw the back door open, and stepped inside.

"You make another sound and I'll kill you," Deeds growled from the next room.

Morgan moved cautiously to the door and looked around it. Deeds held a woman from behind and rested a kitchen knife on the woman's throat. He looked up when Morgan stepped into the room.

"Well, well, Mr. Morgan again. Looks like we have a standoff here. Drop the six-gun or this woman dies."

Morgan shrugged. "So what? I don't know her. The minute you cut her, you die. You want that?"

The logic of it seemed to hit Deeds. He blinked, then nodded. "Hell, don't make much difference. I had my run of good luck. Couldn't last forever."

"Deeds, why did you kill those three women?"

"Wanted to. Always do what I want to do. It's the ultimate in sexual gratification. It happens when the woman reaches her climax and I get mine and at the same time she dies. Nothing like it in all the world. Sometimes I faint dead away."

"Why Lottie? You didn't have to rape her."

"I never raped any of them. They wanted to as much as I did. I seduced them, not raped them. So it's just as much their fault."

The woman he held had been getting more and more angry. She was a hefty female, nearly as tall as Deeds and heavier. Suddenly she grabbed the arm that held the knife and arched her face down and bit it. Deeds bellowed in pain, dropped the knife.

Morgan fired. The round hit the man in the now-exposed shoulder and spun him around, blasting him back against the kitchen table. He roared in pain and stumbled and fell to the floor.

The woman who had been in danger of dying

moments before bent, grabbed the knife, and stabbed Deeds five times in the chest, screeching in anger and fury and pent-up hatred with each thrust of the heavy knife.

Morgan caught her arm after the fifth stab and held her gently.

"Enough, enough. He's already dead," Morgan told her. The woman stared at him with fury still etched on her face. She looked down at Deeds and his blood-soaked chest and slowly the rage faded from her face.

"My God!" she whispered, and dropped the knife and began to cry.

Morgan picked up the knife. He looked at the place where the handle met the blade. There he saw the stamped outline of a pelican.

Chapter Twenty-Two

It took a half hour for Morgan to get the woman calmed down. He told her the man was the rapist killer who had cut up the three women in town.

"I've got to go bring the sheriff," Morgan said. The woman looked at him. She'd told him she was Mrs. Younger.

"I won't stay in the house with that dead man," she said. "I'll go with you. Mr. Younger won't be home for hours."

They walked to the sheriff's office on Ferguson and 19th Street. The sheriff listened to Morgan, then talked to the woman.

"I'll bring around a buggy and we'll head back out there, Mrs. Younger."

By the time the sheriff was done with his cursory look at things and Morgan got away from the house, it was a little past midday. He had a meal, and decided to go back to his hotel room and get his things ready to travel with first light in the morning. Both his small problems here had been wrapped up to his satisfaction.

Sheriff Goranson had taken down the statement by Mrs. Younger about what she'd heard Deeds say admitting the deaths of the three women. Morgan had confirmed the confession. The sheriff hadn't been pleased that someone else had solved the three murders. He'd said Mrs. Younger would not be charged in the death of Thurlow Deeds. She'd been defending herself.

She had gone to a neighbor's house and the undertaker had come and hauled away the body.

Now Morgan could concentrate on the problem of getting Harold Bishop away from the Cheyenne. Even if Harold had at last decided he wanted to leave, it was still a matter of getting into that larger Cheyenne village and rescuing him.

Morgan was thinking about the Cheyenne when he unlocked his door and stepped into his room. He didn't make a quick survey of the place as he usually did. He closed the door, and had just unbuckled his gun belt when he heard movement. He spun around and found Shirley sitting on his bed.

Her hair was mussed and she had her blouse half off to show one breast. One of her hands massaged the orb, and she smiled at Morgan. "About time you got back here."

"Shirley."

"That should be dumb, stupid, bitchy Shirley. I've come to apologize and do what I can to make it up to you. I finally figured out that you saved my life."

"Don't see how. Didn't you sleep with Deeds last night?"

"Yes. He's an inventive lover."

"I still don't see why he didn't kill you the way he did the other three women."

"I'm not sure. Maybe it was because he didn't have to rape me. Then too, I kept him guessing just how I would do him the next time. I guess I was such a great lover he couldn't give it all up by killing me." Shirley shivered. "You going to stand there or give me a hug and tell me I'm safe now?"

Morgan grinned and sat down on the bed, and she melted into his arms and he hugged her and kissed her cheek.

"Morgan, I know you can do better than that."

He kissed her lips gently, then harder, and their mouths opened and the kiss lasted a long time. When she at last pulled away, she sighed. "Oh, glory, but it's good to be alive. He was such a gentleman. Said he should be going back to Chicago, but now that he'd found me, he'd stay a couple of more days. Two days he took me out to dinner and supper, and then we went to the opera house both nights and he just gave me a little peck on the cheek at my door. Never even touched my titties.

"Then last night I asked him into my room and he came and didn't leave. Oh, I did him good. Best fucking of my life. I guess I must have known if I wasn't fantastic, he'd kill me. I kept him guessing until he fell asleep.

"Then you hit the door and it was daylight and we both woke up and it was too late for him to do me. So he hid behind the door and clubbed you with his six-gun when you came in."

"Sounds like you saved your own skin."

"Not so, Morgan. He would have got me on my back this morning and then killed me, I'm sure. It's all over town how Mrs. Younger killed him. She's a regular hero. All the women love her, you can bet on that. She should get a medal."

Shirley slipped out of the blouse and let her big breasts push hard against his chest.

"How did you figure out he was the killer?"

He told her about the pin and the picture of the pelican and how he'd had the answer right in his pocket all the time and never made the connection.

She unbuttoned his shirt and massaged his hairy chest. "Mr. Lee Buckskin Morgan. Right now I want to tell you there is nothing I won't do for you. Any way, anywhere. You just name it and I'm yours, upside down and backwards or inside out."

"Standing up?"

"Hell, standing on my head if you want me that way. I owe you, Morgan."

Morgan let a slow smile creep over his face. "Yes, that's true, Shirley, you do owe me. And I intend to collect today and tonight for just as long as I can hold out!"

"I like the way you talk, Morgan. Now start proving that you're not only just talk."

Morgan took off the skirt and bloomers she wore. He stripped down the pink bloomers an inch at a time, kissing them down her belly around her blond muff and along the inside of her upper thighs until she crooned in excitement.

"Morgan, no man's ever got me warmed up that way before. Damn, but you are good. You get extra points. Now hurry up and get to the poking."

"Hey, bitch in heat. This is my party. You said anything I wanted. First we go slow. You're going to be screaming for it before I get that far. I want to test your patience."

Shirley pulled open the buttons on his fly and undid his belt and pushed open his pants. She caressed the lump that was imprisoned there. Slowly she massaged him through the tight, white underwear.

Morgan bleated in surprise.

She bent and blew hot breath on his erection, then pulled down his drawers and grabbed his big tool as it swung up.

"Gotcha!" she said. Shirley bent and kissed the purple tip of him, licked around and round the head with her tongue, then kissed the tip. Slowly she let her lips part and forced him into her mouth.

She moaned in delight as she mouthed him. Tiny bites pinpricked the head of his penis as she nibbled delicately.

"Woman, you are a witch," Morgan said, lifting his hips to force more of him into her mouth.

She moved as well, and then sucked in most of him, and he sighed and began a soft rhythm of movements with his hips. She countered with her head, and soon they established the pattern.

"You're just trying to get me so excited I can't stop, Shirley. I know your tactics." But he didn't stop her. He worked the thrusts a little more and a little more.

Then Morgan moaned and his fists tightened and his legs stretched and it seemed to him that every muscle in his body tensed.

"You ready, Shirley? You want it there?"

She bobbed her head and he felt the release far upstream. His hips pounded upward and she compensated and held on to him as he went faster.

A moan crashed from him and he felt his hips bucking and the seed spurting and he roared in the age-old sound of the male as he worked to perpetuate the species.

Shirley swallowed and gulped and swallowed again as fast as she could, taking all he had to give.

His hips jolted in one last thrust, then he sighed and settled back on the bed. She came away from him and stretched up beside him and kissed his cheek.

"Gonna make me wait, were you? Ha. I know men better than that. It's your party, but the first round goes to me. I won that one. The next one is your choice."

She rolled off the bed and picked up a picnic basket and put it on the bed between them.

"Figured we'd have an all-day session so I brought some emergency supplies." She opened the wicker top and took out a bottle of wine and handed it to him.

"Open," she said.

She found some small finger sandwiches and put out a half dozen between them, then a plate filled with wedges of orange cheese.

"This is a start. After we get going, we'll really get hungry."

They sampled the wine, ate the small sandwiches and the cheese, then tested the wine again.

Kit Dalton

"What a great idea, supper in bed," Morgan said.

"Food and fucking, what could be better? Food while you're fucking maybe. We'll try that too."

She pulled his boots and socks off, then his pants, and took care getting his underwear off. His manhood was limp and wormlike.

"What a poor baby!" Shirley said. "Bet I can bring him back to life. He must have died." She bent and rubbed her hanging breasts against the limp member. His penis jerked but remained soft.

"Get on your hands and knees," Morgan said with huskiness shading his voice. He slid his head under her and attacked her hanging breasts with his mouth. She gurgled in delight, dropping one, then the other breast into his mouth.

"Oh, Lordy, but that is sweet!" Shirley said. "So good. Just don't chew them off. I might need them someday."

"Hope you do," Morgan said, coming up for air. He moved behind her while she remained on her hands and knees.

"Back there?" she asked.

"Which one?"

"You might as well do a three-holer. You already got the hardest one."

Morgan went to his knees behind her and eased forward.

She looked at him over her shoulder. "Which one?"

"Whichever one I hit."

She arched her bottom higher, and he hit a tube and slid in like he was in a whirlpool.

"Think you found one."

Morgan stayed on his knees, leaned forward

against her back, and reached around and found a breast with each hand. He hung on and began the slow dance that would end with glory.

"Faster!" she said.

"Then you help."

She thrust against him then, her breath coming in gasps and gulps as the fires flamed outside her body. She whined and then crooned and lunged at him again and again until she bellowed in joy and delight and soared into a climax that flattened her on the bed, and Morgan dropped heavily on top of her. She kept spasming and vibrating and keening in intense ecstasy for another minute.

When she tapered off she turned and her smile was radiant, overflowing with total joy and wonder. She tried to say something, but the words wouldn't come. She just shook her head and kissed his arm.

He began to move slowly then. They were still pinned together. Shirley lifted up enough so he had room and he powered off in six quick strokes, then collapsed on her, and they both came close to dropping off to sleep.

Morgan came back to full consciousness and rolled away from her. At once she sat up and sampled the wine straight from the bottle.

"Oh, damn!" was all Shirley could say.

It was a half hour before she could talk coherently. Then the wonder of the experience still overwhelmed her. They had been nibbling at the cheese and he found a sack of crackers, and deeper in the basket cold fried chicken and some salt.

Morgan dug into it before he realized she had stayed with the wine.

"Don't want to forget that time," she said.

"You won't." He watched her. She sat there, naked legs crossed, staring out the window at the Wyoming afternoon.

"Sure you're all right?"

"Not sure at all, Morgan. I almost got myself killed this morning and last night. Damn, I would have been number four. Nobody would have even missed me. You know that? I almost damn well got murdered!"

"But you didn't. That's the important part."

She shook her head. Her long blond hair swung from side to side, and so did her breasts.

"No, not the goddamn point. I almost got killed *because I was fucking around, like this.* I was just fucking around. Not being careful, not doing anything *productive.* My old daddy always used to say a person had to be productive. I been living off Slade. Now he's gone. I can dance and make a living, but I'll still be fucking around, looking for some man to keep me. Hell, no, no more!"

She uncrossed her legs, slipped into her blouse, and pulled on her skirt.

"Respectable. That's what I'm going to be from here on out."

"You can get a respectable job in some cafe for five dollars a week."

"I'd get my meals free."

"You'd be bored to tears in a week."

"I'd be productive."

Morgan chewed on another piece of chicken. Shirley finished dressing and picked up things from the basket and put them inside.

"I probably won't be seeing you again, Mr. Morgan. I'll be on the morning train. I have a sister in Chicago. I'll stay there and she will help me get a job. One of these days I'll get married. It won't be all that hard, not in Chicago."

She picked up the basket and walked to the door. "Oh, I won't be needing this." She opened the basket, took out the half-filled bottle of wine, and set it on the dresser. "It's all yours, Mr. Morgan. If you're ever in Chicago we might see each other."

She nodded, went out the door, and closed it gently.

Morgan snorted. He'd never seen a woman get religion so fast. She'd be back on the road within a month. Unless she snared some rich man in Chicago.

Morgan dressed and checked his watch. Two-thirty. He was due on the train first thing in the morning. He wasn't sure he'd be back in town to stay. He might be going through to Grand Island with Harold Bishop, he hoped.

Morgan checked with the livery stable and paid for a rented horse, then went to the bank.

The president was busy at the moment. He sat in a stiff wooden chair and waited. A couple came from her office a few minutes later with some papers and a smile.

Morgan went to the door and she glanced up.

"Madam President, I wonder if I could have a moment of your time?"

Sarah Everett's smile blossomed and she stood and held out her hand. "Good to see you, Mr. Morgan. I hear you found our murderer. I'm just so proud of Mrs. Younger. It must have been terrible for her for a while."

"I don't know why I didn't tumble to the pelican trademark before. I carried a small penknife with the picture on it."

"Half the households and businesses in the county probably have a knife with that picture stamped on it," Sarah said. "I'm just glad you figured it out before anyone else was hurt."

She motioned for him to sit down.

"We have all of the repairs made. Even a new plate-glass window. It came in from Omaha last night and I had it installed. Feels more like a bank now."

Morgan watched her and became aware of an awkward silent time. They both began to talk at once and laughed. She motioned for him to go ahead.

"Just wanted to say I'll be going to Laramie in the morning. Right now I don't know how long I'll be gone or if I'll be back through here."

"Oh." She looked disappointed. "Well, like I told you once, you won't be here long enough to break my heart."

"Wish I could stay longer."

She moved and arranged some papers on her desk. "If you do come back, I still owe you that roast beef dinner I promised you. Can I count on that?"

"Yes, if I come this way." He stood. She watched him and lifted her brows.

"Well, it was too good to be true anyway. What my father always used to say. If something seemed too good to be true, it probably was."

He went around the desk and leaned down. Her face reached up to his and he kissed her lightly on the lips, then moved away from her.

"Sarah Everett, you get yourself married. A downright waste having such a pretty lady like you running around without a proper husband."

She smiled. "I'll try, Lee Morgan. Didn't do

312

much good this time, but I'll just keep on trying."

He turned away just as he saw a tear slip out of one eye and run down her cheek.

Morgan was never good at good-byes.

That night he slept well, and made the early train with five minutes to spare.

When the train pulled into Laramie it was an hour late. A small washout had had to be repaired before they could pass. Morgan saw Jim Breed pacing beside the station house.

They met behind the building as before and Jim shook his head. "We got problems, Morgan."

"What kind of problems?"

"Cheyenne on the move. Both bands. Working north. Also Army ready to send troopers."

"Where from?"

"Right here. Fort Laramie. Lieutenant go tomorrow, with fifty mounted troopers."

"Chasing Gray Owl and the new band?"

Jim nodded.

"How far away from us are they now, Jim?"

"Thirty miles, west."

"Heading north?"

"Fast."

"No problem, Jim. We'll leave now and beat the Army to them, get Harold, and be gone before the Army gets to them."

Jim laughed.

"Our only chance. We'll angle across and cut them off. Maybe. Where can we get some good horses and supplies for the trail?"

It took them an hour to get the horses and the camp gear and trail food. They headed out of Laramie on a northwest route over fairly level ground.

"We've got a chance. We're thirty miles from

them. If they ride thirty miles north, and we head at them at a forty-five-degree angle, then we need to ride about forty-three miles to find them thirty miles north of their present spot." Morgan mentally checked his arithmetic to make sure he had the correct hypotenuse.

"When are they leaving?"

"This morning, daylight," Jim said.

"How far can they drag those travois a day?"

"Twenty-five miles."

"So we should be able to cover forty-three miles today. We'll be in position to intercept them early in the morning. We'll be with the Cheyenne when the Pony Soldiers are just leaving Fort Sanders."

"Maybe," Jim said.

"Why maybe?"

"Cheyenne might change plan. Cheyenne maybe ride more to east."

"Right, maybe. Chance we'll have to take. Was Mighty Dawn still being held as a prisoner?"

"No. But they watch him. Watch horse. No chance him get away."

"Afraid of that. Let's ride, Indian. We've got forty-three miles to cover before we stop. That means we're going to have to be riding well into darkness."

Chapter Twenty-Three

Morgan moved the horses out at a fast walk. The nags could cover four and a half miles in an hour that way. At that rate it would take them ten hours to do the ride with no stops.

After the animals were completely warmed up two miles from town, Morgan lifted his brindle mare into an easy lope. Jim picked up the pace and came alongside him.

"This is a natural gait for lots of horses," Morgan told Jim. "A horse can keep up this lope for a long time, much longer than a flat out gallop. We're doing about six miles an hour now. That's covering ground fast for a horse."

"How long?"

"We'll do the lope for three miles, then slow to a walk for a mile, then go back to the lope for another three. These two mares should be able to keep that up for eight to ten hours without breaking down."

Jim nodded. He turned his head and watched a jackrabbit bounding away from them. "Meat?"

"Go," Morgan said.

Jim wheeled his mare to the left, pulled the Spencer carbine from the boot, and rode hard for their dinner on the fleet feet. Morgan had heard that big jackrabbits never run in a straight line. They take up residence in a given area, make a nest, and don't like leaving it.

When threatened they tend to run in a circle. An experienced dog will learn this quickly and start cutting off the circle and soon catch the rabbit.

Morgan saw Jim start to do the same thing.

A few minutes later he heard a shot and the big jack tumbled into the dirt and lay still.

Jim came back with the dinner entree smiling. He tied the rabbit to his bedroll to keep it off the hot skin of the horse and they kept riding.

Two hours out of Laramie, Morgan figured that they had covered more than ten miles, even though they had walked the first two.

Now and then they saw a trail to the left, and then Morgan remembered the track that led northwest from Laramie to a little settlement called Medicine Bow. They swung over and used the trail, which made the going easier.

Soon they crossed the Laramie River for the last time as it swung to the right and due north. They let the horses drink, washed the dust out of their hair and faces, and filled up canteens.

A few minutes later they had the horses again at their lope gait and moved ahead smoothly.

At four o'clock, they took a break near a small stream and Jim skinned and cleaned the rabbit. He got a small fire going and placed two quarters of the rabbit over the fire on green sticks to roast. Morgan dug out salt and made coffee. He took out some hard rolls, and when the rabbit was done it was a good meal, the best they might have for some time.

"Maybe rain," Jim said as they packed up and got ready to ride.

"Won't help things a bit," Morgan groused. At least they weren't following any tracks that would be washed out.

The rain went around them to the north and they kept riding.

At sunset Morgan estimated that they had put behind them a little over 35 miles.

They paused when the sun went down and let the horses rest for a half hour. Both had held up well. The two men had no grain for them, but they would graze where they could.

Morgan checked the pocket compass he had brought from the store and got his sighting. Things would look much different after dark. He watched his landmark closely and made certain it was the one he had sighted in on. It was a bluff that showed on the skyline five miles ahead.

By nine o'clock that night Morgan called a halt.

"We're on or near the line where the Cheyenne will pass if they keep moving north," Morgan told Jim.

"Jim look around to south." The Cheyenne vanished into the darkness. Morgan stretched out on his blankets. He'd hobbled the horses in some greenery where they could graze if they wanted to. Almost at once his brindle had moved into a moping stance.

Her back feet were braced and locked. Her front feet were slightly extended to the side and forward and locked. It gave her a solid foundation to support herself. Slowly her head and neck came down until her muzzle nearly touched the ground. She was resting, perhaps even sleeping on and off.

Morgan wanted to start a fire, but out here in the pure, fresh air, even he could smell camp-fire smoke five miles away if the wind was right. He couldn't take the chance.

Jim Breed slipped into the small camp an hour later. Morgan cocked his six-gun. The click made a jarring sound in the stillness.

"No shoot, it Jim."

"Figured. See anything?"

"No. See no fire, no smoke. Smell no smoke. Wind blow toward us. Cheyenne ten miles south. Maybe more."

"Good, we can sleep in."

By daylight, Morgan was up making a fire. The wind was blowing to the north so it wouldn't give them away. Jim came alive and fixed a bundle of tough green willows to make a roasting rack for the last half of the rabbit.

Morgan figured it might be a little ripe by now, but a good roasting would kill all the bad bugs in it. Besides, he was hungry.

Soon they had their fire out, and moved due south to a small hill Jim had found. It produced some grass and sage and a ponderosa pine here and there. It made enough concealment for their safety. They found some cottonwood and aspen brush on the near side and hid their horses there, and sprawled out on top of the ridge with sage-brush to conceal them.

They could see south for seven or eight miles. This time Morgan had his binoculars along. They were former Army issue with a 35-mm field and a power of eight. Morgan began scouring the possible trails up from the south. There were two long valleys extending to the north. One passed a half mile to the west of them.

Jim took his horse and rode down the hill to the south. He wanted to see how far he'd have to go before he could smell smoke. On the trail this way, the band would stop for the night and would fix food before leaving this morning.

Jim was back three hours later. He had probed five miles south, and from the top of another small rise he had caught the scent of wood smoke. Someone was down there, and it wasn't a settler. They had seen no sign of white men since leaving the road that continued on into the small settlement of Medicine Bow five miles to the east.

The two men lay in the soft shade of the sage and waited. Both had saved part of the roast rabbit, and now chewed on the cold meat and nipped at their canteens.

"Waiting is the hardest thing I do," Morgan growled.

"You see Indian move in plain sight?"

"I have. I never believe it. You lay in the open and move an inch or two every ten minutes. Might take you three hours to cross an open spot six feet wide. But anyone watching that place from time to time can never catch you moving, and before he knows it you're across it and chasing up his backside."

"That is Indian way."

Kit Dalton

Morgan's eyelids drooped and he fought to keep his eyes open. Once he drifted off, but came back when his head dropped sharply forward.

Morgan went back to the binoculars. He concentrated on the first part of the valley he could see to the left. It came closest to the ridge they lay on.

For ten minutes he scoured the farthest opening of the valley. Even the trees were tiny sticks from this distance of about four miles.

Gradually he saw a change. Movement! He looked away, then returned to the same spot.

Horses and riders. Indians or Cavalry? He watched again and soon saw a travois behind a lead horse.

"Our guests are arriving," Morgan said. He passed the glasses to Jim, who had used them before. Jim looked and nodded. "Indians. Maybe Cheyenne, maybe not."

"We'll know before long."

An hour later Jim nodded. "Gray Owl and the other band."

"I haven't spotted the boy yet. What kind of pony does he have?"

"Brown with four dark spots."

The combined band of 80 warriors and families stretched out for nearly a mile. There were 80 travois, each pulled by a horse, often a large horse. Morgan knew some of them were Army mounts.

The band came to the head of the valley and scouts were there, showing the way over the ridge and down to the next valley below that led generally north.

The line of march was less than a half mile from the two watchers.

"There he is!" Morgan crowed. "I've got him. He's riding his horse. Stays behind a travois. The other warriors are out on the sides of the line of march."

"Shows Mighty Dawn isn't trusted. Keep him inside."

"Makes it harder for us. What will they do with him tonight?"

"Don't know. Trail camp, no tipis."

"All in the open. How hard would it be for you and me to slip into their camp, free Mighty Dawn, and get out of there...alive?"

"Damn hard."

"I was afraid of that. At least the Army isn't here yet."

"Maybe help."

Morgan looked at the Cheyenne half-breed. "Help? I see. They will be running from the Pony Soldiers and will be stretched out and worried about the soldiers. Might give us a chance to slip in and get the boy."

"Maybe."

"That wouldn't be until tomorrow, maybe tomorrow night or the next day. That's too long. Too much could happen. We have to do something tonight."

"You play Indian?"

"If I have to. We'll shadow them and see where they stop. There's got to be a way to get him out of there."

They lay quietly watching the stream of ponies, travois, and walking women and children pass over the ridge below them. One warrior rode up the ridge toward Morgan and Jim, but turned around 50 yards from them and went back to the line of march.

For the rest of the day they played cat and mouse with the end of the marching line. But the Indians didn't know they were being followed. They had no rear guard, not even a youth on his pony.

Morgan saw an old woman straggling behind. Twice a younger woman went back to help her and hurried her forward toward the end of the line. The third time the old woman faded to the rear she sat down in the dust, put a scrap of a buffalo robe over her head, and turned toward the sun.

"She isn't moving," Morgan said.

"Death song," Jim said.

"I remember," Morgan said. "She will never move again. Today or tomorrow, maybe the next day, she will still be sitting there. Every adult in a Cheyenne band must pull his weight, must be productive for the band. If not, he or she is left to die."

"Son probably killed by Pony Soldiers," Jim said. "No warrior to hunt for her, protect her."

"So she sits down by the side of the trail and sings her death song and dies," Morgan said. "Not a loving way to treat an old woman."

"It is the way of the Cheyenne people," Jim said.

They rode past well concealed. At the closest point they could hear her wailing death song.

The two bands of Cheyenne came to a small stream and some heavier growth of Douglas fir and ponderosa pine along with aspens. It was about four in the afternoon, and they stopped and made their quick trail camp.

The long line of marching Indians compressed

into a quarter mile, spread under the good cover and heavier growth of trees.

"What protects them also shields us from them," Morgan said, thinking out loud. "We have to get closer."

Jim Breed had stepped down from his mount. He took the saddle off and hoisted it to Morgan's horse behind his saddle and tied it firmly in place. He took off the leather halter and bridle and replaced it with a rawhide hackamore from his blanket roll.

A moment later he slipped out of his shirt and pants and put on a Cheyenne breechclout.

Morgan grinned. "Now I see how we can get closer. With so many new faces, neither group of warriors will know everyone. You can ride into camp as soon as it gets dusk and no one will think twice about your being there."

"Maybe lucky," Jim said.

"Find out where Mighty Dawn will be tonight and where the guards are. Check if they have lookouts or sentries."

"Watch for guards," Jim said, and grinned.

They waited three hours for dusk. When it came at last, Jim mounted his horse bareback and kicked the mount with moccasined feet. Morgan hadn't seen him replace his boots.

They both rode forward until Jim raised his hand. A youth of 15 sat on a rock near the stream watching down the trail the Indians had carved through the wilderness.

Jim whispered for Morgan to go back 50 yards and keep out of sight. Jim rode into the slope away from the sentry, and then headed back to the water and the first small cooking fire he saw 20 yards ahead.

Kit Dalton

Morgan eased back into safer territory and tied his mount's muzzle closed with a kerchief. He didn't want his brindle to horse-talk with another animal and give him away.

Waiting was always the hardest part. With any luck they would snatch Harold Bishop and be 20 miles back toward Laramie before daylight came and the Cheyenne discovered their good-magic young warrior was missing.

Morgan found a stick and whittled on it without seeing it. He used the new penknife, and was lucky he didn't slice his finger off.

Just upstream he could hear the Cheyenne making camp, cooking the evening meal, tending to their horses. A woman screamed and a man laughed. Children played in the dark even though they were tired after the long walk.

He could smell the wood smoke, and now and then caught a whiff of some meat cooking. It didn't make him hungry. He was wondering just how he could walk into a Cheyenne war party traveling camp, get away with a hostage . . . and still live.

Chapter Twenty-Four

First Lieutenant Russell Zedicher angled his 50-man patrol toward the small community of Medicine Bow 55 miles northwest of Laramie. He had left Fort Laramie near the town of the same name at five P.M. His orders had told him to move out "as soon as practical, to pursue a band of Cheyenne heading north out of the Medicine Bow mountains."

Lieutenant Zedicher was a career officer who had been in the Army for six years. At Fort Laramie he commanded the Lightning Troop. In the past six months he had built a reputation as having the best average of finding and engaging hostiles of any officer at the fort.

His unit was unusual for the Army. It was not a "regulation" outfit. He had handpicked the men. First he asked for volunteers for a new unit, one that would travel light and fast, with Indian scouts who would help them live off the land to reduce their provisions.

He put the men through a tough physical test of running, marching, rope climbing, and then riding.

Half the volunteers dropped out. In the end he chose the 49 men he wanted. None was over the age of 28. He had two sergeants who were the best of the lot. He did everything that he demanded his men do.

First came equipment. The normal Calvary trooper carried a hundred pounds of equipment when he went into the field. That included his saddle, food, and grain for his horse.

The Lightning Troopers cut that equipment down to a sparse 50 pounds. The saddle alone weighed 15 pounds. They carried no sabers or slings, no saddlebags, no rations, no extra clothes, only one blanket, no saddle cover or watering bridle. They cut everything to the absolute necessities. On most of their trips they didn't take any grain for their horses. This saved three pounds per day.

The men themselves had gone through extensive marksmanship drills with live firing. In the Army, most of the generals considered target practice a waste of ammunition. Lieutenant Zedicher had been trained by his long-time friend, then Captain, now Colonel Colt Harding. Harding had created the Lightning Companies in his fights with the Comanches on the Texas plains back in the late sixties.

Now the system had spread and Colonel Harding gave instructions to groups of interested officers. Every man in a Lightning Troop had training in knife-fighting from friendly Indians, and had found out how the Indians used knives and how to guard against them.

The 50-man troop took special field training, learned to live off the land from the Indian scouts, learned tracking from the scouts, and practiced special riding techniques the Indians used, such as riding off the side of a horse and firing a revolver under the horse's neck.

Every man in the troop had to pick up an unhorsed rider with his horse at a gallop, and in turn had to be picked up by another trooper.

The training was tough, and interspersed with regular fort activities.

Troopers didn't like to change companies. Many of the men had been in the same company and same regiment for their whole enlistment. But the lure of the fast-action group drew a lot of volunteers. The reputation the Lightning Troops were building up in the Army helped.

One of the first requirements for the volunteers was a tough two-mile run. Colonel Harding believed that if a trooper could run two miles with his pack and his Spencer carbine, he would be in good enough shape for the rugged riding coming up.

Now, as Lieutenant Zedicher thought back on his training and the subsequent training of his troopers, he knew that it was the right way to function.

The proof came in the ability of the Lightning Troop to travel fast. He could move his men at six miles an hour all day. Once he had ridden with his men 72 miles in a 13-hour day. When they arrived they had rested an hour until daylight, then surprised a band of 20 Sioux raiders and killed ten and captured the rest.

The system worked. The whole Army should be set up that way, Lieutenant Zedicher thought.

Now he could smell the smoke of the small town ahead. It was nearly three A.M. by the looks of the Big Dipper where it circled the North Star. His men had been riding for nine hours with a one-hour break at midnight. Now they were in position to cut the Cheyenne trail and move up it.

He ordered the men to halt, take care of their horses, and then sleep. The men knew that their mounts came first. They were watered at the small stream, allowed to graze on a short picket rope, and inspected. When the troopers were satisfied that their horses were cared for, they each rolled out their one blanket and slept.

At seven o'clock, half the men were up. The smell of roasting rabbit had awakened them. The six Kiowa Indian scouts had been hunting half the night and bagged six big jackrabbits. Now they were roasting them on steel spits that the Indians carried. The spits hung from forked branches at the sides of several small cooking fires.

With daylight, Lieutenant Zedicher had been up conferring with his chief scout, Walks Funny. The Kiowa was about 30 years old and had a deformed foot, but he could walk and run and ride better than any of his Kiowa friends.

The scout rode off with one other man soon after daylight. He wore only a pair of cut-off Army pants and carried a Spencer repeating rifle.

Zedicher sat and drank his cup of boiled coffee. Officers on the Lightning raids were no better off than the men. No officer tents. No special privileges, no special rations or gear. There was never, ever, a bugle along with a Lightning operation.

By eight o'clock all the men were up and fed and had their horses saddled and ready to go. He told them to have one last cup of coffee, that they were waiting for the scouts to come back.

Lieutenant Zedicher made it a rule that the troopers knew as much about a patrol as he did. He told them exactly what the colonel told him.

On this run they were trying to cut off and punish a band of Cheyenne who had recently been discovered in the Medicine Bow Mountains less than a day's ride from the fort. Now they were moving north, about 60 tipis, which would mean a broad trail that would be easy to cut and follow.

Zedicher had heartily approved the Lightning Troop policy of traveling at night. The dust trail of 50 troopers' horses could be seen for ten miles. There was no better early warning to an alert Indian band that the telltale dust trail.

Whether they would ride during daylight today or wait until after dark would depend on how far the Cheyenne were now ahead of them.

The scouts came back shortly before noon. Lieutenant Zedicher took the report. The band was larger than estimated.

"Eighty warriors," Walks Funny said. "One day ahead. Move twenty miles a day."

"So they're in no rush, they don't know we're here. Good. Sleep. We'll push off at four o'clock, find them tonight, hit them in their camp with sunup tomorrow."

Sergeant Larry Casemore came when the officer beckoned.

"Tell the men they can get some more sleep. We'll be eating at three, and moving out at four o'clock. The scouts cut the Cheyenne trail and we're about a day behind them. We'll catch them before morning."

The two Kiowas designated as hunters for the day brought in 12 pheasants and three larger grouse. The birds were all cleaned and the heads cut off, then the birds, feathers and all, were lathered with a layer of mud from the nearby creek and set aside.

The Kiowa then dug a trench a foot deep and built a fire in it along its ten-foot length. They let the fire burn for an hour, then put the mud-coated birds directly on the coals and covered them with the dirt taken from the ditch.

An hour later they dug up the birds and pulled the layer of dry mud off them. It pulled off all the feathers and skin and left the pheasants and grouse cooked to a delicate brown.

They were cut into quarters and one given to each of the 50 men.

"Best damn pheasant I ever et," one of the troopers said as he licked his fingers and threw away the bones.

The troop moved out shortly after four o'clock. Four miles to the west, they cut the Indian trail and turned north. Then they urged the ponies along at a lope, eating up the ground at six miles an hour. Zedicher had been amazed at what a natural pace the lope was for most horses. Any mounts that could not sustain the pace were weeded out and replaced in the training period.

Just before dark, they came to the spot where

the Cheyenne had camped the night before. Now the quarry could be no more than 20 miles ahead.

With the darkness, they slowed a little, but not a lot. These men and horses were used to night riding. It was nearly midnight when Walks Funny rode back and the troop stopped.

"Found camp. Two miles. No lookouts."

Lieutenant Zedicher walked the mounts the last mile. The troop stopped half a mile away and Zedicher, Sergeant Casemore, and Walks Funny rode silently up to evaluate the situation.

There were no tipis set up. Only a few trails of smoke came from camp fires.

"At least they're still there," Lieutenant Zedicher said. "Looks like they're strung out about a quarter of a mile down there."

"Which way will they head out in the morning?" Sergeant Casemore asked.

Walks Funny motioned to the north. "Up valley, over ridge."

Lieutenant Zedicher nodded. "So we split our troop and hit them from both ends at the same time. Casemore, you take twenty men and seal off the retreat. I'll hit them at the point to the north and work down the camp."

"Run into woods both sides," Walks Funny said.

"Let the women and children run," the officer said. "We only want the warriors. By the time the little boys grow up old enough to fight, we'll have them all on reservations. No shooting the women and children."

"Time?" the sergeant asked.

"We'll pull out at four o'clock, walk our mounts up this way, split, and I'll take the thirty along this ridge until we're well past the camp.

331

Then we'll move down to the creek and back along it until we can see the hostiles. At daylight, I'll fire my six-gun twice. That's the signal to do a mounted charge into the Cheyenne."

They looked at the peaceful site for a moment more. Then Lieutenant Zedicher turned and rode back toward their own camp to the rear.

They moved like ghosts. The three horses had their muzzles tied shut with neckerchiefs to prevent them from horse-talking with the Indian ponies and any captured Army mounts the Indians might have.

The horses could still breathe normally, but they couldn't make much noise without opening their mouths.

Twenty minutes later back at the Cavalry camp, Lieutenant Zedicher watched his troops. Most of them slept. A few cleaned weapons and sharpened knives. One man wrote a letter by the light of his treasured candle.

Zedicher wouldn't sleep until the fight was over. He'd been up for 48 hours many times. He felt he was just as precise and effective the 48th hour as he had been the first.

He grinned. Slipping up on a band of Indians, especially the Cheyenne, was something most Army units would never try. They couldn't do it. With the Lightening Troop it was second nature. They had trained for just this type of action, and Zedicher knew they were good at it. After all, he was the one who'd trained them.

He nodded once, stirred his small fire, added more ground coffee to his tin-can coffeepot, and soon had more of the steaming brew ready to drink. It wasn't quite gone when the troops were roused and made ready to ride. At four A.M. the

Lightning Troop moved out in a column of twos toward the Cheyenne.

A half mile from the end of the Cheyenne camp, Jim Breed sat his mount and watched an Army company ride past. They were moving quieter than any Army unit he'd ever seen. No jangling rings or gear, no talking or yelling. It was spooky to the Indian.

When the 50 men had passed him, he edged away from them and rode to where Morgan waited. Morgan was less than 100 yards below the camp. He found the white-eyes and motioned that they should go.

A half hour later, Jim reined in and nodded when Morgan came up. "Find boy. Has two guards. One awake. No chance tonight."

"What about tomorrow? Are they going to move?"

"Yes. Move shortly after dawn." Jim frowned. "Big problem."

Morgan looked up sharply. Jim had never said the word problem before. "What is the trouble, Jim?"

The half-breed told him about the 50 soldiers he had seen moving like ghosts through the night. "Will attack at dawn."

"Damn! What can we do?"

"Watch, wait. Pony Soldiers kill only warriors. Maybe Mighty Dawn live through attack."

"What will the women and children do during the attack?"

"Run, hide. Go into heavy woods this side of water."

"Let's get down there. Maybe we'll have a

chance to get Mighty Dawn out before the attack."

"Must kill both guards, quiet."

Morgan set his jaw in the faint moonlight. "That might be a whole lot easier than trying to find Mighty Dawn once the Cavalry has scattered the whole band and killed half of them. Anyway, we can't be sure that Mighty Dawn would live through the attack. Let's move!"

Chapter Twenty-Five

Lee Buckskin Morgan and Jim Breed tied their horses' muzzles and led them as they worked up the slope behind the Cheyenne Indian camp in the brushy hills. They followed the river along the slope 50 yards above the sleeping Cheyenne.

They made no noise, moving slowly, keeping the horses with them because they could need them if they could get Mighty Dawn or if they had to ride out in a rush.

Jim held up his hand and both men stopped. He pointed. There was a bend in the creek, and inside the loop of the small stream in shafts of moonlight he could see six sleeping forms.

Jim pointed to a tree close by. A shadow moved there, stood from a squat and stretched, then eased back into the lower position.

"One guard awake," Morgan whispered. "Where is Mighty Dawn?"

Jim pointed to the middle form rolled in what looked like a stolen Army blanket. He was between two longer bodies also covered by blankets in the chill night air at 7,000 feet high.

"Me, guard." Jim said softly, pointing at himself and then at the shadowy Cheyenne. They tied their horses. If they got Mighty Dawn out, he would ride double with Jim since Jim weighed less than Morgan and the pony would have less weight to carry.

They edged toward the camp. It was the longest 50 yards in Morgan's life. One broken stick, one cough or misstep, and he might find himself head down over a Cheyenne ceremonial fire.

They made it to the near side of the stream and paused. The Indian on guard seemed to be sleeping. Jim held a rock twice the size of his fist. It would silence the guard.

Morgan stared at the sleeping forms. How could he wake Mighty Dawn without his making some cry or noise? He would have to get his hand over the boy's mouth as soon as he could.

Jim was ready to ease across the water. He would go first, knock out the guard, then Morgan would come across and the two of them would rouse Mighty Dawn.

Jim put one foot in the six inches of mountain cold water and started to take a second step, when the Cheyenne guard stood again, walked toward the sleepers, counted them, nodded, walked to the other side of the group, and sat down with his back against a sturdy cottonwood tree trunk.

Jim hesitated, brought his foot out of the water, and squatted beside Morgan. He pointed downstream, the way the guard had moved, and they faded ten feet into the brush and worked downstream making not a sound.

Somewhere a baby cried. Farther away a dog barked twice, then yelped in pain. Now Morgan could see the remains of a fire near the sleepers. A few coals glowed in the darkness.

They worked back to the very edge of the water, both kneeling in the lush green grass. Now they were slightly behind the Cheyenne guard against the tree.

Jim stepped into the water. He still wore his cut-off pants and his moccasins. Without a sound he took another step. Four strides later he reached the far side and squatted on the bank near some aspen. One of the sleepers groaned and half rolled over. A form beside him pushed away.

Morgan tried to see if the smaller one was Mighty Dawn, but there was no way of telling in the gloom.

Morgan had checked the Big Dipper the last time he could see it. He figured it was getting close to four in the morning. Even if they grabbed Mighty Dawn now they would have little nighttime to use to hide.

Jim Breed took three quick steps toward the other Indian, then turned away.

Somewhere far off a nighthawk cried twice. Jim heard it and turned back to the creek.

Morgan saw the Cheyenne guard jump to his feet. He looked at his charges, then stared away to the north from where the sound came. It was repeated. The same wild cry of the nighthawk sounded from downstream.

The Cheyenne warrior now held a rifle. He went to each lump on the ground and checked to be sure all were there, then paced in front of his post, waiting.

Jim Breed ghosted downstream until he was shielded by brush from the guard. Then he crossed. Three minutes later he crouched beside Morgan in the covering brush across the small stream.

"Trouble," Jim whispered. "Two nighthawk cries mean danger. The warriors gathering. Soon something happen."

Morgan scowled. "Somehow they must have found out that there are Pony Soldiers getting ready to attack. How could they know that?" Morgan asked.

"The way of the People," Jim Breed said, and grinned.

Two warriors came out of the night and talked with the man near the sleepers. The two men hurried away and the guard leaned down and cuffed the silent forms, waking them. He spoke softly to each one.

"No hear," Jim said to Morgan.

Within a minute of the first movement by the guard, the six were up and pulling the pieces of buffalo robes and Army blankets around them. Then all six walked to the creek, crossed it, and hurried directly up the slope of the hill into the denser brush and woods. They passed within 30 feet of Morgan, but didn't see him.

When they were away, Morgan touched Jim's shoulder. "Was Mighty Dawn one of them?"

"Maybe yes," Jim said. "Move up hill with horses."

They found the horses where they had left them, and led the animals higher on the slope until they were 100 yards from the stream. Now

Morgan could see through the trees at the sky. The Big Dipper showed that it was almost five A.M. It would be dawn in half an hour.

"They expect an attack?" Morgan whispered.

"Must. Send women and children out of camp. No time to pack. Time to get ready for Pony Soldiers."

Morgan tried to hear something in the brush around him. A band of 80 warriors would have how many women and children? Two wives and two children each would make nearly 400 Cheyenne in the camp! How could 320 women and children vanish into the woods without a sound? He asked Jim.

"They are Cheyenne," the grinning half-breed said.

After that it didn't take long for the action to start. Morgan sensed it coming. Just as the first real streaks of dawn broke the eastern hold on the blackness, Morgan heard two quick pistol shots from the north, upstream and not too far away.

Two shots answered from the south.

Morgan could feel the pounding Army horseshoes as the 50 horses charged into the Cheyenne camp. There were only two more shots. Then it was light enough that Morgan could see through the trees. The Cavalry troop charged through the deserted camp, along one side and back the other.

Slowly the movement slowed, and at last the 50 troopers sat on their mounts near the center of the camp waiting for orders.

Before the lieutenant in charge could say a word, the Indians opened fire with their captured rifles from somewhere up the far slope maybe 100 yards away. Evidently they had gathered there on their war ponies, and they poured a murderous fire into the exposed Cavalrymen.

"Charge the hostiles!" someone called over the sound of firing. Six troopers were unhorsed in the first volley, and before the rest turned and rode into the enemy fire, three more went down. Horses screamed as they were hit, and after some 150 rounds, the Indian fire stopped.

The Cavalry charged the position where a small cloud of blue smoke from the black powder had developed. But by the time they arrived, the Cheyenne had retreated to another point. Just as the Pony Soldiers arrived where the hostiles had been, they were met with another barrage of Indian rifle fire.

"Leading them away from the women and children," Morgan said softly with admiration. "No wonder the Army is having such a hard time getting all of the Cheyenne into the reservation."

Jim motioned up the side of the ridge and they worked their mounts in that direction, leading them through the heavy brush and trees. On top they paused and looked down the other slope. They saw half a dozen Cheyenne women herding twice that many children ahead of them.

They had left everything they owned back at the river. Jim pointed at the women. "Two hours women come back with ponies, hitch up travois, and haul away."

Morgan laughed softly. "Neat little strategy. But now, with all this going on, how in hell are we going to find Mighty Dawn? We should do it as soon as the women leave the kids alone down there. But where will they be?"

Jim grinned and led his horse over the ridge

and down into the cover of the brush and trees.

Morgan snorted and nodded at Jim. "Yeah, Jim. Right. I guess we follow them and see where they go."

An hour and three small valleys and ridges later, Morgan and Jim settled down at what Jim figured was a point almost due north of where the Indians had been camped. The kids were playing in a ravine barely 50 feet wide that had a trickle of water through it. The band couldn't camp here.

As Morgan watched, one after another of the women slipped away from the children and went over the ridge back the way they had come.

"Plenty time tie ponies in woods," Jim said. "Now go back, bring travois before Pony Soldiers can burn them."

Morgan chuckled. The warriors had pulled the classic move of a bird faking a hurt wing and enticing a cat away further and further from the nest of her young.

"Now is the time to get Mighty Dawn, before the women get back and especially before the warriors ride in," Morgan said.

Jim nodded. "I find."

He held up his hand to have Morgan stay where he was, and ran lightly through the trees toward where the young Indians played. Morgan watched him go. He might bring the boy back himself. It depended on who else was in the camp and how many older boys had come with the smaller children.

An hour later Jim stepped from behind a tree and sat down beside Morgan.

"Didn't hear you coming," Morgan said.

"Boy with six older boys. Two have bows, arrows."

"We have guns. Let's go get him."

"Hard." Jim motioned and they walked toward the Indian children.

Ten minutes later they watched the site where the women had left the small ones. The youngest children played in a circle in the center of the area. Around them sat the older girls, and the oldest boys stood in the circle around the girls. It was a small fortress.

"But Mighty Dawn is one of the ones on the outside. Will he come with us willingly?"

"Yes, but other older boys will see and chase us."

"We have horses, and guns. Let's go get him!"

Chapter Twenty-Six

Jim and Morgan moved with their horses as close as they could to the group of Indian children, then left the mounts in brush and worked ahead on foot. Far off they heard the ominous sounds of rifle fire. It came in a short burst, and then another one, then quieted.

One last woman left the children and hurried to the south up a ridge line and out of sight.

Morgan and Jim lay in some weeds and low brush 30 yards from the playing children. Jim had moved them both around the circle, which was now breaking down into more of an irregular oblong, until they were opposite where Mighty Dawn stood. He looked outward from the center in the classic guard's pose.

He wore only a breechclout and moccasins. He stood there with authority, and somehow seemed older than he had when Morgan saw him only a few days ago.

Morgan looked over the area as well as at the other larger boys. Only one had a bow and arrow. They had been pulled out of their camp while still asleep.

"We'll go straight in, I'll call to him and see if he'll run toward us, then I'll use my six-gun if I have to, firing over the heads of any who object. After that, we run to the horses and get the hell out of here. Let's ride due east, then turn south when we find a good valley. Clear?"

Jim nodded.

"Let's go."

They stood and ran forward. Some of the children saw them and shouted. Morgan caught Mighty Dawn's attention and bellowed at him.

"Harold Bishop! This way. Run this way. We've come to take you home."

Mighty Dawn frowned for a moment, then must have recognized Morgan. He looked at the other boys and shouted something, then charged forward toward the two rescuers.

Morgan checked the other large boys. Two of them didn't move. One notched his arrow, but he never got a shot off. Three other boys started toward Mighty Dawn, but he shouted at them and they stopped.

Then he stopped running. He looked at a pile of goods to the left and turned and raced that way. Morgan and Jim followed him. It was a stack of the children's goods and blankets. Mighty Dawn pawed through the pile a moment, found his Army saddlebag, and came up grinning.

"Can't forget this," he said, then ran with Morgan and Jim toward the brush.

An old Indian woman rose up from where she had been resting and shouted at the trio as they ran past her into the trees. Morgan had no idea what she said. They crashed through the brush until they arrived at the horses. Jim vaulted on board his and held his hand for Mighty Dawn, who grabbed his arm and with a much practiced vault reached the back of the animal.

Morgan mounted and they charged up the rest of the slope, over the ridge, and out of sight of the youths below.

Morgan turned due east, climbed another slope, and ahead saw a valley that ran south. He ignored it.

"We need to get more distance from the Cheyenne," he told Jim. They rode steadily for a half hour, pushing the horses as hard as they could.

By then it was time for a stop. Morgan unrolled his blankets and took out a pair of pants and a shirt and handed them to Harold.

"Should come near to fitting you. You can put them on now if you want to or later."

Tears brimmed Harold Bishop's eyes. He knuckled them away. "Thanks. Thanks a lot. I really appreciate...."

Morgan waved it off.

"You just needed a little help. Jim told me you tried to ride away but Gray Owl stopped you."

"They said I was good medicine. Looks like I wasn't much help today. Did the Pony Soldiers attack our village?"

Morgan told him how they had been fooled.

Harold grinned. "That's Red Feather's doings.

345

He's a smart man. A good warrior. I hope none of the warriors were killed."

Twice more in the next two hours they heard faint sounds of rifle fire, but it was a long ways off.

Jim scouted ahead and found a good valley, and they turned south. In the open, they moved the horses faster, but soon the one with the double load slowed.

Harold moved to Morgan's horse and they walked the animals for three more hours.

"Time to eat something," Morgan said. He investigated their trail food and came up with a tin of beef stew and a tin of canned meat. They stopped, built a fire, and heated the food in the cans, then ate.

Harold frowned at first, then grinned. "I haven't had real food like this for a long time. I've got to get used to it again."

When the food was gone they drank from a small stream, then mounted and rode south and a bit east.

There was no great hurry. With the Cheyenne running from the Pony Soldiers and the women and children trying to get their travois away safely, there was no one to chase after one boy warrior, even if he was good medicine for the band.

When they stopped late in the afternoon, Harold pointed at Morgan's six-gun.

"If you'll loan me your shooter, I'll bring back supper," he said. "I've learned how to hunt."

Jim nodded and Morgan handed over the weapon and watched the young man fade into some brush and trees. Ten minutes later they heard two shots. Soon Harold came into camp with a rabbit in one hand and a pheasant in the other.

They ate until they could hold no more of the fresh roasted meat.

At the camp fire that night, Morgan asked Harold why he had decided to come back to the real world.

"It was because of a term the Cheyenne use that Jim knows. They do anything they want to and then say it's all right because that's 'the way of the People.' I got so tired of hearing those words that I wanted to scream at them.

"I saw a warrior capture a white woman on a stagecoach raid. Then he realized that she was wounded and out of her mind and thin and sickly. He tried to sell her to the other warriors, but when none wanted her, he slit her throat as if she were an unwanted dog and let her die."

"Must have been hard to take," Morgan said. He paused a moment. "What's the story on the saddlebag? It's marked U.S. Army."

Harold nodded. "Now it doesn't seem so good, but at the time I was Cheyenne and we were fighting for our lives. We had a small Army patrol pinned down on a little ridge and we couldn't get to them. I started the grass burning and it forced them off the hill and into our warriors on the other side.

"I wanted a saddlebag to keep stuff in. That small battle was why they thought I brought them good magic, good medicine."

They sat watching the fire.

"I guess mostly why I decided to come home was because it looks like the Cheyenne are doomed. I mean, the Army is hunting them, the buffalo are gone. They have nowhere to run except into Canada, and even there they won't be safe for long.

"After a while I realized that the Cheyenne warriors have only one job. That's to be fighters, to kill their enemies. They don't even help put up the big tipis or take them down or pack things.

"That's women's work and beneath them. I decided that I didn't want to be a warrior, a killer, for the rest of my life. I'm much more interested in the planets and the solar system and the stars and galaxies. I want to be a scientist."

Morgan grinned. "Well, now, nothing wrong with that. I'm sure your father will send you to any school and college you want to go to. He's got enough money to do that."

Harold nodded. "Yes, he told me that. One thing I hate is that my mother was killed. It wasn't an accident. That trooper deliberately rode her down. So I killed him. He deserved it. I think in another month or two she would have been ready to come back to Grand Island too. Indian women work so hard I couldn't believe it. She worked too hard and got sick, but Wounded Elk still didn't think she did enough. She wasn't well at all there toward the last."

Morgan went to check on the horses. When he came back, Harold and Jim were talking quietly in the Cheyenne language. Morgan settled down near the fire, put his head on his saddle, and tried to relax.

Most of it was over. Now all he had to do was get the boy back to Laramie without meeting those Cheyenne again, and wire his father.

He grinned. The tough job was going to be telling Sarah Everett, the lady banker, good-bye. He had grown fond of that lady and after only a few sweet kisses. He shook his head. He'd work on that problem when he came to it.

Jim caught Morgan's attention. "Harold have problem. Want talk."

Morgan sat up and put some more sticks on the fire. The flames lit up Harold's face, which was troubled.

"I guess I broke the law and I don't know what to do about it. On that raid I went with the warriors when they attacked the stagecoach, I found something. Now I'm not sure what to do with it. It came from the stage. Should I give it back to the coach company or what?"

Morgan settled back and lifted his brows. "Well, Harold, I guess you could say you were illegal just being with the band that raided the stagecoach. If you found something there that belonged to someone else and took it, that would be the same as stealing it. Is that the way you see it?"

Harold let out a long sigh. "Yeah, afraid so. I thought I could have something of my own."

"But it really wouldn't be yours if you found or stole it, would it, Harold?"

"You're sounding a lot like my father, Mr. Morgan, but I guess that's all right."

"Sometimes people who are right tend to sound alike," he said, grinning. "What did you find?"

Harold pulled the saddlebag from beside him and opened the flap. He took out the treasured stacks of greenbacks and sat them all in a row.

"I found these. There was a lot more, but the warriors didn't know what it was and threw them in the air so they scattered."

Kit Dalton

"Cash money," Morgan said softly. "You know how much is there?"

"A little more than ten thousand dollars. I counted it one afternoon."

Morgan put two more sticks in the fire. This might take longer than he figured.

"So what do you think, Mr. Morgan?"

"You do have a problem. The money looks like it was going to a bank somewhere, maybe start-up cash for a small bank. So it was federal cash or belonged to the bank."

"But who could I give it back to?" Harold asked.

"That's the real problem. If you admitted you were there on the raid, some sheriff would want to throw you in jail. You were just an observer, so I don't think he should do that. Then the other problem is trying to find out who the money belonged to. You said it was just part of it. How big a part?"

"Must have been five times as much scattered around. I said I wanted it to use playing a game."

"If they've lost forty thousand, another ten isn't going to hurt them. It could hurt you. So I'd say you don't have to worry about giving the money back to the stage line or some bank somewhere."

"Good." Harold nodded and put two small sticks into the fire. "Course, that doesn't figure out what I should do with the money."

"You could keep it."

"But you said it wasn't like I earned it. I stole it. Besides, my father has a hundred times that much money. He'll give me all I that I need to go to school. I just don't *need the money*."

Morgan grinned. "I see what you mean. Well,

it's a nice kind of a problem to have. You sleep on it, and tomorrow we'll be back in Laramie and send your father a telegram and meet him in Cheyenne. You can have some good food and a real bed to sleep in, and then you can decide what to do with the money."

The 14-year-old nodded. His head sagged and his eyes slid shut and he snapped them open.

Morgan chuckled. "Hey, Harold Bishop. You don't have to be a mighty warrior any more. Just relax. If you want to go to sleep, go ahead. Nobody is going to charge out of the brush screaming or blowing bugles at you.

"Come on, Harold. You're back in the white-eyes world and we're here to see that nothing happens to you until you're safe and happy back in civilization."

Harold grinned, nodded, and eased backward on the grass. He went to sleep instantly with his feet to the fire. Morgan bet that a nighthawk's call would bring him wide awake in a second. Harold Bishop would always be part Cheyenne.

Chapter Twenty-Seven

The three rode into Laramie about three o'clock the next afternoon. Morgan stopped in at the telegraph office and sent a wire to Alonzo Bishop in Grand Island. It said:

"HAROLD RESCUED, IS SAFE, WELL, UNHARMED. WE WILL MEET YOU IN CHEYENNE AS YOU PREVIOUSLY SUGGESTED. WE'LL LEAVE TODAY, BE THERE TOMORROW, MONDAY."

They turned the two horses in to the livery man in Laramie. While they were waiting for the evening train, they had a supper and a half in the middle of the afternoon.

Harold had a steak dinner with three vegetables, mashed potatoes and brown gravy, and three slices of bread with butter and jelly on it.

For dessert he had a piece of gooseberry pie, then one of cherry, and finished with a cut of lemon chiffon pie.

Harold borrowed a 20-dollar bill from his saddlebag and walked the streets for two hours shopping. He never bought a thing.

"That's more fun than I've had in six months!" he said when he met them at the depot.

The 6:34 train heading east was on time and the three boarded it, gave their tickets to the conductor, and settled down for the 50-mile run to Cheyenne. It should take about an hour and a half, Morgan knew. It was most of two hours before they arrived.

Morgan took Harold directly to the hotel, where he booked a room for him, and got his word that he would go right to bed and to sleep.

"Oh, any idea about what you'll do with the money?" Morgan asked.

"Some, but not for sure yet. I need to ask some more questions."

As soon as Harold was settled, Morgan went by the saloon where Shirley had been dancing. Her picture was still on the bulletin board on the outside door. She put on two performances nightly at eight-thirty and at ten-thirty. Morgan grinned. He was sure that she hadn't been frightened enough by her close call with the killer to reform. She was a dancer and she would stay a dancer, plus working for what other income she could on the side. He had no wish to see her. He waved at her picture as he passed it and closed that chapter of his life.

Morgan meandered past Sarah Everett's house, but walked on by. He did want to see Sarah again, but it would not be proper to call at a lady's home uninvited. Morgan had lost track of Jim, who'd vanished as soon as they hit town. Morgan had paid Jim the 20 dollars he'd promised him, two dollars a day for the ten days.

If Jim followed form, he would be half drunk by now and getting into trouble in a bar. Morgan checked in the bar near Jim's shack, but he wasn't there. He wasn't in the shack either. That made Morgan wonder, but not worry. Jim could look out for himself. Jim had promised to be on hand the next morning when the night train from Omaha got in.

Morgan guessed that Mr. Bishop would catch the first train out of Grand Island that he could get that afternoon or evening, and should be there in Cheyenne sometime in the morning.

Morgan stared at Lottie's Cafe. It was still locked up. No one had bought it yet. He shook his head. What a waste. Thurlow Deeds had had demons of his own, but he was free of them now. He had created a lot of hell for a lot of women before it caught up with him.

Morgan gave up and went back to his hotel. He had a cup of coffee in the dining room just before it closed, then went up to his room. He opened the door cautiously, but no alluring naked lady sat on his bed.

He was bone-weary from all the riding and sleeping on the ground. A good bed would feel perfect about now. Morgan slept better than he had for a week.

The next morning, Morgan was up at six and shaved closely and dressed, then roused Harold out of his bed. They had breakfast in the dining room before they hurried to the train station to meet the 8:10 steamer in from Nebraska.

It came in five minutes early and was a mixed train, four boxcars and two passenger cars. The steam engine raced into the station, then screeched steel wheels on steel rails as it stopped. Porters hurried out with step stools for the passengers to come down on.

The sixth person to get off the train was Alonzo Bishop. He saw Morgan, then spotted Harold beside him and ran forward. He threw his arms around Harold, who let out a squawk of surprise and embarrassment.

"Wonder of wonders!" Bishop said. "I never thought I'd see the day!" He stepped back a minute and studied Harold. "You've grown four inches. You look like a little old man, so serious, so tanned and brown, and so thin. We'll get you new clothes, go to Omaha for them if you want."

He looked at Harold and smiled. "I know I was a little reserved with you before, Harold, but that's all over now. I can see you're practically a man. You'll be treated fairly and with love and compassion in our home. Welcome back.

"Now, I understand the next train back to Grand Island isn't until nearly noon. We'll plan on taking it if that's all right with you, Harold." Bishop paused and watched his son, who nodded. "All right then, in the meantime I'd like some breakfast. Is there a passable restaurant where we might have something to eat and we can transact some business?"

"One just down the street that isn't half bad," Morgan said.

Harold looked beyond his father, saw something, and darted that way. He came back with Jim Breed in tow.

"Father, I'd like you to meet Jim. He's half the

reason I'm here. He talked to me when I was still in the Gray Owl band, and helped to rescue me."

Alonzo Bishop held out his hand. "Jim, I'm glad to meet you. Thank you for helping save my son's life. I hope you were adequately paid."

"No, he wasn't, Father. I think you should pay him, oh, at least five hundred dollars."

Alonzo looked down at his son in surprise. "Well, I'm sure that can be arranged. Jim, come and have something to eat with us."

"Already did," Jim said.

"Well, we'll talk on the way. What do you do here in town, Jim?"

"Odd jobs."

"But Jim has a new idea," Harold blurted out. "He likes to work with leather, and he told me he made a saddle once just by looking at an old one. Jim wants to open a saddle shop here in town, but he can't."

Alonzo looked puzzled. "Why can't you, Jim?"

"Father, this is the West. An Indian, a breed like Jim and me, can't own property."

Alonzo shrugged. "No problem. Show me the store you want and I'll buy it and let you use it, give it to you. Nobody can stand against that. You picked out a store?"

Jim nodded.

"Well, let's see it first. Harold wants to help you, so let's get it done."

An hour later, Alonzo Bishop had inspected the store, a frame structure with room enough for a workshop and a small area in front to show leather goods with a counter across it. In back there were three rooms that had been used as a residence.

They found the property agent who had the

building for sale, and Alonzo Bishop wrote a bank draft for the entire amount: $450 and filing fees at the county clerk's office.

Harold turned to his father. "Thank you. Jim thanks you. Now I have another small problem." He showed the small paper bag that he had been carrying to his father. It held the $10,000.

"You robbed a bank," his father said.

"Almost, Mr. Bishop," Morgan said. "It's a long story, but Harold decided that since he found the money it really isn't his and he can't keep it. The cash can't be traced back to its true owner, so he has to do something else with it."

"I'm going to give it to Jim so he can start his leather shop," Harold said in a rush.

Jim's eyes went wide. He knew the value of money. He shook his head. "No. Do enough already."

Alonzo watched them both. His eyes sparkled. "Jim, you only have a store. You'll need equipment, stacks of leather, tools, dyes, all sorts of things. Let's go to the bank and open an account for you there. We'll put in five thousand now and the other five thousand later so the bank doesn't get jittery. I'd bet you'll be the first Indian in Cheyenne with a bank account."

A few minutes later, Sarah Everett looked up quickly as the four men walked into her office at the Cheyenne Territorial Bank.

"Gentlemen?"

"Sarah, some friends of mine," Morgan said. "This special friend on the end is Jim, you might have seen him around town. Jim's opening a leather goods and saddle shop here in town and he needs a bank account. He has five thousand dollars as an opening deposit."

Sarah lifted her brows. "And you other gentlemen are here to support and back him, I would expect. Don't worry. We have accounts here for Irishmen, for a Chinese couple, for three Mexicans, and two Negroes. I'm proud to have an account for an Indian."

Harold got busy sorting out five thousand dollars. He had taken the bands off the bundles so they couldn't be identified. Sarah counted it all, then had her head teller do it again. Sarah showed Jim his book and told her to come see her when he needed money. She took out a hundred dollars and put it in a small purse for him. She must have known he had never had that much money before in his life.

She thanked them, and Jim thanked her, and they headed for the street.

When the others left, Sarah motioned for Morgan to stay. She pointed at the others. "This was part of your business in town?"

He nodded.

"And your business is about over?"

"Yes, my work here is finished."

"You still have to collect that roast beef dinner I promised you. Would tonight be too short a notice?"

"How about six-thirty?"

"I'll be ready."

Outside, Morgan caught up with the others. Alonzo was telling Jim where he could get tools for his shop and what he'd need. At last he stopped.

"Jim, I think I better stay over another day and help you order what you need out of Omaha. I know some people there and I'll vouch for your credit. You should have everything in a week or so."

He turned to Morgan. "Now, you and I have some business. Let's wander up this way."

When they were away from the other two, Alonzo took an envelope out of his pocket. He handed it to Morgan. Inside was a bank draft made out to Lee Morgan in the amount of $10,000. Morgan read the figures, saw it was signed and proper, then put it his shirt pocket.

"I'd say our business is finished, Mr. Bishop. It's been interesting working for you. I'm sorry about your wife. I talked to her a few days before the attack. She was still determined to stay with her people and to keep Harold there."

"Yes, Willow was a strange woman in many ways."

Morgan shook hands with Alonzo, then went back and shook hands with Harold.

"You surprise me and go to Harvard and discover a new star or something. I'm counting on you."

"Do my best, Mr. Morgan," Harold said, and grinned. Jim and Alonzo headed for the telegraph station, where they would wire Omaha and get the supplies started.

Morgan found a chair in front of the Underwood Groceries and Provisioner store, leaned back in it, and dropped his hat over his eyes. Morgan relaxed.

Ten thousand dollars, the double bonus Bishop had promised him. Good pay for a short job. That was more money than he'd had in some time. He'd leave most of it with Sarah's bank. Nice central spot here in Cheyenne, so he could get it whenever he wanted to.

He opened the account after snoozing for a half hour. Damn, but this felt good! No worries, a couple of dollars in his pocket, and nobody pushing him to do anything.

Sarah had been surprised by his deposit. He told her he wanted an account he could write bank drafts on and she arranged it. She looked up when he said he wanted a thousand dollars in cash.

"To carry with you? Isn't that dangerous?"

"Only if someone knows I have it. I'll get a money belt and keep most of the money in hundred-dollar bills."

That evening he rang the twist bell on the Everett home promptly at six-thirty. Sarah met him at the door. Her cheeks were slightly flushed and her brown eyes were dancing.

"Oh, good, I was afraid you might not come." She opened the door and stepped back. When he was inside she lifted on tiptoes and kissed him on the cheek. "That is just for fun. Now come out to the kitchen. I need you to move the roast out of the oven for me."

The dinner was delightful and delicious. Sarah acted like a young girl with her first beau and Morgan enjoyed playing his part. When the food was gone and the delicate dessert finished, she led him to a wooden porch swing in the backyard. They sat there swinging gently as it grew dark.

"I know that you're heading out of town soon, Lee Buckskin Morgan. I wish you weren't."

He held her hand and then lifted it and kissed it softly. "At times like this, I wish I were a banker or a merchant or something so I'd settle down."

"But even if you did, it wouldn't last long. Would it?"

He grinned, and then his face sobered. "Not for long."

She pushed toward him. "Then kiss me and lie to me and then I'll see you to the door. I'm not going to let you break my heart. I simply won't."

The kiss was gentle, soft, with lips barely touching. She sighed when it was over. Then she leaned in and kissed him harder, and she let out a soft moan as it ended.

Sarah stood quickly, caught his hand, and led him straight to the front door. Gently she urged him outside and swung the screen door closed. She stood there, a tear working its way down her cheek.

"Lee Morgan, stop by and see me from time to time. Now get out of here before I start crying!" She smiled through her tears as she closed the front door and shut him out.

Morgan stood there a moment, then lifted his brows. It was traveling time. He wasn't sure where. He'd wire Denver. There might be another job offer waiting for him. If not, he could always do some fishing. There were some trout streams near Denver he never tired of testing. Yes, trout fishing. He'd get the first train out in the morning heading down the branch line to Denver.

He knew this old guy in a shack about 20 miles from Denver who made artificial flies. Little bits of string and colored yarn so they looked like real flies or moths or gnats and each one had a barbed hook right inside.

Morgan hurried as he headed for the train station. He wondered if there was a night train down to Denver. That was his most important job right now. As Morgan walked to the station, a pleased, satisfied smile came across his face. Just thinking about catching those trout lifted his spirits.